Charles

Kentucky Dreams

by Marlene Worrall

Blessings & Love

Marlene

ISBN-13:978-1-946939-90-6

Dedication

Thanks to Almighty God, the prayers of the saints and the wonderful, brilliant Cynthia Hickey.

Acknowledgement

Jesus Christ who gave me the gift and joy of writing for His honor and glory.

Chapter One

Dana and Graham settled into wedded bliss...but not for long. Though she'd had many reservations about just how well daily life with Graham would work out, she was thrilled and delighted to discover that it was much better than she could have hoped for. "Good morning, darling." Dana nuzzled close to her handsome, new hubby. It gave her an incredible high just being in close proximity to him. She gave him a peck on his cheek.

In seconds, Graham's lips were on hers. Passion engulfed them as they soared to new and glorious ecstasies. When they finally came up for air, Dana bounced out of the luxurious bed, slipped on her lavender silk robe that lay strewn on a chair and hummed a tune, soon bursting forth into song. *"If ever I should leave you...it wouldn't be in winter, for seeing you in winter, I never would go...your hair soft as sunlight, your lips right as rain..."*

Graham joined her in song as they harmonized dancing around the room together as though they were rehearsing for a musical. He twirled her around the room, despite being clad in his white, terry robe.

Dana's spirit soared to new and glorious heights. Heights she never could have imagined. "So this is love! " She flashed him a huge smile. "You want to know something...really, totally amazing?" Dana's heart was as light as a feather.

"You have to ask?"

"Just...checking. Well...God...I guess I would have to say...the Holy Spirit, which is the same thing... has been pouring out incredible songs of praise and worship to me...I mean... just raining them down on me... I could be riding one of the thoroughbreds... when suddenly this supernatural...anointing falls over me and I burst into song...the music and lyrics just rain down from heaven! I mean...I can't tell you how incredible that is!"

"Amazing! I hope you've recorded...or remembered the words and the tune...I realize that might be a challenge when you aren't expecting the... outpouring."

"Well that's just it. It's happening more and more...so I know God wants me to get back to singing..."

"*Back* to singing? I didn't know you were ever a singer."

"Well...not for long. It was while I was in college...I didn't really know what I wanted to do...except that I knew it wouldn't be conventional. I was looking for a back up to horse training...in case for some reason that went sour..."

Graham laughed. "I think God has a divine sense of humor...because we both know the arts are anything but predictable..." He moved toward her, taking her in his arms. "Dana...Oh Dana...I can't keep my eyes off you...and I can't keep my hands off you...I just can't..."

"You don't have to..." She moved closer to him,

whispering in his ear. They slid back under the covers. It was dusk when they awakened to the sound of pounding on their door. They could hear the muffled sounds of Will and Jay through the locked bedroom door.

Graham leaped to his feet, pulled on his robe and moved close to the door, talking through it. "We'll be right down, guys. How about making us a pot of coffee?"

"Sure, Dad." Their youthful voices harmonized.

Downstairs, in the kitchen, Graham and Dana's faces beamed with radiant joy.

Violet winked at them when the boys weren't looking. "Ah. Wedded bliss. You leave for your honeymoon tomorrow morning, right? So...there are a few things we need to discuss before you travel." Violet poured the gourmet coffee into two mugs. She handed Graham his mug, reading the print on it, aloud. "Good morning, handsome." She smiled. "I didn't know you cared."

"Good morning, gorgeous." Violet read the print on Dana's mug.

Dana and Graham peered into each other's eyes, mesmerized. After a short while, Graham turned. "Where are Will and Jay?" He glanced around the rambling, old country kitchen.

"Playing chess in the games room... probably." Violet's eyes flashed from Dana to Graham.

"I've made a light supper...snapper with a cold veggie dish... ratatouille. I even found a dry white wine in the cellar to compliment the dish."

"It better be good. We don't want any cheap stuff at the start of our honeymoon." Graham winked at Violet.

"After all, I want Dana to know that we will always live in grand style...as the Lord provides..."

Dana nuzzled Graham's neck. "You better make sure. If I discover you aren't treating me like a countess, like you promised, there will be...necessary corrections." She peered into his eyes, fighting to keep a straight face.

"Yes, countess."

Violet raised her eyebrows. "So...your flight leaves at 7:00 tomorrow morning, correct?" She stood near the table, topping up their coffee. "Dinner will be served in the dining room at 5:30. I'll eat with the boys in the kitchen." She winked at them. "You need your privacy... at least for the first while."

AT THE DINING TABLE

"So...you're sure you want to go back to Freeport...despite everything that went down?" Dana eyed Graham across the table.

"Absolutely. It's paradise. I don't allow the bad guys to deter us." Graham uncorked the wine pouring a small amount in the crystal glasses. "See if you think it has travelled well, Dana." He tossed it around in his mouth, with an imperious air.

How pretentious, Dana mused. But as she peered over at Graham, she realized he was serious. He swirled the wine over his tongue, paused to savor the taste before making his pronouncement. "I think it's excellent, Countess. What do you think?"

Dana tried hard not to laugh, but she couldn't help herself, she burst out, chuckling. "If it's good enough for the Count...it is good enough for the Countess. I shall defer to your judgement, darling."

Graham and Dana ate heartily.

Violet brought in the desert, setting it down at their place settings. "Prune whip. I know y'all love it."

Graham grinned at her. "Thanks, Violet."

"Wonderful, Violet. Thank-you. I have a tough act to follow when it's my turn to cook."

"Gee, thanks. Glad y'all enjoyed it. I've made a pot of cinnamon apple tea...and I brought my list."

"Sounds good. The Good Lord was smiling down on me the day I hired you, Violet. You're like family."

Violet handed him a list.

He glanced over it, adding a few items and then handing it back to her. "Here's the deal, Violet. We'll just be gone a week...as you know. Sybil will be staying here and I've left her in charge of interviewing a new ranch hand...what I'd like *you* to do...if you will...is to just give her your take on them... and don't be afraid to offer your opinion to Sybil...I trust your instincts; and I've always believed that two heads are better than one. Don't be afraid to ask the prospective ranch hand questions. They won't suspect that you have anything to do with the hiring...so they might let their guard down around you and start talking." He grinned. "Serve them homemade peanut butter cookies, and...be your...usual, friendly self...you just never know what you might learn."

Chapter Two

FREEPORT, BAHAMAS

Dana and Graham towelled off after a long swim and then kicked back on the lounge chairs. "Did I ever tell you that you're the most gorgeous woman on the planet?" He nuzzled her ear.

"More...more. Don't stop there." She flashed him a sexy smile, her eyes dancing with unspeakable joy. *Lord, thank you for hearing my prayer. You have done above and beyond what I could ever think or imagine. Your timing is superb. You are a great and mighty God. There is none like you. Praise your holy name, Jesus.* She whispered the prayer to the Almighty with a grateful heart. She had prayed for years to find a hubby, finally coming to the point that she almost didn't care if it ever happened. She'd watched a couple of girlfriends meet great guys, soon showing off their engagement rings and walking down the isle. Reluctantly, she had come to believe that maybe marriage wasn't in her future.

"If it doesn't happen for me, Lord, that's okay...because *you* are enough. I'm finally at that place,

Lord. Truly, *you are enough.* Oh, I fight twinges of something like...jealousy...and I fight longing...longing for companionship, intimacy... the comfort and joy that only marriage can provide. Only in that secure place is there a chance of getting to truly know someone and deeply love them... now suddenly it's happened. It's almost too good to be true. You pray... you wait...and you hope...and then one day God rains down a blessing upon you...and you can barely contain it. *Thank-you, heavenly father, for all that you are...for all that you've done...for me...and all mankind. I stand in awe of you.*

"Does dancing sound like fun tonight?" Dana cast an admiring glance at the hunk seated a few feet away from her. *This man belongs to me. He's my hubby. This is heaven on earth, no doubt about it. All those barren years I hung onto the scripture "If you delight yourself in me, I will give you the desires of your heart."* Psalm 37:4 had been emblazoned on her mind and heart for ages. She'd tenaciously clung to God's promises. *And she'd been rewarded.* God had brought her dream man into her life!

"Whatever the Countess desires." He grinned and twirled her around, stopping suddenly. He pulled her close to him, holding her tight.

She was breathless. They were so close it was scary. *Could she even breathe?*

"I'm glad we decided to come up to our honeymoon suite after dinner." His voice was husky as he nibbled on her ear. "My angel... my princess...my countess...my...wife... I love you...so... so much." He whispered the words of endearment into her ear as he caressed her neck, face and body and then his lips came down on hers.

Her heart leaped for joy. This truly was heaven on earth. *Thank-you, Lord.*

They danced to a live orchestra that night, taking advantage of the events outlined in the promotional brochure the travel agency had given them. Dana felt every inch the Countess. Dressed in a white jersey, strapless dress, she wore gold pumps and accessories. *I never want this to end, Lord. I want this to go on and on forever...and yes it will. Because the Word says that we will know each other in the great beyond, we will recognize each other there...so really... this time of joy is merely a prelude to eternity with Jesus in a place called Paradise. There, we will reunite with our loved ones.* She peered into his eyes as he swirled her around the room gaily, laughter tittering from her lips, eyes sparkling and heart soaring on a cloud floating high in the heavens.

Breakfast on the patio at the hotel was perfect. She'd thought so until she spied a gentleman clad in expensive, casual Bermudas and blue designer cotton T- shirt. He dined alone, his face buried in the newspaper. That didn't bother her. That was normal. What disturbed her was the way he glanced their way furtively and once eye contact was made, he quickly turned away *as though he were avoiding them. Why? Who was this man? And what was he hiding?*

Dana waited until they were out of the cafe and alone in their suite. "I'm sure you noticed that blonde guy that was sitting at the next table...alone."

"Of course I noticed him...and I think there was something... off base about him. I mean...did you notice the shoes?"

"No. What about the shoes?"

"Very costly. I happen to know about shoes. A buddy of mine was the CEO of a major shoe company. He wore pricey shoes but his clothes were bought at Walmart. It was... incongruous. Now with this guy...it struck me as odd that he kept his face turned away from us... and when I glanced his way, he turned his head totally away, as though he didn't want us to register his features. He avoided making eye contact. I have to wonder if that is because he did not want us to identify him...which of course raises red flags. I mean...what is the guy up to?"

"I don't know...but I'm going to try to figure it out, Dana. You know, when I was in business...in commercial real estate...I would mull over a deal in my mind. Sometimes, I did not arrive at a conclusion I was comfortable with. I used to go to sleep and then wake up in the wee hours of the morning with a solution. I know that sounds odd, but actually...it made me a lot of money. Sometimes the players in a deal or the complicated factors in a large deal were not always apparent...thus, I began letting my subconscious solve the issues. It was weird. I would wake up in the middle of the night...and suddenly...voila! A solution would pop into my mind. Once I realized how successful the method was, I deliberately allowed my subconscious to aid me."

"Interesting. So maybe in the wee hours of the morning... you'll nudge me and you'll know what the secretive guy sitting alone at a table was up to. Maybe you'll figure out his hidden agenda."

"Maybe. I'm wondering if we've met him somewhere before. Maybe he's in the horse racing industry."

"I've never seen him before. I always remember a face." Dana shook her head.

"So do I."

The lovers strolled hand-in-hand, basking in paradise, their love soaring higher and higher with each new day, with every breath. Graham leaned closer, whispering in her ear. "I'm so crazy about you I might want to spend one whole day a week just praising God for his goodness in bringing you into my life. Two awesome women in a lifetime is surely the gracious hand of the Almighty."

Dana smiled, peering into his eyes. Momentarily, she glanced up. "Look at that! A vivid red Parakeet just swooped past us. The way I feel right now, I would gladly scrap the work and dedication involved with training a potential Derby winner and trade it to bask here in paradise... with you... forever."

"And what about the boys? Just forget about them and let them do their own thing?" Graham smirked.

She swatted him. "Honeymoons are like living in a fantasy world. Can you blame me if I never want it to end?"

"No...I can't blame you, gorgeous. I confess that thought actually crossed my mind, too." Graham smirked, pulling her close to him and kissing her passionately. "Great minds think alike."

"What do you want to do for the rest of the afternoon?" Dana winked at him.

Dinner was superb. They gazed into one another's eyes as they glided around the dance floor, buoyed by their heady love and the balmy, tropical climate...coupled with the joy of having no responsibilities or chores.

Graham seemed to snap to his senses. "I need to call home. Check on the boys right away. Mind if we...take a breather." He took her hand leading her off the floor.

They plopped down on the luxurious sofa in the lobby. Graham got on his cell. "Hey, Sis. What's goin' on?"

"Great timing. I was just going to call you. There's no easy way to say this, Graham. Will has disappeared. He's not responding to text messages or voice mails."

Graham's heart was in his throat. He took a deep breath. "Wh...whatever do you mean, Sybil?"

"Just like I said...the kid has vanished. Right after lunch he said he was going for a ride on his bike...I told him not to be long...this was three hours ago. I keep phoning and texting him...all to no avail."

"Call the sheriff. I know he's not missing until 24 hours has elapsed; but given the whole bizarre charade with Tanner and Troy...he might make an exception...and start the search immediately."

"Okay. I'm on it. Meanwhile...I suggest you drop everything and go into serious prayer. Meditate on the Word...don't just read it...meditate on it. The power the Word contains is far more effective than the sheriff and police department."

Graham was in shock. The words Sybil spoke sounded surreal.

"What we perceive and see with the natural eye, and understand with our heart... is light years behind the spiritual power and authority contained in the Word."

"You *did* glean something from your studies, after

all. The Masters of Divinity you earned was not in vain."

Without a word between them, Dana knew this was a crisis involving one of the boys. She waited until he ended the call. "What's goin' on, Graham?"

The color had drained from his face.

Oh Lord, what now?

"Will has gone missing. We need to...plug into God's power...meditate on scripture...and pray." Graham was sombre.

"I guess that explains why a lot of people who think they're seeking God, just because they quickly flip through a few scriptures each day...become mystified when their prayers aren't answered." Dana bowed her head.

"Well, Dana...let me put it this way...I used to be like that...before Myrna died...it took that tragic illness and eventual passing to wake me up to the reality that I was just plugging in God, the way I plugged in a lot of other things...I wasn't *pursuing* him with all my heart and mind and soul...and yet the scripture spells out that that is what we need to do...I mean... if we are to love the Lord thy God with all our heart, mind and soul...surely that would translate to study and focus... as opposed to a quick read through."

"Absolutely. I'll tell you what, Graham...maybe I'll invent a new game. How about you pick a passage from the Bible; I'll do the same. We'll go off and study it thoroughly. We'll find resources, access the internet and truly meditate on it...then...once we have that knowledge under our belts, we will conduct a study. Obviously, the person who focused on a particular chapter will ask the other person questions, reflections, observations...etc., and then by digging into it, we will ferret out nuggets of wisdom. The reason I want to do this is because I have a tendency...probably like everyone...to do a cursory read. But since God instructs us to *meditate* on the scriptures, we *must* do it." She arched her brows for emphasis.

"I'm proud of you Dana. You should get back to teaching Sunday school. You have a gift for teaching. Come on, let's do intercessory prayer. We need to seek God fervently and believe for the safe return of Will."

"Yes."

"We'll go back to the room and pray until the burden is lifted...even if it's 3:00 in the morning."

The bed side clock read 3:00 a.m. "I can't pray anymore, Dana. Let's get some sleep. First thing tomorrow morning, we'll call the prayer chains."

"You don't think Sybil is already on it?" Dana sighed, glancing over at Graham.

"Probably. But she's got a lot on her plate...with running the farm. It might have slipped her mind. You know, Dana...a lot of things are coming into focus. For example, when we were training Flaming Bullet we...I think we actually became so obsessed with winning the Derby that we...left God behind. Oh... not totally... of course. But I think we would be wise to remember that God is a jealous God. He demands first place in our lives...he must be our first love...far above and beyond everything else...every other enterprise we get involved with."

"True, Graham. Life is about learning lessons. Ironic isn't it...just when we sort of get everything figured out...it's time to say good-bye to earthly things...and all the knowledge we gleaned here..." "But when we are ushered into eternity, what we have learned thus far...goes with us, right? I mean...when we get there we won't just be reclining on a cloud like a cherub or angel, we will continue working for our Lord and Master, right?"

"That's my understanding. We will be designated jobs...and responsibilities...I suspect there will be a kind of hierarchy in heaven. We want to enter the Kingdom on a high tier..." He smirked over at her.

"You're too much, Graham. I don't know if all this stuff is true. God leaves a lot to our imagination... "

"Are you up for a game of chess?" Graham peered over at her.

"You're joking, right? I don't play chess. You have to know I don't play chess...and, actually, I'm not inclined to take it up."

"Okay. I'm just teasing. I knew that. I'm not really in the mood to play anyway. I don't know why I brought a set with me. Why don't we go for a stroll around the hotel grounds?"

"Let's do it." Dana glanced at her watch. "We have at least an hour before dinner."

They strolled, hand-in-hand through the vividly lit hotel grounds, basking in the tropical weather and watching, mesmerized at an array of tropical birds, including two, exotic, colorful Herons strolling by them. As they walked past a water fountain adorned with a mermaid, water sprouting from her belly, they almost bumped into an elderly gentleman.

Tall and bespectacled, he was milling around the fountain, throwing pennies into the water below. "Good evening." He grinned, nodding to them, then turned back to continue dropping pennies into the fountain.

"Good evening to you." Graham matched his formal tone. "Making wishes?"

"I am. Oh...might I ask you a small favor?" The older man peered over at them, leaning on his cane.

Instantly, Graham was on the alert. Something about the man sent up red flags. "What might that be?" He didn't try to conceal his skepticism.

"Well...I...would like you to come closer...I'd like to show you something..."

Graham was curious by nature. Not this time. Something was off base here. But what? He didn't move. "What's the favor?" Graham peered into the man's smoky, grey eyes, struck by his gloomy countenance.

"You must come closer." The man turned his face away from Graham.

"No. We were just leaving. Come on, Dana...let's go." He hustled her along. "I'll get someone from the hotel to assist you."

"That won't be necessary." Suddenly, the old man swirled toward them aiming a Colt 45 at Graham. He peeled off a mask revealing none other than Tanner. "Pretty stupid to come here for your honeymoon. I own this town...and the people here. You're a nobody in this place...I could murder you both right now and not be incarcerated. People owe me favors...people in high positions."

Graham shot up a prayer for supernatural protection and boldness. He turned to Dana. "Come on, let's go. I'm not real fond of the company here." He'd made the instant decision to call the man's bluff. If he wasn't bluffing they were dead anyway, unless God intervened.

Dana had been silently praying as soon as she'd spotted the odd man. There had been an unsettled feeling in her spirit, prompting her to seek God.

They sprinted toward the brightly lit entrance of the front door of the hotel, breathing a sigh of relief, when the doorman ushered them in.

Graham reported the incident to Walter Manning, the hotel manager

"I'll page security." In minutes, two burley guards hurried to the fountain, escorting Tanner off the property. "There will be no charge for your hotel stay. I know you're on your honeymoon and we pride ourselves in the security of the hotel. The suspect has been apprehended. Dinner is on the house tonight. The Grand Palace dining room has some splendid specials I'm sure you'll love. Enjoy the rest of your stay here."

Graham and Dana peered at each other. *No hotel bill? And a free gourmet dinner tonight? "Wow!".* Graham smirked. "God is so good."

"Let's head to the room and praise God. It looked for a minute there that we were going to be ushered into heaven a whole lot sooner than we anticipated."

Chapter Three

The idyllic honeymoon was cut short. Dana and Graham flew out of Freeport back to Lexington, Kentucky, the next morning. Will was still missing.

At the sheriff's office, they were given sombre looks and little encouragement. "Okay. So it's twenty-four hours...Will is officially missing...and we have no leads...I don't know what else to tell you, Graham." Sheriff Brady wore his concern across his features. "History has proven that disappearances are usually connected to someone you've encountered along the way, or someone you know. In your case, of course, Tanner and his boys spring to mind. They're at the top of our list. After shutting down his illegal operation with the stolen Thoroughbreds, they're probably out for vengeance." The sheriff shook his head in disgust.

"That's what I was afraid of. Those were among my first thoughts. But there is something we haven't thought about..." Graham said.

"Which is?" Sheriff Brady peered over at him.

"Well, it's hardly a secret that Will is fascinated by horses. Maybe he went riding and...rode too far out... and got lost..." Graham was grasping at straws and he knew it.

"Have you checked the barn? Are all the horses there?" The sheriff asked.

"Yes. They are all there. Unless..." Graham was somber.

"Unless what?" The sheriff peered at him.

"Unless...Juan... the new ranch hand drove Will somewhere."

"Like where? And why isn't Will answering his cell?"

"I wish I knew the answers." Graham shook his head. He knew he was grasping at straws.

Dana and Jay sat next to him. Silent. Praying.

"Let's work together to assemble a team to hunt for Will. You may want to contact your church and see if there are men there willing to be part of a search team." The sheriff's countenance reflected grave concern.

A search team was rapidly assembled.

Twelve hours later.

At the sheriff's office. "We've come up empty. I don't know what to say." The sheriff sighed.

Graham and Dana were pale. Neither of them spoke, as they sat across from the sheriff at his desk.

"Go home. Get some rest. And pray. And pray...and then pray some more. Only God can help you." Sheriff Brady fought back sentimental tears. He was fond of both Graham's son and had no sons of his own.

That night at dinner, Violet prayed fervently, aloud. Then Sybil prayed. The group sat around the formal dinner table. Graham had invited Violet to join them for dinner.

After dinner, they all joined hands, saying a group

prayer. The prayer meeting lasted a couple of hours.

Graham's eyes filled with tears. "Only God can help us. Only He can find Will. We need to lean on the Everlasting Arms." He was overwhelmed with emotion. "God knows exactly where Will is and when he will return home. I'm thinking that we should join hands as a group, read the 91st Psalm aloud...it's the Psalm of supernatural protection... and ask the Lord to bring Will safely home... and then praise Him and believe that God will supernaturally bring Will back. I mean...I don't know what else we can do." He peered over at the sheriff." It occurs to me that Billy might have a hand in this."

"Yeah. I wouldn't put anything past him. Maybe he's still hanging out at the secret ranch; despite the fact that it is now defunct. He might have slipped onto Sugarbush farm undetected. Maybe he bonded with Will, while the two of you were on your honeymoon. Maybe he's cooked up a scheme to get his hands on some cash." The sheriff peered over at Graham and Dana.

Billy knew that if he was ever going to find a great broad, he would need to have a solid nest egg to impress her with. A fancy sports car would be good. He grinned. He'd keep it shiny and clean. Use the old truck for work. He needed to spruce up his wardrobe and have his teeth fixed. He had to look sharp because the bar was high for the kind of broad he had in mind. Dana wasn't good enough for him. If she couldn't see his potential and didn't appreciate his earthy, sexy, good looks, and opted for that wimpy cowboy wannabe instead of him; then who needs her, anyway? He was moving on to greener pastures.

Billy had planned everything out perfectly. He'd been watching Will with his binoculars from his secret hiding place. Every day after school Will and Jay hopped on the school bus that would take them home. Saturdays, the brothers often practiced soccer in the fields adjacent to the school. He'd been watching them for a couple of months, using his binoculars, mostly. Though, sometimes he took a seat in the bleachers where parents sometimes watched their kids. It had been a stroke of luck that Jay had jumped on the bus, while Will remained on the soccer field. He spotted a couple of bicycles. He was pretty sure one of them belonged to Will. The kid had a gift for sports. He admired that.

It was the perfect opportunity. Billy had always been detail-oriented. It had kept him out of jail. It would always keep him out of jail. He'd scraped up the money to buy a really beautiful Palomino. That would be the bait. He was fortunate that neither of Graham's sons had visited the secret ranch. They couldn't identify him. When the big sweep had occurred, Billy had his Palominos safely tucked away on a couple of acres which his old buddy Roy lived on. The Palominos were owned by him.

Billy had carefully mapped out his plan. The time had come to implement it. He drove his friend's horse trailer with the two Palomino beauties inside. He waited patiently until he could see that the soccer game was over.

Billy made his move. The soccer players were quickly dispersing as their folks picked them up. Billy pulled his truck alongside the soccer field. He opened the back of the trailer and let the magnificent palominos out just as Will sprinted to his bicycle. "Hey, young man...a little birdie told me you live at Sugarbush Farm. I'm wondering if you could put in a word about my Palominos. You need to see how gorgeous they are."

"My Dad makes those decisions. Not me." Will was only a few feet away from his bike, which was parked in the bicycle rack.

Billy pulled down the ramp. A sleek, creamy tan colored Palomino appeared.

"He is a real beauty. Have you got my Dad's phone number? Maybe he would be interested." Will was transfixed to the magnificent Palomino.

"You must have ranch hands out at the farm. If you want, I could help you out...I could put the bicycle in the trailer and drive you home...that way your ranch hands would be able to see how gorgeous they are."

"Nah. That's okay. We'll just wait 'til Dad gets back from his honeymoon. Mom and Dad will make that decision." *Something about this guy disturbed him.* He hurried toward his parked bicycle.

"Sure. I could do that. But then again, they might be sold by then. I need the money for...a new truck I'm buying...yup, these beauties will be long gone by then..." He turned on his boyish charm. "Tell you what... you're a good kid, so I'm going to do you a favor. We'll drive out to Sugarbush and see if the ranch hands agree that these Palominos are among the finest out there. I'll leave them there until your Dad gets back, by then you'll have fallen in love with them and your old man will buy then." He grinned, turning on the charm. "Hop in, kid. I'll drive you to the farm."

Will didn't have a good feeling about this guy. Seemed like God was warning him against the cowboy. He hesitated.

With a deft move, the speed of lighting, Billy snatched Will's cell phone, shoving him into the cab of his truck and locking the door from outside.

Will was caught off guard and overpowered. He yelled for help, but it useless. He'd seen the last car parked by the soccer field roar off with his school mate. No one else was around.

Billy had no intentions of driving to Sugarbush. Instead, he drove the horse trailer to his buddy's farm. He chuckled when the kid protested, driving faster. Soon, he drove onto Horseshoe Ranch and stopped the trailer there.

His buddy, Shane, had been waiting for him. He was nervous. He'd never done anything like this before. He was scared, too. He'd never been in jail like Billy had. He followed Billy's instructions. He went outside to meet Billy and Will when he saw his truck and trailer drive up.

Billy grinned confidently, as he unlocked the door for Will. Shane stood by the driver's seat like he'd been told to do.

"Sorry, Kid. You won't be inconvenienced for long. Soon as we get our cash... we're gonna set you free." Billy handcuffed the kid so fast Will's head spun. Billy turned toward Shane. "Easy pickins' So far... everything's goin' accordin' to mah plan."

"Come on, move." Billy wasn't known for his patience. He wanted the kid in the house where they could keep a close eye on him. Once there, they tied him up, sealing his mouth with duck tape. They stuck him on a chair in the kitchen. Though they weren't expecting an answer, Billy glanced over at his buddy. "I'm bettin' his old man will cough up the million-dollar ransom real quick."

"I sure hope so." Shane was nervous. *What if something went wrong? He didn't want to go to jail. He shouldn't have gotten involved in this hair-brained scheme. He'd been makin' an honest livin' until fast talkin' Billy showed up. Him and his clever plans.* "Let's hope so. The kid seems real nice." Shane had mixed feelings about Billy's plan. Still, he was desperate for cash, so he'd agreed.

"Hey...don't wimp out on me. We're in this together, buddy." Billy snarled.

"Yeah, yeah, I know." *But he was wimping out.* Shane resented Billy calling the shots. It was *his* ranch Billy was hiding out at and the Palomino's were *his* horses. True, the scheme was masterminded by Billy, but they didn't have the money yet and he sure hoped Billy knew what he was doing. He was tired of scrimping to make ends meet. This money would change both of their lives...unless his old buddy decided to double-cross him. He wouldn't put anything past slick Billy. Still, they'd been buddies for ages. He'd just have to wait and see how it played out.

Despite numerous attempts to reach Graham, they had no luck. They removed the duct tape from Will's mouth. "Where is your old man? Why isn't he answering his cell phone?" Billy wanted answers.

"If you give me my cell phone back, I'll speed dial him and get him."

"Not so fast, kid. We're not going to deviate from

the plan. I'll reach him soon enough."

Billy plastered some new duct tape on the kid. It was always possible that the ranch hand would come up to the house or some unexpected visitor might show up.

The buddies took shifts watching the kid. He seemed to be praying. He was surprisingly calm considering the circumstances.

The next morning, Billy's phone rang. "Hey, Graham, it's your old buddy... Billy Jones... from the secret ranch. You didn't quite shake us off. See...the way it is now, I'm gonna need you to put up a...just a million bucks... to pay the ransom for your kid. Will. He's here with me. With us. I want the cash delivered in small bills...twenties and fifties..."

Graham held the cell away from him so Dana could hear, also. He felt the color drain from his face. *"Lord. No."* He wanted to scream, or cry or stamp his feet. Anything, but respond calmly to the outrageous demand. *Instead, he prayed silently.*

Dana was already on her cell, calling the sheriff.

" We got a tip from somebody who spotted Will in Billy's trailer. They thought it was suspicious. One of his soccer buddies saw him get in the truck, but it seemed like he was coerced. We don't know where he's staying though."

Billy intended to play hard ball. He'd been bullied by his Dad and Uncle Henry when he'd been a kid. Nobody was ever going to bully him again. He was callin' the shots. That's the way it had to be. The kid goes home when the ransom is paid. Not before." His voice was cold steel. He was in control. He was calling the shots. He would always be calling the shots. *Nobody would push him around ever again.*

Billy got on the phone with Graham demanding a million dollars cash for the safe return of his son, Will.

Will was still praying. His head was bowed in silent prayer, as tears tumbled down his cheeks. *"The steps of a righteous man are ordered by the Lord."* Will believed in miracles. He always had. Because he read the Bible, and it was full of miraculous accounts. He believed in a miracle rescue for himself.

Chapter Four

Danielle had slept poorly. Sleep had eluded her ever since Dana had married Graham, her dream man. Her *secret* dream man. She still hadn't met an alternative despite attending all the Christian activities around town, faithfully showing up at a Bible class at church once a week, and attending church every Sunday. *Where are you, God?*

She heard his voice. It was audible. "*My precious, precious daughter. I have not forgotten you. It is you who has forgotten Me. Until you truly meditate on my words, you cannot hear my voice all the time. You do hear it sometimes; but not enough. I want you to forget about your own desires and focus on Me. Then I will make your way prosperous and wonderful. Trust Me. Trust Me with all your heart, and mind and soul. I am all you need. And until you come to that place...just as your daughter did...I cannot give you the desires of your heart. I am a jealous God, my daughter. My heart is brimming to overflowing with love for you. Trust Me. Trust Me with all your heart and mind and soul and lean not on your own understanding...*"

"*The world is filled with disobedience, violence and*

wrong doing. Even some Christians are using my name in vain, and hide among the church members, while nursing secret, evil agendas. Watch out for them. They are wolves in sheep's clothing. Stay in my Word. Meditate on it day and night. Then you will see answers to your most fervent prayers. Trust me, daughter. Trust me and love me with all your heart and mind and soul, and lean not on your own understanding."

And then it was gone. Danielle hurried to the mirror, shaking her head. She spoke aloud. *"*The voice of God! I...I heard the voice of God!" Tears welled up in her eyes. She felt instantly ashamed. *How could she be jealous of her own daughter? And yet she was.* They were in crisis. But she had a life...sort of. It was time for her to turn her back on Graham and Dana. She would yield to the constant harping of her girlfriend Mavis and join her for Happy Hour. Mavis swore by Mama Gina's.

It would get her out of the house at the very least. She would have her quiet time with God tonight. But right now, she would find out if there were any red-blooded males on the prowl. She speed dialed Mavis. "Mavis? Hey, thanks for the invite. Sure. I'll meet you at Mama Gina's at 5:00 tonight."

"You're joking, right? We need to meet at 4:00 if we're going to get a seat."

Danielle glanced at her watch. "Really? That early? " Quickly, she mentally ran through her schedule, swiftly changing a couple things. "Okay. See you in an hour."

Danielle gussied herself up. It was Friday night and according to Mavis, the place would be hopping. She flipped through her closet looking for something exciting to wear. Her eyes landed on a recent purchase.

A fuschia-colored dress. It was short, flattering and sexy. She slipped into her white Manuelo pumps. Shoes she kept for special occasions. Adding some chunky, fun jewelry, she checked her image in the mirror. "I look fantastic, if I say so myself." She turned to the right and then the left, finally giving the mirror thumbs up.

She knew about the disappearance of Will and had prayed for his safe return. She'd already figured out it was probably a ransom holdup. Getting out of the house would give her a new perspective on the situation. She couldn't do anything more than pray, anyway.

Danielle spotted him right away. Dark, curly black hair and a wicked smile, the man had smouldering dark eyes. *Italian?* She caught him glancing her way a couple times. Soon, he sent over a glass of wine. Not just any wine. Fine wine. She knew that as soon as she took the first leisurely sip.

"To a beautiful lady." He grinned, raising his wine glass in a toast, despite sitting two seats away from her. The woman sitting next to him left in a huff. The handsome, burly guy moved onto the seat next to her. "Hey, lovely lady. What's your name? I'm Dario Rizzo. What brings you out tonight? Haven't seen you here before?"

"Haven't been here for happy hour before." Danielle flashed him a big smile. "Danielle Lockhart."

They made small talk for a few minutes. His eyes roved over her appreciatively. He grinned, slyly. "Join me for dinner tonight?"

"Well...I..." Danielle was flattered but stunned at how fast the guy moved.

"I'll make reservations for us in the dining room...if you tell me you'll join me for dinner." He grinned again, showing perfect, white teeth.

"Well...I *do* have to eat. I love the food here. And I guess I'm about to find out if you're good company." She threw caution to the wind. God was giving her an opportunity to meet a new man. She had to grab it.

Dario was bright, witty and charming. An ideal dinner companion. *Or was she missing something? Why wasn't he married or in a relationship?* The male company was a gift. She found herself laughing at his jokes while she basked in the male company.

"May I have the pleasure of seeing you again?" His dark eyes danced with life and mischief as he grinned, walking her to her car after dinner.

Her heart lurched. She wanted to scream YES! YES OF COURSE YOU CAN SEE ME AGAIN. She took a moment, composing herself before she dared speak. "That might be fun." She flashed the charmer a big smile.

He handed her his card, giving her a peck on the cheek. "Text me with your number."

She did as instructed, texting him as soon as she got home. She didn't get a text back from him, though. That was irksome. Three days later, when she'd practically written him off, her cell chirped, and she recognized his number flashing on the screen. She read the text. "Meet me for steak dinner tonight. Angus Steak House on Charles Street, downtown. 7:00."

She showed up. They had great fun. Soon, a whirlwind courtship began. While she was making a pot of coffee in her kitchen after dinner, Dario stunned her by crouching down on bended knee and proposing.

Danielle was over the moon. She accepted, naturally. She could hardly believe her good fortune.

He suggested flying to Vegas and tying the knot there. It would be fast, simple and cheap.

They flew in to Vegas the following Thursday night. She shopped in the hotel and found a gorgeous dress and accessories. He rented a Tux. In a few hours, they were husband and wife. Following a very elegant dinner out, they pressed the elevator that would take them up to their luxurious Honeymoon suite.

Their brief honeymoon in the swanky hotel suite was blissful. Elegant, private dinners served with fine wine or champagne followed. His company was terrific. It was heady stuff.

Soon they flew back Lexington. She'd insisted on a prenuptial agreement because she had a healthy bank account, as well as substantial equity in her house. Decades of hard work and diligent saving had paid off. With her Masters in business, coupled with a strong work ethic, she'd amassed a nice little nest egg. She'd never told any of her suitors about her bank accounts; and she wasn't about to tell her new hubby much either; just in case things didn't work out.

Dario told her he that he used to own an Italian villa, which was located on the outskirts of town. He drove her by the opulent villa. It was perched high on a hill, the tile roof shimmering in the sunshine. "The villa has been in my family for over a generation. My grandmother moved here from Palermo as a child. She lived there with my grandfather."

"So...who lives there now? Do you live there?"

"Yes. Also my rich, eccentric aunt Gloria lives there, with her new hubby. She now owns the villa. My folks are deceased. She bought out the other family members. Although she owns the villa, family members are always welcome to stay there. It's a massive house. Aunt Gloria and Uncle Martin throw a lot of dinner and cocktail parties. We'll go to some of them."

Danielle was in seventh heaven. Never in her wildest dreams did she think she would be lucky enough to hook up with a gorgeous hunk like Dario. Witty and bright, he kept her on her toes. She couldn't wait to meet his aunt and uncle and see the opulent villa. It looked incredible from the street.

She'd come home early, unexpectedly, from a meeting with her business partner. Peering around the house, she couldn't locate Dario. Finally, she opened the door to her private office. She watched with mounting horror as her new hubby rifled through her files. His back was to her. She'd slipped, noiselessly into her office. Outraged, she confronted him. "What...are you doing?" She stood at the door to her office, hands on her hips. Livid.

He swung around with the speed of lightening. His eyes were steel, devoid of any warmth or humor. His tone was ice cold. "We are married. Why do you want secrets from me?"

"Who said they were secrets? I want to know what you are doing meddling in my files!" She was irate.

He moved toward her, suddenly becoming violent. He snapped her hands behind her back. "I'm the head of this household and you are not allowed to keep secrets from me. I was merely trying to gain an understanding of your various businesses. You have not been forthcoming about them. It was time for me to take matters into my own hands."

"How *dare* you? Who do you think you are? We're married. That doesn't mean you *own* me! And it doesn't mean you get to control my businesses, either." Her mind was racing. Something was very wrong with this picture. "I think we need to have a meeting with my attorney present." Her voice was steel, despite the fact that she was shaking inside and felt like bawling.

He morphed back to Mr. Charm. "Hey...hey... hey, honey...relax. I just wanted to find out a few things so I can help you..." He moved closer to her and grinned, pulling her close to him as his lips came down on hers.

She was a goner. One heady whiff of Dario's after-shave was all it took. Basking in his masculinity, she melted. It had been much too long since a man she found attractive had held her close, made her feel like a woman...desirable and beautiful.

They made love. She was putty in his hands.

A couple hours later, he knew everything about her businesses and had begun urging her to tear up the prenuptial agreement. "There are some things in life more important than money," he assured her. He kissed her again.

Suddenly, nothing mattered to her but the intense passion they shared and the love for him that was blossoming.

In the cold light of the next morning, Danielle was sure she needed her head examined. And actually...she did. She had willingly signed off on the prenuptial. They now jointly owned everything together. *What had she been thinking?*

Danielle met her closest girlfriend Gigi for lunch at a popular cafe in town. As they picked on their Cobb salads, Danielle fessed up that she'd been desperate for a man and was putty in his hands.

"Am I supposed to be surprised?" Gigi shook her head.

"I was so desperate that I turned a blind eye to his faults. I suppose one could argue that I bought him. Because actually... I guess I did... as pathetic as that is."

"Okay. Now what? Surely you're not going to divorce him after signing over your assets to him, are you? You've bought yourself a husband. Enjoy him."

"I wish I could, but it isn't that simple." Danielle burst into tears. "He's filing for divorce as we speak." She couldn't stop the flood of tears cascading down her cheeks. She choked back powerful emotions. "I'm in love with him...I knew what he was up to...of course...but I guess I was willing to pay any price to keep him...to have a man. Pathetic, isn't it?"

"Danielle. Maybe now is a good time. Maybe God allowed all this stuff to happen to get your attention. When did you last attend church?"

"Come on, Gi Gi. Give me a break. You know I'm a believer..."

"A backslidden one..."

"Gi Gi. Why are you being so hard on me? I've just been through major trauma and you're pushing religion on me?"

"Wrong." Gi Gi pushed back wisps of wavy, unruly

hair from her face. "I'm just sayin' that if you had been walkin' close to the Lord, you would have heard his still, small voice warnin' you of wolves in sheep's clothing."

"Spare me the lecture, GiGi. I need a friend right now. You've always been there for me...and I'm grateful for that..."

"Thanks. And since I *am* really your friend, I need to share some truths with you. If you continue down the path you're on, I don't think your life will come together the way you want it to."

"Give me a break, GiGi." Danielle stood up. "The last thing I need right now is a lecture."

"Sit down, Danielle. How long have we been best friends?"

"Uh...around twenty-five years, isn't it?"

"Twenty-six, to be exact. Here's the deal. Ever since Rolf died...what...about...fifteen years ago...?"

"Fourteen."

"Well, ever since he died, you've been on a manhunt. You finally got married to a taker. We both know he's not the real deal."

"Where are you going with this?" Danielle sighed, frustrated.

"My dear; if you had spent copious amounts of time in the Word, attending the Bible classes, studying the Word diligently, like I do, and mingling with the folks at church, I bet anything you would be married to a great guy by now. I mean...look at you...you're gorgeous, smart, witty..."

"Don't forget rich. *Used to be rich.* Give me a break, Gi Gi, I had enough religion crammed down my throat as a kid...to last me a lifetime. You know that's why

I'm turned off the women's Bible studies and that sort of thing..."

"I want you to admit that you've failed. Miserably. Throw yourself on the mercy of God and start over. Get down on your knees and ask God for a miracle. You worked hard for that money and I really hate to see this taker grab it all. I'm thinking maybe the deal can be reversed, because you signed it under duress. Get yourself a good attorney to rep you. I just happen to know one."

"You, of course."

" No. Not me. I'll give you the name of an attorney who specializes in these kind of cases. His name is Bart Herzog. You should offer him a percentage. It will be worth it for you."

"Okay. I guess you have a point."

"I'm not through yet. If you spent as much time studying the Word as you do hunting for men online, I believe that God would have brought you your dream man."

"Isn't that a bit niave, Gi Gi.? Do any of us know what God would actually do?"

"We have a strong inkling of what he might do. Check out Ephesians 6 verse 10. *"If you delight yourself in Me, I will give you the desires of your heart."* She smiled. "Okay, that's it "

"After that lecture, I don't need to go to church. I've already heard the sermon. But, guess what? I'm not going to do that. If God doesn't love me enough to give me a man, based on the fact that he created me to need one and he knows what would make me happy...so I'm going to give the church thing a pass."

"Okay. That's your choice. I'm done." Gi Gi was

silent for a few beats. "I'm going to shake the dust of my feet and stop witnessing to you. I'll get the bill." She signalled the waiter. "Oh, that scripture is found in....."

"I'll get this lunch. I invited *you*, remember?" Danielle smiled, her dimples showing.

"No. I insist. I'm so sorry...but I need to end this friendship right now."

The waiter arrived with the bill. GiGi grabbed it.

"What on earth are you talking about?" Danielle was stunned.

"I have spent many years trying to wake you up spiritually. It's time for me to move on. There are millions of hungry souls in the world, spiritually speaking. They're anxious and willing to drink of the deep well of water God offers... willing to study... to show themselves approved." She stopped for a moment. "We've been over this territory for many years. And you never change... never grow...when it comes to the Word. I'll leave you with one scripture. *"I would that you were hot or cold, but because you are luke-warm, I will spue you out of my mouth."* "Do you really want God to spue you out of his mouth?"

"I can't believe you're abandoning me when I need you the most!"

"Frankly, darling. It's because I *do* care. I care deeply about your spiritual life and I love you. That's why I'm walking away from you. It might be the wake-up call you need."

Danielle slapped down her credit card. "This is the worst month of my life. First, the marital disaster... now my best friend turning her back on me..." Tears trickled down her cheeks and she sniffed, pulling out a Kleenex from her purse.

"Come on, let's get out of here." Gigi fished in her purse, pulling out the card for the attorney. She handed it to Danielle. "Here's the attorney's card. He just might be able to reverse the damage your new hubby caused. But, you'd better move fast. Call him right now. Request an appointment at his earliest convenience. Tell him it's urgent. Time is of the essence. Do you think your hubby might have packed up and vanished before you even return home?"

Danielle smirked. "No. I think he'll want one last roll in the hay. And that little weakness on his part...might just be the extra time I need to get my case together." Danielle signed her Visa, grabbed a copy of it, and punched in the numbers for the attorney, reading them from the card, as they moved toward the front door. "It went directly to voice mail." She glanced over at Gi Gi. "This is Danielle Lockhart. GiGi Olson recommended me. It is urgent that I see you as soon as possible It's a marital dispute...financial. I signed over my assets to my hubby under duress." She left her phone number.

"If I were you...and I know I'm not; I would find a church and get down on my knees and pray. You've worked hard all your life...and amassed a nice little nest egg... and for that..."Toy Boy"... to sweep in and snatch up your hard earned cash... well, it's obscene."

Danielle was bawling, as they walked together from the restaurant to the parking area. Gi Gi wrapped her arms around Danielle, comforting her. "I'm not going to reneg...no matter how hard you cry. Because I deeply care for you...for your well being...for your soul, I need to move on. At the risk of pushing it...may I share some gems of biblical wisdom with you?"

Danielle sniffled. "Why stop now?" She smiled through her tears.

"Malachi 9. It talks about a curse over your finances. That happens when you're not tithing or at least giving generously to the work of the Lord. That may be at the root of this...that and a Satanic attack. The adversary used your weakness in desiring a man...to the point of being obsessed... and because you are not walking closely with the Lord, your judgement was off and you made a grave error...by marrying this guy... and then allowing him to take advantage of you financially..."

"What am I supposed to do now? The damage has been done."

"Fall on God's mercy. Seek Him with all your heart, mind and soul...and don't lean on your own understanding. In all your ways acknowledge Him and he will direct your paths. That's paraphrased from the Good Book."

"So...I should go to church and pray...I guess I'm ready to do that...I've got nowhere else to go." Danielle dried her tears.

"If I were you, I would spend the rest of the day on my knees. Start by thanking God for all that he has given you. Praise Him for the miracles in your life, for Dana's new hubby and the countless blessings you receive from his generous, loving hand every day." GiGi glanced at her watch. "I have a meeting to get to. I've got to race out of here. Bye. I'll be prayin' for you."

Chapter Five

Dana and Graham were greatly disturbed. They made an appointment to see their minister, requesting emergency prayer. "Please ask the prayer warriors to pray for Will's protection and his safe, speedy return. We'll be fasting and praying, also."

Tobias Chalmers, their minister, prayed with them and assured them that he and the prayer warriors would continue to pray diligently for Will's safe return.

Three Weeks Later

Graham had been sleeping sporadically ever since Will had disappeared. The rest of the time he and Dana were on their knees praying for his quick, safe return. Still, there was no break in the case. He was bone weary.

So was Dana. They had just finished lunch. Dana had made Mexican food, in the hope of stimulating Graham's appetite. It worked. Graham loved hot, spicy food. She'd been concerned about his loss of appetite. Not that hers was much better. They were finishing their coffee when Dana laid down the law.

"Graham...we...we can't go on like this. We need to trust in the Lord and not lean on our own understanding..."

Graham finished the scripture passage for her. "In all your ways, acknowledge Him and he will direct your paths."

"Honey, we've fasted, we've prayed...and we have sought God with all our hearts and minds and souls...and still, we have heard nothing. What are we going to do? We've got to get Will back." Dana burst into tears. Somehow, she thought this was her fault...somehow that recurring thought kept niggling at her.

Violet puttered around the kitchen and family room, watering plants. "Why don't the two of you go for a drive? Just don't forget your cells. I'll hold down the fort. Jay and I are very capable of doing that. Wilbur and Pete will take care of the farm. Go for a drive and have lunch out. As long as you have your cells with you, you're good."

"Okay, okay. I know when I'm outnumbered. I can't pray anymore, anyway. I'm all prayed out." Graham covered his face with his hands and bawled like a kid. "I'm sorry, Dana. I just couldn't stop the urge to cry."

She held him in her arms. "Cry, my darling, cry. God hears you. God knows how broken your heart is...let it all hang out. Somehow...maybe when we least expect it...Will is going to show up at the door with a big grin on his face...and tell us about his...hairy adventure." Dana forced a smile.

"Do you really think so, honey?" The glimmer of a grin formed on his lips. "You're not just saying that?"

"No, Graham. I'm not just saying that. The Holy

Spirit has impressed on me that he is going to walk in that door...soon."

"Then...shouldn't we be here... waiting for him?"

"No. I think God wants us to step out in faith. We prayed. We've sought him with our whole heart...now we need to trust that He heard our prayer and will answer it. The God who created the universe...who formed us fearfully and wonderfully...that same God will cause Will's miraculous return. I can just see it. *I have seen it in my spirit*." Dana smiled at Graham. She wanted them both to keep their spirits up.

"Then why should we take a drive? Shouldn't we stay home?" Graham raised his eyebrows in question.

"We'll step out in faith. We'll have lunch out and wait for the call and the instructions."

"Okay, Dana....we'll do it, if you feel that strongly about it. I know you're as upset and devastated as I am about Will's disappearance...so, yeah...let's go for a drive. We've been holed up here for days without leaving the house...it will probably do us both a lot of good...to get out...enjoy the drive and the sunshine and get our minds off the horror of it all. Maybe...the fresh air will give us a fresh perspective."

Graham put the top down on his Jeep. They drove out to Villa Da Vinci for lunch.

"That balmy breeze is so stimulating, Graham. I'm glad we got out of the house."

"Me, too. It was the right choice." Graham kept his eyes on the road until they reached the Villa for lunch.

Graham's cell chirped just as they drove onto the parking lot. A male voice, authoritative and laced with power barked out a message. "A million bucks and you get the kid back. We've got him. Wanna hear his voice?"

Graham was relieved and disgusted. "Put him on, please."

A few beats later, Will was on the phone, his voice shaky. "It's me, Dad. I'm okay. They want money. Lots of it."

"Take it easy, son. I'll pay and you'll come home..."

"I'm...not sure they won't double cross you, Dad..."

He could hear the phone being wrenched away from his son; but not before he'd warned them. If they just knew where he was, they could deal with the issues as they came up. "Where are you, son?" Graham yelled.

Before he could answer, the phone was wrenched away from him. The thug was back on the line. "Meet us at Lone Creek...do you know where it is?."

"Matter of fact, I do." Graham said. "We'll watch for you at exactly 5:00 p.m. tonight. If our count verifies one million bucks, you get your son back, unharmed. You pull any pranks. *Any* pranks, and we give you no guarantees about your son. Bring the cash in twenties and fifties. A guy calling himself Bart will do the exchange. We'll be real close by, so don't try any pranks. If we see a sheriff or the police, or if you try to muck around in any way, all bets are off; and we won't guarantee the safe return of the kid. Only if you do *exactly* as we say, will you get your son back. You got that?"

"Yeah. "

"We look forward to makin' the exchange." The man with the cold, brittle voice spoke loudly and evenly as he barked out the instructions.

Graham got chills.

She jumped into the Jeep next to Graham as he drove away from the driveway of the ranch.

Graham had worked hard for his money. He'd been frugal, made good investments including his recent purchase of Sugarbush. Dana was sure he couldn't afford to lose a million dollars. She whispered a prayer to the heavenly father. *"Lord, help us. Is there any way we can get Will back without paying the ransom?"*

Like lightening, it hit her. She smirked and turned to Graham. "These guys aren't geniuses, though they think they are. If we can get a suitcase and fill it with fake bills and get the sheriff and his men hiding nearby, maybe we can nail these bad actors and get Will back without handing over a million dollars to them." Dana peered over at Graham to gauge his response.

"We can't chance it. If they figure out the bills are fake, they could become irate...and God only knows what they might do to Will, then. No, we'd better do exactly as they say. They're not playing around; and we can't either."

"Well... what about the sheriff and his boys? How close can they come?"

"Not very. These guys are pros. They've probably pulled this scam before. Their men will be watching for anything off base."

"Are you sure they will give us Will back?"

"No. It's a chance we have to take. They will guess that the sheriff and his boys will be hiding nearby. Their modus operandi might change at the last minute. If it does; we have no choice, but to go along with it."

"I wonder why they chose the secret ranch for the meeting place."

"Who knows? Anyway, they likely have some goons standing by, in case there is any trouble."

Dana's mind flashed back to Billy. *Could he be involved? She wasn't about to bring up his name, though.*

Chapter Six

Danielle was beside herself. She really
didn't want to spend the afternoon praying at the church
like GiGi had urged her to do. Maybe she would stop
by and have a brief prayer though, before she headed
home to deal with the issues at hand. She parked her car
on the church lot. She'd remembered that the quaint,
white church on the hillside was open during the day
for prayer. She'd seen the sign when she'd driven by.

She opened the church door, glancing around the
room. She spotted her husband instantly. He was on his
knees, his head bowed, praying fervently.

A couple of older woman were crouched on their
knees near the back of the sanctuary.

She moved noiselessly toward her hubby, taking a
seat in the pew behind him. She hated herself for
listening in. He was praying aloud, in a hoarse whisper,
pleading for forgiveness. Though his voice was barely
audible, somehow she could make out every word he
uttered. "*Lord, I have sinned. I have used the lovely
woman you brought into my life. I stole her money,
Lord. Forgive me. But Father, you know the dilemma
I'm facing...you know the pressures I'm under...you*

know the sorrows and burdens I have...forgive me, Lord. But I'm taking the rest of the cash and leaving tonight..."

Danielle stopped herself from gasping. *This was a warning from God.* Swiftly and silently, she moved out from the pew she'd intended to kneel at, hurrying to the exit door at the rear of the church. She let herself out as quickly and noiselessly as she could.

She hurried over to her Mercedes in the small parking lot. Opening the door, she slid into the driver's seat, and spun out of the parking lot, her emotions running wild.

Letting herself into her house, she faced another shock. The entire place was in utter chaos. Every paper, every document, every file had been rifled. The small safe which held emergency cash was open. The cash was gone. "Lord, what have I gotten myself into?"

She couldn't call Dana and Graham. They had their own problems. Besides, she was persona non grata with them. The Good Lord knew they were in the midst of their own crisis. She couldn't call Gi Gi. They were no longer friends, so she'd told her at lunch. Who could she call? She quickly sifted through her friends in her mind and came up empty. With her two best choices off the boards, she decided to call the minister at her church. The church she rarely attended; Sunny Acres Evangelical Church. A recording came on after a couple of rings. She waited until it ended, and then left a message. "I have an urgent prayer request...and an urgent matter to deal with." She left her cell number. "I'll be lucky if I get a call back." She spoke the words aloud, flopped down on the sofa, and poured herself a glass of good Cabernet. Miraculously, her scoundrel of a hubby had not touched the wine cellar. *I guess he has bigger fish to fry.*

The wine would relax her while she waited...and prayed for a miracle. She took a sip of the fine wine quickly realizing it wouldn't solve anything. She was in deep, deep trouble. *Only God Almighty could help her.* She threw the wine down the sink and knew it was time to repent. Repent of her apathy toward God. Repent of her jealousy toward Dana. Repent of running ahead of God and grabbing a Toy Boy in desperation. Repent of...so many, many things. Tears gushed from eyes like the overflowing of an artesian well.

The repentance came from somewhere deep inside. From some hidden, private place that only God understood. "Lord, I'm sorry. I know I've been running from you. I've been running fast and furious, determined to avoid you." She sobbed. "I'm done running Lord. I can't make it without you. I admit I'm a failure. I confess my sin of apathy...of being lukewarm...of not following you...Lord... I am so... so sorry. Please forgive me." Once the tears started, they wouldn't stop.

"I...hated Dana when she hooked up with Graham! Hated her so much...I almost felt like...murdering her...Oh Lord...I can't believe I've sunk this low. If Dana knew...she would be heartbroken, if she knew the depths of my jealousy toward her...if she knew that I secretly wanted Graham for myself...oh Lord, how have I stooped so low? How did I get to this place?"

She heard him speak then. His voice seemed audible, though it was actually a voice in her spirit. *"My precious, precious daughter. You have wandered so far, but you have come home...and just like the prodigal son, my arms are open to embrace you...to welcome you home. I love you. I died for you. You are precious to me. I have allowed all these setbacks and disasters to overtake you, because of my great love for you. And now, my daughter, I forgive you, because I know your repentance springs from deep in your soul. You have come up from the bowels of the sea. And I am here, waiting for you. I've been waiting for you for a long time. I sent my people across your path, but you did not embrace them. I kept sending them, but your heart was hardened. You wanted to go your own way. So I had to let you. You have free will. I knew you would return to me. And I knew what it would take. And so, my precious, precious child, my arms encircle you, my love overflows for you. And I have a little surprise for you. If you will share your faith with your new husband...really share your faith...he will find Me in a new and deeper way, and then I will cause the two of you to live together in harmony. Do not worry about the money you have lost. Do not give it any thought. If my people just knew how inconsequential money actually is, they would be amazed. They think life is about amassing a fortune, or making money and living the high life. They do not realize that the highest and most glorious life is the life I have called them to. A life of devotion to Me. A life of sacrifice, joy, abundance, generosity and great, great favor. A life that only I can provide. And so, my precious, precious daughter, enjoy your evening. Embrace your life. Enjoy your new husband. I will take the rocky road you started out on and turn those rocks to smooth stones, as smooth as glass. And when you next look in the mirror you will see...not just YOUR face but you will see ME. reflected in your eyes. You will know a softness you've never known before. A gentleness you often admired in others. That quality has not manifested itself in you because of your sins."*

Suddenly, the outpouring of the Spirit was gone and Danielle was in a state of utter and absolute amazement. "Lord, what happened?"

The door opened ushering in her hubby. He was grinning as he moved toward her, soon taking her in his arms. "I'm sorry, gorgeous. I really am."

She found him exciting. Sexy. She had from the moment she'd laid eyes on him. "I'm just...I'm okay. How are you?" *Was she really going to ignore everything that had happened between them? Only a few feet away stood the safe which was now empty.*

"I'm good. I went shopping at the supermarket. Do you like Italian food?"

"You have to ask?" She raised her eyebrows.

"I'll start boiling the water for pasta. I'm making you clams linguini."

"Impressive." She peered over at him, stunned. "I'll... set the table and... fix a salad." *I'll ask him about the money from the safe, later.*

Chapter Seven

Zero hour.

Graham held the suitcase containing the small bills.

Graham and Dana had been on their knees for a couple of hours, having risen at 4:30 this morning. They'd called every prayer chain they knew about. It was 7:00 a.m. They'd both taken a quick shower before heading into the kitchen for breakfast.

"Breakfast is ready and waiting...waffles with sour cream and fresh strawberries." Violet smiled, as she served them.

"Yum." Jay appeared at the table, taking a seat."Save some for Will. He'll be home today." Jay smiled brightly. He was about to dig in when he spotted Graham peering at him. *The blessing, of course.*

Graham bowed his head. "Lord, we give thanks for this food; and we give thanks for the safe return of Will.

Dana and Jay bowed their heads also.

They ate in silence.

Graham peered over at Dana, finally speaking. "How dare these gangsters demand a million dollars for the return of my son?"

"Well, thank God you managed to raise the cash, anyway." Violet hovered over them with the coffee pot, topping up their mugs.

"It's a lot of cash. It cut sharply into my savings account and... investments." He'd raised the cash, of course. But it grated against him that these thugs were confident they would get away with this. He would teach them a lesson they would never forget. *I'll get fake bills. I'll need to move fast to set that up. How would they know until they tried to cash them? Fake money was pretty much identical to real money. Dana was right.* He'd checked it out carefully. Even the experts had trouble identifying the bills to determine their authenticity. It was a cinch. He wouldn't tell Dana that he was taking her suggestion. Not now anyway. He wouldn't tell anyone.

Graham forbade Dana to join him on the drive to meet the kidnappers and make the exchange.

"I'd like to go with you, Graham." Dana took a sip of the coffee, peering over at Graham.

"No way, Dana. I'm not going to worry about you. You're staying right here. Please."

"I wish I could go. But I know I can't." Dana sighed, wistfully. She was gradually learning to obey most of Graham's orders. Still, she did not want to sit at home waiting to hear word that Will had miraculously returned home. She was a front lines person. She'd been that way all her life. Not even her new hubby could restrain her. Yeah, she knew she was a lot like her feisty Thoroughbreds. They chomped at the bit to be part of the action, whatever it was. And as a former Show Jumper, she'd been   front and center.

Where the cameras were.

Where the action was.

A leopard didn't change his spots.

Graham didn't like to keep things from Dana. He cherished being able to share pretty much everything with her. But the fake bills would be a secret for now.

Graham had filled the suitcase with cash. He'd left it by the front door. He would pick it up on his way to the Jeep.

The sheriff and deputy sheriff would be escorting him on the mission. They would be undercover and hiding nearby, since he was instructed to come alone when the exchange took place.

Graham had hired a marksman, though he hadn't confided that to the sheriff. The sniper would already be stationed at a strategic point near where the exchange was to take place. "It's up to the Lord from here on in. We've done everything we know to do, it's up to Him to deliver Will back to us and capture the bad guys." Graham's voice took on a somber tone. *But his conscience niggled at him. Was he really so obsessed with his money, that he was willing to gamble with his son's life? Get thee behind me, Satan.*

"God doesn't want me throwing my money away." He whispered to himself. *But even as he uttered the words, he knew he had made a grave error. Hadn't he promised the kidnappers he would give them a million dollars for the safe return of his son?* He'd flat out lied. He had fake cash in the suitcase, and had convinced himself that it was okay, because the kidnappers had no right to demand his hard-earned cash. *They'd taken his youngest son and held him up for ransom. They were the scum of the earth.*

"Something...is going to go wrong...I don't what...but the Lord is showing me that." Dana's voice was somber, as she walked with Graham toward the front door, where the suitcase filled with cash was ready and waiting.

Graham's hand was shaking as he picked it up. He had been told to come alone, of course. Still, they would expect that he'd have law enforcement nearby. He regretted weakening and allowing Dana to join them, once she'd leaned on him. *What had he been thinking?* The Sheriff and Deputy Sheriff had been adamant about Dana not joining them. They'd specifically forbidden it.

Dana insisted she could handle herself. And he had to admit she knew how to handle a gun. She could take care of herself. She wouldn't take no for an answer, anyway. She'd insisted on being where the action was. He didn't want to fight with her. Not so soon after their glorious honeymoon.

Graham and his entourage drove to the ranch. They were approaching the property when his cell chirped. "There's been a change of plans. Meet us at trailer #7 at Willow Tree Trailer Park. We know you've been there before. So don't play like you don't know where it is. 3:00 sharp. Do not be late. And make sure you come alone. Or you'll regret it."

Graham shook his head. *Like he's going to be late for this event? An event he prayed would end with him getting his beloved son back.* "Right. I know where it is. I'd like to speak to my son. I want to make sure he's all right."

"You're pushin' your luck, Hot Shot. But you're

lucky I happen to be in a good mood today...so I'm gonna grant you your wish."

He heard voices in the background. "Will....´Seems your old man wants to hear your voice. Wants to make sure you're alive." He dripped sarcasm. "You're lucky you've got someone who cares."

Will was crying and shaking. His captors had pushed some scrambled eggs in front of him earlier that morning, but he'd had no appetite. He'd barely eaten anything in days. "Not hungry." His face was drained of all color and he'd lost some weight. The mobile unit they moved him to was quite nice. He remembered his dad saying he suspected it was a stash house.

"You should be happy, Kid. You get to go home today. I never had a home. Lucky you. Somebody cares enough to put up a million bucks to get you back. From what I've heard, it won't even make a dent in your rich Daddy's finances."

"Don't believe everything you hear." Tears tumbled down Will's cheeks. He sniffled.

"Don't be a smart ass, Kid."

"Sorry, I..."

"Come on. Say a quick hello to your Dad on my cell. Then, we're outta here."

"Where are we going?"

"You'll find out soon enough."

The exchange did not go well. Graham hadn't slept much since the ordeal began; though he was prayed up. Still, apprehension churned in his gut. *There's going to be a complication. I don't know what it is, but I know there's going to be one.*

Graham wasn't nervous. He was steady as a rock. He

strode out to the marked location, suitcase in hand. He saw the captor from a short distance. Will was with him. *What could possibly go amiss?* "Okay, you give me my son — you get the cash."

The sniper he'd hired grazed the kidnapper's shoulder. He screamed in pain. Angered and caught off guard, he reached for his gun.

In that split second, Will rushed toward Graham, as though it had been carefully orchestrated. There was no time to embrace. No time for emotion. He didn't trust the captors, of course; and didn't know what to expect next. Sure, he had back-up. But would it be effective? "Let's go, Will. Run." Graham had Will and the suitcase stuffed with the fake bills.

The sniper downed Billy. He screamed and writhed in pain. He was on the ground. Shane, his accomplice ran off.

But as Graham and Will raced to his Jeep, he realized Dana was not there. "Where is Dana?" He was fighting panic. He peered at the sheriff and deputy sheriff who were in their vehicle, right next to his. With mounting horror, he screamed her name. "Dana! Dana!"

Dead silence.

His heart was in his throat. What had he done? Tried to save a million dollars; and tried to placate his wife. He'd lied to the kidnappers. Maybe God hadn't protected them. Because Dana had disappeared.

So much for his hair-brained scheme of bringing fake bills. Dana was...gone. They'd taken her. Outsmarted him. He'd double-crossed *them* because he felt justified. *But he'd still double-crossed them.* While he focused on getting his son back, the kidnappers snatched Dana.

"They've taken Dana! And when they realize the bills are fake, they're going to be ten times harder to deal with!" He called her name over and over again. Panic seized him as mounting horror soared through him, bringing tears to his eyes. *Lord, what have I done? What was I thinking?*

The tires had been shot out on his jeep. He glanced at the sheriff. "I know...I know, you did your job...you warned me not to try to outsmart them. And I blew it. Though it's a moot point now, I thought we would be able to pull it off. I never should have allowed Dana to come along."

"We both know Dana wouldn't have taken no for an answer, if that's any consolation." The deputy sheriff sighed.

"Well, the good news Graham... is that they will want to keep Dana alive while they make their outrageous demands. They're bound to ask for two or three million now. That's my best guess." the sheriff shook his head, sadly.

"They'll want to keep you alive to make sure you deliver their cash. Maybe Will can shed some light on their operation." The deputy sheriff sighed. "Which...they will doubtless change totally...if they try this again."

Will was blurting out information about the gangsters a mile a minute. "Well...like Dad...they were actually quite nice to me. Like...they fed me cool stuff...the one guy...the nicer one...well, he liked to cook. He made spaghetti and a really amazing sauce. He said he used to be a chef."

Graham grinned. It was great to have his son back.

Thank-you, Lord. Will always chattered incessantly when he was nervous or excited.

"I've called for backup and sent an All-points bulletin calling for roadblocks...." The sheriff's voice droned in his ears.

It was a bad dream. A nightmare. He would wake up any minute and Dana would smile and bat her aqua green eyes at him. "Gotcha! Just kidding! I'm right here...watching an old black and white movie on TV." But she wasn't going to be at home. He had allowed her to go on this mission against his better judgement. He'd been preoccupied with the money and the goal of getting Will back. "Lord, I blew it! I'm in really, really big trouble. Only *you* can help me. Only *you* can lead us to Dana. I repent of not honoring the arrangement I made with the kidnappers. Lord, please forgive me and bring Dana safely home. I know I need to give them real cash. I really...really blew it." He put his hands over his face and sobbed bitterly, as he slumped down in the back seat of the sheriff's unmarked vehicle.

The sheriff and deputy sheriff sat in the front of the car. "We'll call a tow truck for the Jeep." The sheriff was on his cell organizing it.

"I need to get Will home." Graham was overcome with emotion.

"No. If we're going to have a chance of picking up these thugs that have kidnapped Dana, it's going to be right now." The sheriff drove out of the trailer park and down Holt Road which led to the main artery. The secret ranch was only a few miles down the road. "They might be at the ranch. Maybe they still live there. Cowboy by day — crook by night? Who knows?" The sheriff shrugged.

"I wish it was that easy. No. My best guess is that they will take Dana to a remote location a long way from here. I cringe to think what they might do...what they might try. You get a bad guy angry and you open a hornet's nest..." The deputy sheriff spoke from decades of experience. He gazed heavenward. "I guess...all we can do is pray that God will lead us to them" He shook his head in dismay. "And cause a miracle to happen. We have to believe God that she will be set free without any harm done to her."

Chapter Eight

It wasn't possible. It was a bad dream. A ghastly nightmare. His beloved Dana could not be missing. Graham wanted to bang his head against the wall. *What was I thinking? Lord. I am so, so sorry. Whatever made me decide to use fake bills? How could I have opened a Pandora's box with these bad actors?*

The roadblocks turned up nothing. He kept calling her, despite knowing the futility of it all.

"It's 11:00 P.M. Graham. We have no tips. Nothing. The best thing you can do is to go home and...pray...I don't know what else to tell you. My best guess is that you will hear from them within 24 hours...maybe 48. They want to make you sweat...they'll figure that gives them more leverage."

"Have you...been involved with many kidnapping before?"

"A few."

"And how they did they play out?"

"Not always good, I'm afraid. We had a case where the targeted man was not as rich as the kidnapper thought. Turns out his credit wasn't good, either. The

man   couldn't   raise   the   money."
Graham didn't want to hear the upshot. Still, the
pragmatic side of him wanted to know. Knowledge was
always power. Maybe one little thing he learned could
open his window of opportunity. One little piece of
information might make the difference. Who knew?
"So...he didn't get his kid... or wife back...or whoever
was kidnapped?"

"He almost got his wife back. One of the kidnappers
had a heart. The other one didn't."

"So what happened?"

"You don't want to know."

Graham could feel the color drain from his face. "He
never saw his wife again?"

"Yeah." The sheriff nodded, sadly.

Chills ran up and down Graham's spine.

"If we can find out where they are, we'll send in a
SWAT team in and get Dana back. You'd better pray
for a miracle.

Graham's cell rang. He picked it up. It was Dana.
"Dana! Where are you?"

"I'm not allowed to say. They're standing over me.
I've got two minutes with you. They want three million
in ransom."

Graham's heart sank. He'd worked hard all his life.
Sure, he'd come from a monied family, but there were
many expenses and financial obligations in his life.
Sugarbush was in a negative cash flow every month.
He'd lost a small fortune last year when Flaming Bullet
had been tampered with. That dream was gone...for
now at least. He had ranch hands to pay, horses to feed,
sons to raise and a wife to take care of ...until recently.
Three Million Dollars! He wasn't sure if he could raise

that much money on short notice. But he had to try. No, what was he thinking? He had to get it. As outrageous as the request was, he had to get the cash.

Graham reluctantly put in a call to his father. "Dad, I'm in a crisis. Your grandson was returned to me, as you know; now they have Dana and they're demanding three million for her return." Graham hadn't cried since the passing of his late wife, Myrna. But he was sobbing now.

"What in heaven's name are you talking about?"

"Dad... Dana's been kidnapped. They want three million for her safe return."

The silence was deafening. It was some time before his dad responded. "Son, I don't have that kind of cash available...few people do. How did they get her? What's going on? We need to get the press involved. What about hiring a private investigator?" His mind was racing a mile a minute. "Didn't you just cough up a million to get Will back?"

He couldn't lie to his dad. He'd been brought up to be truthful. He felt foolish and ashamed. "Dad...I...I blew it... big time."

"What are you talking about, son?"

He had to spit it out. Had to tell the truth. It was the last thing he wanted to do. But it had to happen. "I gave them fake dollars for Will. They grabbed Dana. Now they're furious. I haven't been able to sleep. I don't even want to think about they might do to her. Or God forbid, what might already have occurred."

"Son...you really are in a mess. I told you not to marry Dana in the first place. Your Mom and I both thought she was too headstrong for her own good. She's the wrong woman for you. As far as we're concerned...

she brought this trouble on herself. You told me you tried everything to dissuade her from going with you to get Will back... and she wouldn't listen. What kind of a wife is that? Honestly, I think you should divorce her."

"Dad! We're deliriously happy. You have no idea how wonderful she is! Okay, so she has a character flaw. Don't we all? Are *you* perfect? Am I? Is anyone? Dana has been wonderful...and I love her very deeply. We've bonded. The kids love her. We're a happy family..."

"Enough! I get it. And I also get that she'd blindsided you. Used you. Didn't she just step up in life by marrying you? Wasn't she renting somewhere...and had farmed out her horses? She doesn't sound very together to me..."

Graham hung up. He'd never done that before in his life with his dad. But this was his beloved wife he was talking about. *And the conversation was going nowhere. How dare him trash Dana, while her life and well-being are in grave danger? He had to wonder what was going on with his dad. He hadn't paid attention to his folks ever since Dana came on the scene. He'd better pay them a visit soon. Maybe his Dad felt neglected since Dana had come on the scene.*

He phoned Sybil. "Hey Sis. I should have phoned you sooner. I need to give you an update. The kidnappers are demanding three million for the safe return of Dana. I already told you I gave the thugs fake money...thought I could away with it. It was a...grave error of judgement. I know I have to take responsibility for my own actions...and...I really blew it." Graham fought tears and an overwhelming urge to bawl.

"Brother, dear, I love you so much. No matter how

much I see you, it is never enough. Dana really *is* the right woman for you. You made a sound decision marrying her. And we'll get her back. I know that because I've been seeking God 24/7. I know you're burnt out and haven't slept much...and I appreciate how much you must be suffering..."

"Hey, Sis. How about driving out here and staying for a while. I...really need you. We need to commiserate..."

"And more than that, I may be able to help you...with the money."

He realized suddenly that he had no idea what his sister's financial situation was. He only knew that her late hubby, a business mogul, had left her well-fixed. He didn't know how well, though.

Sybil pulled up to the house an hour and a half later, hopping out of her gray Jeep.

Graham saw her vehicle approaching and hurried down the steps to greet her.

Sybil stepped out of her jeep and into Graham's waiting arms.

"Thank God for you, Sis. I need you...so much." They strode up the front steps of the ancient house, and onto the veranda, soon moving into the house.

Violet greeted them in the kitchen with a warm smile. "I made a fresh pot of coffee and...look at this...sinfully fattening...sweet rolls." She passed the plate of rolls to each of them.

Graham took one. "Thanks."

Sybil took one, also. "Thanks, Violet."

"You always know the right thing to do...the right thing to say, Violet. I'm so glad you're here." Graham glanced over at her.

"Yeah. Everybody says that about me. I told you before...you're real lucky to have me." She smirked and headed out of the kitchen. "Got work to do. Catch you later." She gave an affected wave, akin to royalty and departed.

Sybil smiled.

"Oh...and, uh... I'll pick up the boys after school. You've got enough on your plate..." Violet smiled at her own joke.

"Thanks. I appreciate that, Violet." She really was a blessing and he trusted her judgement. She was one sharp cookie and knew the trouble that had beset him. Nobody would mess with her. He'd been stunned one day to discover she was a crack shot and kept a Colt 45 in her purse. She'd explained why. "Ever since I worked in South Africa, I've kept a gun in my purse. Never had to use it. Hope it stays that way." She'd shot Graham a look. "But let me assure you...guess I never did tell you...my Dad taught me to shoot ever since I was a kid." She'd chuckled. "And that was a long...long... time ago. I've kept up the skill by heading out to the shooting range every season. Didn't do it last year...but I'll get back to it now that I'm settled here at Sugarbush."

Graham took a healthy swig of the iced tea. They had settled in the family room. "Sybil. I'm in big trouble here. I don't know what possessed me to think that I could pull off giving the kidnappers fake money..."

"Yes. It was a mistake. And we all make them. Let's put that behind us and deal with the situation as it is."

"Thanks. What am I going to do, Sybil?"

"Well, big brother...first we're going to praise God that your son was returned with really...relatively little emotional damage. Kids are resilient. This will be an experience that will change him for life. You get that, of course. He'll never be the same. He may even do something remarkable in his life because of this trauma. Perhaps, something he might otherwise not have done. God always turns our tragedies into triumphs."

"You were always wise beyond your years, Sybil. Always so smart."

"Thanks, Graham. So...moving on...we need to praise God for Will as I said and praise Him in advance for the miraculous return of Dana. Because we *are* going to need a miracle. Dana is a gorgeous woman. I don't even want to think of the ramifications if we don't get her back. Fast. The possibilities are obvious and for that reason I won't state them. So, let us pray..."

They praised God and sought him with their whole hearts. An hour or so must have passed and then Sybil spoke. "Okay. God is giving me a plan. And here it is. I'm going to write you a check for a million dollars right now..."

Graham's eyes were like saucers. "You don't have that kind of money, Sybil. What are you thinking?"

"Who said I don't have that kind of money? Do you think I would write you a bouncing check?"

Graham peered over at his sister. "No, of course not. I...just didn't realize you had that kind of cash. I mean you live in a modest house...you drive that old Jeep..."

"What can I tell you, Graham. I have a few bucks stashed away for a rainy day. And it's raining real hard right now..."

"It sure is. But, Sybil...we still need a miracle. We prayed for protection for Dana, we prayed that by a miracle of His hand we would learn where she is...and get her back."

"The sheriff wants us to stop by his office this morning. They have an All Points Bulletin out on Bart Green. They've figured out who he is. Bart Green is an alias of course."

"Of course."

"The guy moves from state to state implementing various scams. He has a real serious record."

"I'm not surprised."

Chapter Nine

The sheriff and deputy sheriff ushered them into a room. "We haven't heard anything yet. No trickles of information. We're dealing with seasoned pros here. These boys aren't novices. We don't know who his accomplice is...but it's just a matter of time until some tips pour in...I'll be on the 6:00 P.M. news asking the public to be on the alert. We'll show photos of Bart, which have been digitally enhanced to reflect how he likely looks today."

"Thanks, I...ah...I need to go. I have an appointment with my banker." Graham turned to leave.

"Of course."

Sybil and Graham shook hands with the sheriff. "This will come out right in the end." The sheriff grinned, confidently.

"From your lips to God's ears."

Graham and Sybil jumped into his jeep. Sybil turned to him. "I would like to accompany you to the bank. Are you still with Bank of America?"

"I am."

"That's my bank, as well. My husband was friends

with the president; Jack Barnes."

"The manager is a hard nose. He's not an easy man to deal with."

"I'll make sure he treats you fairly. He is merely an employee. Jack has been president of that bank for decades. He's got clout."

They hopped into Graham's jeep. He drove out the gate at Sugarbush Farm.

Sybil's mind was whirling. "What about Villa Medici? It's worth a fortune. Couldn't you remortgage it and raise the three million?'

"I wish I could. It's a consortium, controlled by Dad. I thought you knew that. I have nothing to do with the financial aspect of it. It was Dad's generous gift to me. As his only son, he wanted me to have Villa Medici. You see, Sybil... it was his concept, originally. He and Mom had planned to come out every season during the Kentucky Derby and stay there... but as they got older, they lost interest in the sport. They still have a grand social life in Houston...most of their old friends are there. We put everything on hold... as you know... when Myrna's illness escalated. Then after her death, I lost my taste for business for some time...and so did Dad. My folks were so very fond of Myrna. They'd known her since she was a teenager. It was like losing a daughter rather than a daughter-in-law. And then...no one really measured up to Myrna. Particularly in my parents' eyes. Dana had large shoes to fill."

"I knew it was Dad's pet project, of course. But I thought you'd taken it over."

"I have. But only the operation. Not the financial aspect of it."

"Right. Well, don't worry, brother. It's only money.

When God closes one door, he always opens another."

"Thanks, Sis." Graham grinned. How he loved his only sister.

Violet cooked roast beef, serving it with mashed potatoes, gravy and carrots.

Everyone settled into the family room after dinner.

"What am I going to do, Sybil? What in heaven's name am I going to do?" Graham peered over at his sister.

"I don't know. But I know one thing. I'm going to stand with you until we get the money you need. Why don't you try again to reach Bart...maybe tell him you've raised two million and you're about to get the rest of it. Tell him you want to hear Dana's voice." She took a sip of the herb tea Violet had served them.

"Thanks, yeah. That's a good idea. I...I'm not thinking clearly...because I haven't been sleeping."

Sybil smiled and hugged her brother. "Big sister is here, Graham. You need moral support as much as anything else right now."

The meeting with the banker did not go well right from the start. Graham replayed the scenario in his mind. The banker had been burned a few times. He was reluctant to make large loans.

He and Sybil went out for coffee after the meeting. They found a quaint coffee house in the area. "I don't get this. I have a small mortgage on Sugarbush. And I've got three portfolios with a lot of stocks, bonds and commodities. My net worth is probably close to fifteen million...not counting Villa Medici. So what's the big deal about loaning me three million?"

"I don't know the answer. It's odd... to say the least. I know he went through a brutal divorce and his wife left him drained financially. She had her name on everything...for a banker...seems like he was not thinking clearly."

Anyway, call Bart... and...maybe ask to speak to Dana. We need an update. We haven't heard from him in a whole day." Sybil took a sip of coffee.

"Right. We'll get our mind off the financing issue. God is working behind the scenes."

"What about Danielle? She must be in bad shape...if she's not willing to get involved." Sybil raised her eyebrows.

"She is. She's in denial. Says she has her own problems and can't deal with this. She told me I married Dana and I need to take care of her."

"Come on. She didn't really say that, did she? That's the extent of her concern? I'm sorry...but that is...downright shocking. She is a successful businesswoman. I'm amazed she hasn't offered some serious cash to you."

"Well, she hasn't. In fact, I've heard very little from her. Maybe she just thinks I can write out a check...that raising three million is no big deal...all I know is that she's been pretty much incognito."

"Weird. Really weird. I think I should call her." Sybil peered over at Graham. "It's going to work out. I don't know how...but it will. I feel the Lord is showing me that."

"Thank you for that word. And, yes, do call her. Surely she cares enough about Dana to get involved."

Graham punched in Bart's phone number.

"Yeah. This is Bart. Did you raise the three mil?"

"I've got two. I'm workin' on raising the third million. I need to hear Dana's voice. I need to know how she is."

"No contact until you have three. You tell me you've got three; I'll give you the location for the exchange."

The line went dead. Graham phoned back right away.

"You messed with us. You better come up with three real fast. My patience is wearin' thin. You have one day left to raise it. Tomorrow you tell us you have three and you get to hear Dana's voice. You get her back if the bills are real. I'll have an expert with me to verify them."

"You better not have messed with her. I'm warning you. I'll get the money, don't sweat it." But he didn't know how he would come up with that kind of cash. Getting two million was fairly easy. But that last million...*Lord, how can I get it?*

Over coffee and chocolate squares, Sybil egged her brother on. "Call Danielle and ask for a meeting. Maybe she'll kick in some serious cash. Strange we haven't heard from her."

"Yeah. Ever since she got remarried...she's been incognito...and acting very odd." Graham glanced over at his sister.

"I smell trouble with the new hubby." Sybil raised her eyebrows. "I really feel that we should talk to Danielle. Maybe she can help us raise the third million."

"Sybil. I can't tell you how much I appreciate your moral support. Here's Danielle's number." He scribbled it on the back of a card. "Why don't you try her?"

Sybil punched in the numbers and let it ring for a

while. No answer. She left a message. Then she tried Bart. "Bart, this is Sybil, Graham's sister. We're working hard to get your third million. We have two. But we need to talk to Dana. How do we know she's even alive? And we don't know what kind of shape she's in. Call me back, please."

Late that night, Sybil's phone rang. She was staying at the ranch. She knew Graham needed her support more than he ever had.

"This is Bart. Get Graham. I'm puttin' Dana on."

Sybil was suddenly wide awake. Alert. She raced down the stairs and pounded on Graham's bedroom door. "Graham... it's Bart...he's on my cell. He's bringing Dana to the phone!"

Graham was instantly alert and excited. He grabbed the cell. "Dana? My darling ... how are you?" His heart sunk. She sounded weak and strained. He felt the color slowly drain from his face.

"I'm...I'm alive. I'm...all right."

"Are...are they treating you okay?"

Silence. A full minute ticked by. Finally, she spoke. "Yeah. Yeah...they are."

Graham didn't buy it. *She's been raped, Lord. I just know it.* He had to be strong. God was in control and he always would be. "Keep prayin', gorgeous. I love you. I'll get the third million and you'll be comin' home. Fair warning, darling. I'm never going to let you out of my sight again. I love you, beautiful." He fought the urge to bawl.

"I was hoping you'd say that. That's what I want, too. I love you so much, Graham."

Bart cut in on the call. He barked out orders in his

icy cold, brisk manner. "The call is over. You better have all the cash by tomorrow, or you'll never lay eyes on your broad again."

Graham's heart was in his throat. He knew Dana well enough to know that she was not only stressed but he guessed she'd been tampered with. *Lord, please let me be wrong. Please protect and watch over my precious angel.* He had to trust God for a million-dollar miracle and for the protection and safe return of his beloved Dana.

"I'm making a pot of coffee and we're going into prayer, Graham. Then, I want you to call Danielle...yes, in the middle of the night...and ask her if she can help raise the third million. It's her only daughter, after all. Actually, I can't believe she hasn't surfaced and worked with us on this. Okay, we know she had a quickie marriage...but given the magnitude of this crisis, I find it truly shocking that she hasn't surfaced."

"She's a...complex person. I've always sensed she has hidden agendas. I just wish I knew what they were. At one point, it almost seemed like she was flirting with me, but I kept ignoring it and eventually she tired of my lack of response. I sensed it irked her."

"That's really weird. I mean, I know Dana is adopted and all that, but it's still just so bizarre." Sybil shook her head.

Danielle was sleeping soundly despite Dana's crisis. The loud jangle of her ground line startled her awake. Dozy, she glanced at the number on the screen and picked up the phone. "Graham, how's it going?"

"I raised two million. I'm still short a million. Can you help? She doesn't sound good. We need to get her back...fast."

Dana, Dana, Dana. Everything is always about her. I was perfect for Graham, despite the fact that he didn't get that. I would have been lady of the Manor. I would have run things beautifully. I would have been too smart to tag along on a kidnapping quest. Too bad she got herself in hot water. I'm not going to help. I have my own problems. Big problems. Her mind was racing a mile a minute. *I'm sorry, God. I've already given up plenty for her. Don't I deserve some happiness?* "Graham...I don't know what to say. My new hubby just cleaned me out financially and I have a court case pending in the matter. I'm up to my eyeballs with financial problems."

Graham saw red. He rarely got really angry. But Danielle had been revealing the dark side of her character over time, and he was outraged at her reaction. The woman was ruthless, self-centered...and cold. He couldn't fathom how any human being... much less a step mom... could turn her head away from her adoptive daughter when she was facing a crisis of epic proportions. God would surely open another door for the cash. And He would deal with Danielle

.

"I'm sorry, Graham. That doesn't surprise me. I think the woman has some skeletons in her closet. She's hiding something. We need to move on. I'll get my Bible. We'll pray the 91st Psalm of protection over Dana. I phoned several churches, including, of course, your home church and asked them to put Dana on their emergency prayer list. I also requested prayer for us to raise another million dollars. Pronto." Sybil hurried back into the kitchen, Bible in hand. "I'm going to read some scriptures, starting with the 91st Psalm of protection over Dana. Then, we'll ask God to open the door for the rest of the money. Remember...with God nothing shall be impossible."

"Why don't we just praise Him and thank Him for it. We have asked him many times and now I think we should relax, sit in the living room and together just praise his holy name and believe for a miracle answer to prayer." Graham said.

Sybil peered over at her only sibling. "Good idea. We'll worship at his feet and praise him for all that he is and all that he has done for us. And for all the wonderful blessings we've received. And we'll praise him for a miracle."

More than an hour went by and finally Graham grinned, peering at his sister. "You know, Sybil...it occurs to me that perhaps if I go to my bank... and tell them I want to pay out the mortgage on the farm and refinance with another bank...well, maybe they'll suddenly come up with that third million. They won't want to lose a perfectly good mortgage and a perfectly good customer. I mean... given my equity in the farm and the appraisal, they know they can't lose."

"At the risk of sounding repetitive, Graham, the jealousy aspect factors in, also. You blew in from Houston. Nobody knows you here. You buy up choice real estate in Bluegrass country. And that Turn-of-the-Century mansion on it...well... folks might be a little green...with envy."

"I guess you're right, Sybil. I never thought of it that way."

Graham's cell rang. It was the sheriff. "Somebody...called in with a tip. A pizza guy...he was delivering a pizza to the industrial area of town, to what looked like an abandoned warehouse. When he drove up in his van and jumped out, a gorgeous blonde woman peered out through a dirty, cracked window, signaling she was in trouble and gesturing for him to call the police immediately. Then she ducked quickly out of sight. But not before making a gesture signaling she was in big trouble and being held against her will. Well, I may only be a pizza delivery boy but I'm not stupid. And I watch the news like everybody else. I figured it just might be that missing woman...the horse trainer."

"Hey, kid. Thanks. We appreciate the tip. Maybe it's her. You'll get a hefty reward if this tip leads us to the kidnappers and Dana. We're on our way as soon as we assemble a swat team. This tip could be an answer to prayer. She's being held for three million in ransom."

The kid let out a shrill whistle.

"What did the thugs look like? Can you describe them?"

"One of 'em was tall and skinny... dressed scrappy with jeans. Mousy hair. The other guy was kind of a good lookin' clever type. He seemed sharp. The skinny dude paid me. Oh...and I got the license plate of their black SUV." He grinned, proud of himself. He read off the number to the cops.

"Nice work, kid. We'll be in touch. And if this is the real deal, you'll get a hefty reward, of course. Gotta run."

Graham miraculously got the rest of the cash from the bank. It seems the general manager of the bank had a complete change of heart. "We'll be prayin' for Dana.

You'll get her back." He grinned, shaking hands with Graham.

Thank-you, Lord, for this miracle. Thank-you for hearing my fervent prayer.

Chapter Ten

The SWAT TEAM was ready to go. There was a lot of TV coverage about the case. They'd gotten the break they needed, it was time to smoke out the kidnappers and rescue Dana.

"Stand by with the three million. In case everything goes wrong, you'll need to pay. I can't see that happening. And you'll have a bodyguard. But we need to cover all the bases. Prepare for a worst-case scenario. We'll tell you where to park your car. We're going in tonight." Robbie, the SWAT TEAM leader barked out the information.

Sybil and Graham waited in an unmarked car, praying unceasingly. They knew the power of persistent prayer. God would honor their diligence.

ZERO HOUR.

The SWAT TEAM leader blasted out orders over a bullhorn. "You are surrounded! Come out with your hands-on top of your head! You have three minutes. Otherwise, we're comin' in!"

Silence.

Three minutes raced by. Robbie fired a warning shot. "Okay. We're comin' in."

"Crash!" The front door cracked open with a deafening thud. Next, he sent in a robot with a camera inside it, to survey the scene. Then, six men, highly skilled, clad in black, bullet-proof body suits and wearing wires, stormed the place.

Men were positioned on the roof and surrounding the warehouse.

Overhead, the ominous whir of a helicopter spiraling downward hovered over the building.

The kidnappers cowered in a corner of the warehouse. Frozen. Terrified.

Dana was crouched in an arm chair, clad in a man's shirt and jeans. She stood up when the commotion began. "God heard my prayer! This is a miracle!" Her hands were raised heavenward in praise. "I never stopped prayin! Never stopped believin' I'd be rescued...delivered from this ghastly nightmare!"

When she heard the commotion, she'd begun singing and praising the Lord with great gusto. "*Jesus is Lord! You are Lord. You are Lord. You have risen from the dead and you are Lord. Every knee shall bow, every tongue confess that Jesus Christ is Lord. You are Lord. You are Lord.*" She'd taken her inspiration from Paul in the Bible. When he was imprisoned, he sang worship and praise songs to the Lord. Soon, the prison doors were miraculously opened! An earthquake occurred, and he was set free. His friends had all been praying for a miracle and it happened.

The kidnappers fired shots toward the SWAT team guys, despite everything. The bullets bounced off their hardware. The SWAT team swarmed the place. Robbie wrested the gun out of Bart's hand, while Jason, another SWAT team member, snapped cuffs on him.

Bart and his accomplice cursed, squirming...but soon gave it up. "Hey, we didn't do nothin'...the broad liked me...she came on to me..."

"Sure she did." He shook his head in disgust at the lame retort. "Let's go, Bart. Your kidnapping days are over... you're going to be locked up for a long time."

He sputtered and squirmed while the guys grabbed his partner. Less aggressive, the partner put up little resistance. He glanced over at Bart. "I told you I had a bad feelin' about snatchin' that broad. I warned you..." the weaker partner snarled at his buddy.

The Swat team guys glanced at each other, stunned. One guy turned to his partner. "Twenty plus years I've been doin' this and I've never seen this before. Dana was praising God and thanking Him for a miracle...that just happened now. Isn't that something?"

His buddy shook his head in amazement. "It really is. The victims are usually curled up in a ball, weeping uncontrollably..."

"It's okay, Dana. We're here. It's over. We've got them. Your husband is outside waiting in a car."

Tears streamed down her face. She jumped up off the chair, tears of joy cascading down her face. "I knew I'd be rescued. I knew God would make a way. He's never stumped. Nothing is impossible for him. I never stopped praying...never stopped believing for a miracle."

One of the Swat Team guys leaned down, scooping her up in his arms. "It's over. It's okay. You're okay. God has spoken. He has delivered you from this horror show."

Dana managed a weak chuckle through her tears. "Yeah. Yeah... I'm alive. I'm definitely alive. Praise

God. I am alive! And I'm outta here!" She began weeping and laughing simultaneously, her voice laced with hysteria. She glanced heavenward. "Jesus is Lord! He did not forget me. He sent an angel...that pizza guy...heaven sent...gloriously... heaven sent. I want to kiss his face and... reward him financially. I can't wait to give him a hug and personally thank him."

"Let's get outta here." The swat team guy let Dana down but stayed next to her, escorting her outside.

The helicopter whirred overhead, spiraling higher and higher into the sky.

The mission had been accomplished.

Graham thought it was a mirage. She never looked more beautiful to him than she did at this moment. His face beamed with unspeakable joy. "Dana! My darling. It's over! It's really over! And you're safe. I'm never letting you out of my sight." He hugged her and whirled her around in circles.

Sybil had hopped out of the car when she'd spotted Dana with the SWAT TEAM guy heading toward them. She overflowed with joy. "I never doubted for a moment that God would bring you back, Dana."

Graham and Dana were escorted home by a couple of the SWAT team guys. Graham's Jeep had been left at the ranch, like the sheriff had instructed him to do. He had driven to the warehouse with the sheriff in his unmarked car.

Sybil smiled over at Dana and Graham. "I'm going to crash early. I know you two want to be alone." She winked at both of them and headed up the stairs to the guest room she usually occupied.

"I better call Mom." Dana told Graham as she put on a pot of coffee in the kitchen.

He turned to her, kissing her cheek. "Leave all that for tomorrow, honey. Tonight is mine. Ours." He started nibbling on her neck. Soon, he turned off the coffee pot and pulled her close to him. "Dana...oh my darling, darling Dana. How I love you...how I want you...how I need you..." He picked her up in his arms and carried her to their bedroom. He'd told the boys he wanted to be alone with Dana tonight. He'd asked them to save their reunion with her for tomorrow. Tonight she was his. All his.

They slept late. Violet knocked on the door around 11:00 a.m. "What's up, Violet?" Graham asked, opening the door a crack.

"Breakfast. I brought it up on trays."

Violet was a mind reader. He'd been hoping for that indulgence, and here it was. "Wonderful, Violet. Thanks. Come on in."

Violet set the trays on the bed. The newspaper sat on the tray, also. "Enjoy." She smiled and vanished.

Graham picked up the newspaper. The headlines jumped off the page. "Local equestrian, Dana Van Rensellier was miraculously rescued by a SWAT TEAM. Relaxing at Sugarbush Farm after a harrowing kidnapping ordeal and dramatic rescue, she is in high spirits. A SWAT TEAM bombarded a local warehouse where kidnappers were holding her for three million in ransom."

"Police and the local sheriff are to be commended for their swift, professional work in dispatching a SWAT TEAM to the suspected kidnapper's hideout. A local pizza delivery boy will receive an honorary payment for tipping off local police..." The article went to talk about Dana's successful career as a trainer and professional equestrian.

Dana was invited to be a guest on the local talk shows. They wanted a first-hand account of her hostage experience.

Danielle had called the house once. Other than that, she continued to be incognito.

Dana didn't understand what she was up to. She and Graham argued over Danielle. Graham asked Dana not to visit her or call her until further notice. Though she was tempted to jump into her car and drive over there, she didn't. She'd learned a bitter lesson. God was showing her that she needed to obey her husband whether she felt like it or not. She was the weaker sex, and Graham would take great care of her if she allowed him to.

He watched over her like a Mother hen. The experience had rattled them both. That night he held her close to him during pillow talk. "Darling, I don't know if you are aware of it or not, but your Mom got hitched. A quickie wedding. Turns out the guy she married was a gold digger. He managed to steal most of her money..."

"What? What on earth are you talking about? Mother would never be that stupid..."

"Well, she was. Loneliness can do that to a woman. She was so crazy about this Italian guy...that she lost all reasoning power..."

"Well, why didn't she call me? I couldn't understand why she suddenly stopped returning my calls. I was beginning to think something happened to her...now you inform me that she contacted *you* and told you she'd gotten hitched."

"Actually, I didn't pick up the phone, when her number flashed on the screen. She left a message while you were kidnapped. Maybe she was embarrassed. She was always the one to give you advice. Turns out she handled her own love life very poorly. Apparently, the guy cleaned her out...financially speaking."

"So that's why she hasn't called me. She's embarrassed. Too bad she didn't take her own good advice." She peered over at Graham. "So...are they getting a divorce, or what?"

"That's the weird part of this whole thing. She's staying with him. Says she's forgiven him."

"What? She really has gone off the rails." Dana shook her head in dismay. Maybe we can somehow...help her get the money back..."

"Leave it alone, Dana. Your mother is a bright, educated woman. She knows exactly what she's doing. She made her bed. Let her lie in it. And yes, I'm afraid she really is that desperate for a man. Desperate enough that she's allowed him to take all her money and she still wants him. She's a big girl, honey. Apparently, this is what she wants."

"Well...I can't believe she just...like...dropped off the planet the whole time I was held hostage! According to the sheriff, she never called him...not even once..." Dana started crying. "I thought...she loved me. Now, I see that she didn't...she just...put up with me. I guess she's... never... really loved me."

"That's because she's actually in love with herself, darling. Don't you see that? Danielle is in love with

Danielle. That's why she can't face the fact that the man she married isn't in love with her...but only wanted her money...she's in denial. I'm sorry her true character had to unravel while you were in a crisis, being held hostage..."

"I knew Danielle was self-centered. And I knew she was often jealous of me. Little things she would say or do...but I'm stunned to discover how...extreme her character flaw is."

"Something must have happened in her life to cause her to be like this. But we'll talk about that later. Right now, my darling...we have a lot of catching up to do..." He whisked her into his arms, carrying her back to their bedroom.

Late the next day, they emerged. After breakfast, Dana finally began to talk about what happened while she was being held hostage. "Bart liked me and said he kind of hoped you wouldn't come up with the money, because then he would keep me his prisoner; his sex slave until he tired of me."

Graham couldn't hold back his anger and his questions any longer. "Did he rape you?"

"No. Almost; but God intervened."

"How did that play out?"

"Well, late one night, when I was trying to sleep on the mattress on the floor, he crept over to me, and asked me if I found him attractive. I thought about the question and decided I would play him. I said "You're an attractive man, but I'm married. Once I get out of here, I can introduce you to my gorgeous, single girlfriend, though."

"Why would you do that?"

"Because she's smart and tough; as well as beautiful...and she could help you get your life straightened around."

"Why do you care?"

"Because I'm a Christian. God is love; and I love my fellow man. He created you for great and awesome things...not for this low-life you're living...running from the cops...living in the shadows...God has great and mighty things in store for you."

"God wouldn't want me. I've done some terrible things in my life."

"What if I told you that he will forgive every sin you've ever committed or will commit? What if I told you that He loves you with an everlasting love and he wants to fellowship with you?"

"I'd say there's no hope for me. I've committed every sin in the book and even invented new ones."

"You don't get it, do you? Jesus died to save us from our sins. *All* our sins, no matter how despicable, how nasty..."

"I wish I could believe that. I've been on the street since I was nine. My Mom was a prostitute. She's dead...died of a heroin overdose."

Dana's heart had gone out to him, despite the situation. "You can accept Jesus into your heart right here...right now. If you are truly sorry for your sins and you want to turn from them...and if you believe that Jesus died so that you might live eternally with him, then you are a new creature in Christ, born-again!"

"Are you sure? Are you sure God would forgive me and accept me?"

"100% sure. Soon, I said the sinner's prayer with him and by that time, he'd gone off the idea of raping me. It was supernatural. We kind of...bonded, in a way."

"That is nothing short of a miracle." Graham reached over and hugged her, holding her close. "I'm proud of you, Dana. Proud that you didn't fall apart and that you shared your hope...your faith. And it seems like you remembered the conversation verbatim."

"Oh yeah. It's etched on my mind and spirit. God is in the miracle business." Dana smiled over at her handsome hubby. She threw her arms around his neck. "I am so happy to be home. There are no words that can describe my joy."

Graham was bursting with overflowing joy, also. He began singing. *"We'll have a lifetime to share, so many ways..."*

Chapter Eleven

Graham and Dana held hands as they strode to the barn to do their morning chores.

Sybil had insisted on taking the boys for the weekend so they could continue their blissful reunion.

"I think we should go for a long, leisurely ride and then just hang out together. Oh Dana, I don't know what I'd have done if I'd lost you. I wouldn't have been able to stand it..."

"Let's not look back. What are the chances of me being able to lead the master mind kidnapper to Jesus? And yet I did. It was supernatural."

"You know Dana, the longer I live, the more I realize so many things...so much of life is actually supernatural. In fact, all the gifts and talents we receive from the creator are in that category. We didn't give them to ourselves. God bestowed them upon us. Just look at the incredible beauty around us...the mountains, the vast variety of trees... the birds...all God's creatures are amazing. They're all supernatural."

"Love is supernatural, too; when you think about it. I mean you can meet twenty, thirty people of the opposite sex; they can all be attractive in different ways, they all have their share of attributes, etc., and yet... suddenly, you meet someone and bells go off...and then you know; you just know that that is the person God has for you." Dana threw her arms around Graham's neck. "Oh my darling...I'm so happy that we found each other. Life can be lonely...and...less than wonderful when it's lived alone. But He came to give us life *abundantly* and we must hang on to that promise."

Dinner was steak, pan fried potatoes and salad. Violet insisted on joining them. "I want to hear about your harrowing ordeal. I bet you could write a book about it, Dana. It must have really been something. I prayed for you unceasingly."

Dana could hardly believe her ears. "You prayed for me, unceasingly? What about the housework...and the cooking?"

"I let it all go. I told Graham. I said... you can fire me if you want, but God has laid Dana on my heart and I'm gonna pray until she gets released..."

Dana got up, her eyes filling with tears. She hugged Violet. "Oh, Violet, you are so special. I am so grateful for you...and your prayers. You're not *like* family...you *are* family."

Graham winked at Violet. "I'm going to give you a raise, actually."

Violet chuckled. "Don't bother. I don't need the money. I don't have any family...although...who knows...maybe Will and Jay will wind up with a little brother or sister." She smirked.

Dana shrieked with laughter. "You are...beyond outrageous, Violet. The things you come up with..."

"Folks usually like me because I call a spade a spade."

Chapter Twelve

Danielle phoned early the next morning.

Graham peered at the call screen. When her name flashed on the screen, he hesitated but finally picked up the call. "Yes, Danielle?"

"Well... that's hardly a warm greeting. You *are* my son-in-law, after all."

Graham had had enough of this woman. In retrospect, he was amazed Dana had turned out as well as she had. "Dana is busy right now. I'll have her call you back, if she wants to." He'd never been a game player and he wasn't about to start now. Danielle needed a wake-up, and it was up to him to give her one. He had to protect Dana from her ruthless step-mom.

Danielle didn't like being brushed off. Okay, she deserved that for being incognito the whole time her only daughter was holed up with the kidnappers. But what could she do, after all? Graham was her hubby. *He* was responsible for Dana. Not *her*. Of course she knew she should have become more involved, should have at least pretended to find some of the cash Graham needed. But that was all in the past now. Dana was home. *Lucky girl. The kidnapping plot didn't work out the way she'd orchestrated it.*

She was penniless. Maybe she could prove in a court of law that she signed her assets over to her hubby under extreme duress. Maybe it could be reversed. He'd vanished this morning, without even a farewell note. Now, she had no one. *Lord, please let me get back into Graham and Dana's good graces. I know I don't deserve it. But I've lost my best friend, Gi Gi... my hubby...and I cannot lose my daughter and son-in-law, Lord.* She would have to be gracious. Being snippy wouldn't get her anywhere. "Okay, Graham. I look forward to hearing from her. Nice talking to you. How are you after the...ordeal?"

Graham knew she was making nice, of course. He felt sorry for the woman in a way, as deceived as she was. But now that she had revealed her true character, he would be very cautious about allowing Dana to spend any time with her. He did not trust the woman. Sometimes, he even thought maybe she had something to do with Dana's kidnapping.

Three days went by before Danielle finally got a call from Dana. "Hey, Mom. What's goin' on?"

"I wanted to ask *you* that? How are *you* after that horrible ordeal?"

Dana and Graham had discussed her mom at length.

Dana finally admitted, albeit reluctantly, that Danielle didn't give two hoots about her.

Graham had smelled a rat and hired a private investigator to check Danielle out. He'd learned she had a criminal record and had done time in prison.

Dana was stunned. Then, she remembered when she'd been in her teens and had moved in with her aunt for several years. That's when she'd begun taking riding lessons. Danielle was a career crook. The detective opened up the possibility that maybe she hired the kidnappers to kidnap Dana, because she wanted to get rid of her so she would have clear sailing with Graham.

As bizarre as her fixation was, Dana knew it was true. Waves of sadness washed over her. Her step-mom was an ex-convict.

Graham had hired a detective because he smelled a rat. They met for coffee after the detective had called to report that he had some interesting news for Graham.

"The woman came on to me like gang busters. It seems she set her sights on marrying me. She wanted Dana out of the way; as preposterous as that is. I think that was her nasty, little scheme." He shook his head.

The detective took a sip of his coffee. "Danielle Lockhart has a prison record." He gave Graham some printed information about her. "I'm sorry to give you this wake-up call. But at least you know who you're dealing with now."

Graham was in a state of shock. Finally, he found his voice. "Yeah. I sure appreciate the light you've shone on this." Graham picked up the check and the two men walked out together.

That night after dinner, Violet, Graham and Dana said some prayers. "I think, at the very least, Dana, we're going to give Danielle some time off. I don't want to see her at Sugarbush. I don't want to socialize with her... and I forbid you to call her or take her calls. At least, for now."

"Graham. That's outrageous! She's my Mom! She

has a ruthless side; I'll grant you that, but we...can't just...ignore her..."

"Actually, we can. And we will. Dana, this is not up for discussion. As long as I am your husband, I will protect you. And I'm telling you...I'm warning you... you haven't seen the tip of the iceberg with that woman."

Dana's eyes grew big as saucers. "Well...like...what do you think she's up to?"

"I don't know. But I do know that I...we can't trust her, and we can't believe one word that comes out of her mouth...she is a ruthless woman. You might just be surprised at the sort of things she's involved with...and this new hubby? What's that all about? I don't believe for a second that he ripped her off. She's much too shrewd to allow a new hubby to clean her out, financially. I don't believe it."

"Oh fine. So you think she's a liar...and a crook. When and how did you arrive at these conclusions?" Dana was crushed.

"Dana. Don't you see? She *wants* us to fight. She *wants* us to break up. She wants me for herself, as preposterous as that is."

Dana finally calmed down. Women's intuition told her some time ago, that Danielle had set her sights on Graham. She instinctively knew that was true. She was relieved in a way, because she had never felt relaxed when Danielle was around Graham. She sensed that the moment her back was turned, Danielle would flirt outrageously with Graham, as preposterous as that was.

Chapter Thirteen

It was Sunday morning. Graham drove everyone to church.

Dana and Graham spent a half hour in the prayer room while the boys were in Sunday school.

When the service began, they sat in a pew near the front of the sanctuary.

Dana couldn't focus on the message. Her mind was racing in the aftermath of the kidnapping trauma, as well as the startling truth about Danielle's past.

When the service was over, she glanced over at Graham. "I feel that the Holy Spirit wants me to step forward and pray for Danielle. I sense that she is in a crisis."

"Go ahead, honey. I'll be in the lobby with the boys. I'll field some of the inquiries about you. I might as well get that out of the way."

"Absolutely." As Dana stepped forward to pray with one of the three prayer warriors standing at the front of the church, she sensed some kind of disruption in her spirit. *"Lord, what's going on?" She sensed the spirit directing her to the tall man standing at the front of the church. There was a couple next to him.* "Good morning, I'm Dana Van Rensellier."

"Tom Sinclair." He held his hand out in greeting.

"Would you please pray for my mother, Danielle? She's going through a... rough time. I don't think she actually knows Jesus. Oh, she attends church occasionally...and even reads the Bible now and then, but I don't think she has ever actually met the savior."

"Let's go to prayer." Tom prayed with great power, anointing and authority, standing on the Word of God. "Now I feel we need to pray for your protection. I see another attack coming your way. It's no secret that you were kidnapped. You were on the news daily until your miraculous discovery and dramatic escape. I've heard rumblings that your captor has become a Christian and his partner in crime is apparently livid. ABC News announced that both men are being held in the county jail pending their trial. The media picked up the news that Bart apparently asked for a Bible in prison. But...here's the thing that's interesting; Danielle apparently went to visit them. A reporter jumped on that information."

"Mom *knows them!* How is that possible?" Dana was stunned.

"I don't know. I just thought you should know about it. You may not be aware of my background. I was a news analyst and reporter. I'm retired now...used to work for ABC News."

"Thank-you, Lord." Now she knew why the spirit directed her to this particular gentleman. What a great and mighty God we serve!

Graham drove the family out of the parking lot at the church. "Where do you want to go for lunch, Dana?"

She was silent for a minute. "Can we drop the boys at home? I need to talk to you...privately."

"Sure, honey."

"I'll ask Violet to make you guys something amazing for lunch." He addressed the boys. "I was thinking we should drive out to Villa Di Vinci. A leisurely lunch might be nice." Graham grinned at Dana.

"You boys can go riding after lunch. Just make sure one of the ranch hands is around and knows where you are. Call me on my cell when you get back from the ride."

"Okay, Dad. Okay Dana." Jay and Will chimed in unison.

Graham dropped the boys off at the house.

Dana and Graham drove out to Villa Da Vinci to have lunch.

They were greeted by Juan Perez the Maitre D. "Senor Graham, Senorita Dana. What an honor to have you here for lunch; and what an honor to work for you." He grinned as he grandly escorted them to the premier table outside on the patio.

Seated at the wrought iron table, amidst vividly colored, exotic parakeets in cages and a smattering of small Palm trees, Dana thought she was in heaven. It was a wonderful gift after all she'd just been through.

"The specials are on the blackboard. Let me know when you're ready to order." The server stood by. "May I recommend the guava juice...spicy shrimp in hot sauce with taco chips for starters?"

"Sounds perfect." Dana smiled at the waiter and then at her beloved.

"Thanks." Graham nodded to the server.

Dana peered over at her wonderful hubby. *Lord, you are so good to me. I didn't even know a man like Graham existed. And here...you've brought him into my life, we're married and suddenly my life in beyond wonderful.*

A dull ache niggled at her. Who was the real Danielle? She wondered what else they would discover now that the Pandora's Box had been opened. "Graham... the man I prayed with at church seems to think that Danielle...has actually been in prison! He was a reporter, apparently. That couldn't possibly be true, could it?"

"Dana. I've known for some time that Danielle has a secret life. A life you knew nothing about. She might actually have orchestrated the kidnapping."

"What!" Dana stood up. She was outraged. "Come on, Graham! You can't be serious." She peered over at him, skeptically. "Do you know something about her past that you haven't...told me?"

"I just recently learned about it. I connected the dots when she started asking a lot of questions just after you were kidnapped. Then she ducked out of sight. And...brace yourself, honey...she didn't seem to care whether I raised the three million to get your release — or not."

"You mean...she didn't call anxiously...every day... to find out if you'd heard anything...if she could help you raise the money we needed?"

"Dana. I realize this is a cold shower for you. It was for me, too. She dropped out of sight when you were with the kidnappers. She made no effort to help me raise the money for your release; but worse than that...she never once asked about you...inquired as to whether you were still being held captive. She just dropped out of sight."

Tears rolled down Dana's eyes. "All this time...all these years...she was my hero. I looked up to her. I thought she loved me...wanted the best for me...now, I find out...that everything was about *you*. She wanted *you*. She was...ruthless. And...ya...I get it...she wanted me off the scene at any cost, so she could ride off into the sunset with you...fat chance she would have."

"You led your captor to Jesus! It doesn't get any better than that. Maybe God allowed this kidnapping episode...in order to save that one...lost...soul."

"Maybe. God is always full of surprises." Dana smiled. "So...why did Danielle go to prison?"

"The P.I. I hired said she was incarcerated for her significant share in a Ponzi scheme. That was some time ago. She was in a women's prison for over three years. There were a number of charges against her. A murder charge she beat, for instance. She apparently pushed a man off a cliff to his death. She hired a good attorney. The charges were dropped. She swears they fought and he fell to his death. Anyway, she's a convicted criminal, honey. And she was willing to sacrifice you; so she could have what she wanted. Yours truly. Bizarre isn't it?"

"Do you actually believe that she may have hired the kidnappers in the first place...with the idea of getting Will first...and then me?'

"It's a distinct possibility."

"Should I have nothing further to do with her?" Tears sprung to Dana's eyes. "I can't do that. I love her way too much for that. I still want the best for her. I want to have lunch with her and find out what happened with the new hubby."

"I'm not sure she'll level with you, Dana. I mean...I hope she does..."

"I think she will."

"Dana. I'm sorry, but I forbid you to see her right now. Until we get this thing figured out, she's a loose Cannon. And I don't trust her, one bit. Neither should you."

Tears sprung to Dana's eyes. "You're forbidding me to see my own Mother? We don't have all the facts. I'm sure there is a perfectly logical explanation for all this. Danielle is...a wonderful person."

"I wish that were true, Dana. But right now... the facts prove otherwise."

An onrush of tears cascaded down Dana's cheeks. "You don't...really believe...that Mom...set this whole thing up....that she masterminded the kidnapping or orchestrated pulling the puppet strings the entire time."

"Possibly. Maybe we've all been puppets on her string...dancing to her tune. The puppet master had her own secret goals...and they did not include you. In fact, you were just in the way of her plan. That's why she tried to get rid of you...problem is...she overplayed her hand. Sybil knew something was off-base with her when she didn't bother to find out how you were... and when she didn't show concern or offer to help raise that last million I desperately needed."

"Oh, I get it!" The red lights suddenly flashed. They got brighter and brighter. "She was going to keep some of the ransom money. She was in on the deal with the kidnappers..." Dana's eyes widened like saucers. "Of course! Why didn't I see that before? *She* was the mastermind!"

"Maybe, Dana. The P.I. discovered her businesses were doing poorly. She has barely been able to keep the doors open with her beauty salon. The newer, glitzier salons crowded out her little place. And the boutique she owns is just limping by. She needed an infusion of cash. And she needed it fast. She was desperate. Her little cottage was mortgaged to the hilt. She played the *role* of successful businesswoman...and did it very well. But she's a fake, honey."

"I want to call a meeting with Danielle. I find it hard to believe all this stuff."

"Nor right now, honey. You need to take a total break from that women. If our marriage is going to thrive and survive...we need to take her out of the equation."

The next morning, Graham showed Dana the prayer room. "I hope you don't mind that Sybil fixed it up as a sanctuary of worship and prayer to the Lord. Throughout the deep valley of waiting... and praying for your return; and the ransom money, Sybil and I took refuge in this room."

"I love how she pulled it together. The classic photo of Jesus, the Good Shepherd, on the wall, and the Persian rug she laid down..."

"She wanted it to be a special place of refuge. A place to seek the Almighty." He ginned. "She added her own personal touch with the bright, decorator pillows."

"It's eclectic. I rather like that. Anyway, I happen to love pink, lime green and turquoise decorator pillows. It gives the room some panache. And it's great for the prayer warriors. They can comfortably kneel down as they seek God."

She'd placed several Bibles on the small tables in the room, hung a large cross on the wall, and managed to make the room ideal for prayer and meditation. Graham slipped in a disc with classical music. The sound wafted throughout the space.

"It's remarkable that there are two stained glass windows in the room, as well as a built-in bench and an East facing window. Who knows? Maybe the contractor for the house had originally designed this room as a Prayer Room." Dana smiled at Graham, joy seeping into her soul. *I am so blessed, Lord.*

Chapter Fourteen

Dana arose well before the first light of day. She hadn't slept well. The shock of leaning the truth about her step mom was overwhelming. Taking a mug of coffee, she climbed the staircase to the prayer room. She drank the coffee and then fell on her knees as she sought the Lord. Despite her awful betrayal, she loved Danielle. She would always love her. Fraud or not; she was her Mother. "Lord, how could Danielle have sunk so low?"

She cried bitter tears and then sought the Lord with her whole heart. Danielle was the only mother she'd ever known. And she'd utterly betrayed her. She had lied to her and deceived her on many levels. Though she knew she had to forgive her and she would... right now, this deep valley of shock and betrayal that she was walking through could only be shared with God Almighty.

Dana had been in the room praying on her knees for a couple of hours. Finally, she felt a release in her spirit. She knew, of course, that Danielle had serious spiritual issues. She'd only attended church sporadically over the years, and now... with her finances unravelling and the truth spilling out, maybe she would be ready to repent and follow God with a whole heart.

"Lord, you know my heart is broken and my spirit grieved at these new findings. And yet for years I've known Danielle had spiritual issues and was off base; but in my wildest imagination, I never could have guessed that she was verging on bankruptcy. Is she a total phoney? Lord, right now it looks that way." Bitter tears slid down her cheeks. *"Lord...it hurt so much to discover that Danielle did not even inquire about my status while I was being held hostage. And now there are rumblings that she might have been involved. Lord...I don't want to face the fact that there is a ruthless side to her...it breaks my heart. And, still, with all this...I ask you, Jesus...to touch her, to open her eyes to see you, to repent and seek you with a whole heart. And Father, I pray for restoration for the two of us. We were friends. What happened to disrupt that, Lord? Was it really...jealousy... because I married Graham?* Tears cascaded down her cheeks.

It was cathartic. *"Lord, I just want to say thanks. I just want to praise you for bringing me through these dark...choppy waters. They did not overflow me, because you did not allow them to. You are faithful, now and forever. You are a Great and Mighty God. I worship you with my whole heart and mind and soul. And I will not lean on my own limited understanding. In all my ways, I shall acknowledge you and know that you are Lord. You have risen from the dead and you are Lord. Every knee shall bow, every tongue confess that Jesus Christ is Lord."*

Suddenly she knew what she had to do. She rose

from her knees, a plan forming in her mind. She would drive over to Danielle's house; unannounced. Maybe bring her a double Coffee Latte and a little bunch of flowers...daisies perhaps. She would offer to pray for her. There was a spring in her step until she remembered that Graham had forbidden her to see Danielle for a while.

She made a fresh pot of coffee and suddenly had the urge to bake cornbread. Of course Violet would do that if she asked her to; but she enjoyed baking Graham cornbread because he loved it so much. And she absolutely adored him. Graham...her wonderful hubby. She would not betray him. He'd told her to stay away from Danielle for a time; and until he changed his edict on that, she would not visit her. She would obey her husband. He was protecting her, after all. And with everything she'd been through, the Good Lord knew she needed all the protecting she could get.

She was just about to pour a cup of the freshly brewed coffee when Graham appeared. His face lit up when he saw her.

She smiled at him, peering into his eyes. They seemed bluer, brighter than they were yesterday. She threw her arms around his neck. "Did the Thoroughbreds miss me?"

Graham chuckled. "What do you think? They asked for you every day. They were disappointed when I showed up with the ranch hands. They *like* us; but they *love* you. I instructed the Thoroughbreds to pray for you. Whispered it into their ears as I petted them."

"You can make a joke about that all you want, Graham. But you know what? I think they did pray for me." She smiled. "Oh, not in the traditional sense...the way we pray...but horses are so instinctive...they knew I was missing...I think they have a ...sort of a...form of prayer that they do."

"No kidding. Well, I wouldn't put it past them. They're amazing creatures, that's for sure." Graham grinned, peering into her eyes. He winked at her. "Violet drove downtown for the day. She decided to exercise her options. She actually took the day off. Guess you're stuck cooking for us. And we'll need to pick the boys up after school, too."

"Well, I'm glad she took the day off. It's about time."

"Me, too." He grinned at her with male appreciation.

A couple of hours later, Dana finally made the cornbread and served it with salad for lunch. She was riding on billowy clouds. She'd been in that euphoric state ever since marrying her dream man; with the exception, of course, of the kidnappings. Smiling over at him, she had the sudden urge to do a tap dance. And she would have. Except for one thing; she didn't know how to tap dance!

After dinner, Violet returned home. Loaded with colorful, decorator bags, she climbed the steps of the house.

Dana and Graham hurried out to the veranda. Meeting her there, they took the shopping bags from her.

"I went on a shopping spree. Bought stuff for everybody." She smiled. "I still have a few more bags in the car."

"Where did you go?" Dana's eyes swept over the decorator bags.

"I stopped in to Danielle's boutique. There was a big sign in the window. It said CLOSING SALE. I figured i'd find some bargains. And I did. Look at all this great stuff!"

"Looks like you bought out the store."

"Not really. I did buy you a couple of cute outfits, though." She smiled at Dana.

"Was she...in the store?" Dana couldn't resist asking.

"There was a young Spanish gal at the counter. But Danielle came in while I was there." She smiled. "Try the clothes on. I'll give you the scoops later."

"So...let's have a look at what you bought." Dana opened the colorful plastic bag Violet handed her, as soon as they entered the kitchen.

"Nice." Dana pulled out a couple of short skirts; both had colorful, matching tops. "But Violet...you know I never wear short skirts. I always wear jeans..."

"Well, honey...that's exactly why I bought them for you. It's high time you got out of your jeans and wore skirts and dresses for a change. You need to look like a woman. Enough with the horses, already."

"You sound like the Jewish Mother I never had." Dana chuckled.

"That's because I am."

"You're Jewish? I didn't know that."

"Of course I'm Jewish, goofball. How do you think I got so smart? I'm one of God's chosen kids."

"You are too much, Violet. Don't you ever dare leave here."

"As long as y'all let me call the shots and look after

everything on the home front, I ain't goin' nowhere." She winked at Dana.

"Since it's your day off, Violet; what can I make you for dinner?"

Violet rolled her eyes. "I'm not fussy. Whatever you feel like cookin' up. But I want you to open the bags and see the rest of the stuff."

Dana did as she was told. She pulled out the first outfit. "Wow! Look at this. It's gorgeous!" She held up a bright tangerine and pink, floral jersey top. Next, she pulled out two matching skirts; a pink one and an orange one. "I had no idea you were such a fashion diva, Violet!"

Too bad I don't have matching pumps. But she hadn't opened the bright pink bag or the bright orange one yet. Soon, she pulled out two pairs of pumps; pink and orange, size eight. *"Violet. You really are too much!* How did you know my size?"

"Graham tipped me off. We're very tight." She smirked.

Dana modelled the fabulous new outfits for Graham, strolling around the enormous country kitchen.

"This calls for a celebration." She smiled, pulling down crystal champagne glasses from the cupboard and opening a bottle of champagne. "I know you love champagne, Violet; though you rarely imbibe." She poured the bubbly, handing a glass to Violet and one to Graham, who just happened to amble into the kitchen.

Dana proposed the toast. "To Violet. Woman extraordinaire. Thank you for buying me these fabulous togs and shoes! It's your day off and you went shopping for a new mini wardrobe for me. Thank-you!"

Graham grinned at her. "Well, well, well...the

equestrian has morphed into an elegant lady. I knew I liked Violet. But I had no idea what an amazing woman she would turn out to be. She must have read my mind. I kept dropping hints about wanting you to change your style of dressing, but they seemed to fall on deaf ears. Isn't it ironic, that even while Violet was trying to help Danielle by shopping at her boutique, she caused the blessing to fall on us?"

"Well... honey... let's take a look at you! You look stunning. Violet has exquisite taste. Why don't we continue the modelling show in our dressing room?" Graham carried his glass of champagne. The women followed him.

Dana modelled the outfits around the spacious dressing room. "What do you think, honey?" She flashed Graham a big smile.

From his chair in the dressing room, Graham sipped champagne and enjoyed the fashion show.

Violet reclined on the chaise lounge watching the show. "So...Danielle's hubby came into the store. A good lookin' guy...maybe Italian...he strutted into the boutique. Danielle introduced him to me as her new hubby."

"Really? So she's still married to him, then." Dana was surprised.

"Looks that way. Maybe he was in the clothing business at some point. He was busy around the store, doing stuff. Seemed like he was real comfortable with that role."

"Did she ask about me?" Dana peered over at Violet.

"No. She seemed to be in her own little world."

"So...you just guessed at my sizes?"

"No. I cheated. I asked Graham. Told him I might do

some shopping for you. Guess he wanted to humor me...so he gave me your sizes."

"He couldn't have known what an eye for fashion you have." Dana smiled.

"I'm glad you like my purchases, honey." Violet smiled.

Dana moved toward Violet as she reclined on the chaise. She kissed her on the cheek. "Thank you so much, Violet. I am so happy you're here." She fought the urge to sob. Violet was becoming like a mother to her.

Chapter Fifteen

Danielle was fed up with her new hubby. The conflicts had begun right after they'd tied the knot, and they had increased. But what was she to do? He had her money, they'd stopped divorce proceedings and now he'd promised to help her turn her businesses around. She'd bought a Toy Boy. She might as well face it. She just hadn't realized how much it would cost her. She was pathetic. But it was too late to turn back.

He milled around in the kitchen peering at the spices in the spice rack.

"What spices are you looking for?" Danielle asked. "They aren't very organized. But you should be able to find everything you need for the red sauce."

Danielle's conscience niggled at her. She hadn't wanted to walk away from her adoptive daughter. But she had to do what her Italian, dictator hubby demanded. "I don't want you going anywhere near that step-daughter of yours. She and her hubby... that gentleman farmer dude... want to own and control you. They think they're so clever. Well, you don't need them. What has Dana ever done for you? What has Graham ever done for you, for that matter?" He found the spices he was looking for, and set them on the counter, next to the large frying pan and the sauce he was making.

"I didn't know they were supposed to do stuff for me. I've done pretty well on my own all these years..."

He chuckled. "That's a story you've concocted...and circulated. Well...I give you credit for sticking to it. But honey... the boutique should go into receivership, just like the beauty salon. They're both failed businesses." He added spices, stirring the sauce.

"Oh nonsense. I make money on them every year. Just...maybe not as much as I'd like."

He fried some garlic and onions. "Well... I've studied the books. I'm not sure you ever have. You're in bad shape with these two businesses. You should probably file for bankruptcy."

Danielle saw red. She'd had enough of this guy running her life; taking over everything. Dictating to her. She wanted her own life back. He was a taker. A con man. He had already taken her to the cleaners. Now he wanted blood. How in God's creation had she ever allowed this man into her life? *Still, a niggling little voice reminded her that it was too late.*

She hadn't been listening to God closely enough, that's how this had happened. She hadn't been following him and she'd made a poor choice... actually many poor choices. And she would have to live with them for now...because the man wouldn't leave. *Could he actually be in love with her?* She didn't know, because he was so temperamental and moody. *I'm just going to have to see how this thing plays out.*

He was in high spirits today. He hummed a tune as he joyfully cooked up the red sauce.

"Wow! It looks delicious." She moved closer to it. The aroma of the sauce filled the air. "And it smells great, too. Ever thought of becoming a chef?" She would give him mixed reviews for his business acumen; but as a cook, he was amazing.

"I used to be a short order cook...when I was in University."

"I can see that."

Danielle glanced outside at his red Porsche. The man had style. She'd give him that much. She poured herself a glass of red wine and one for him. She knew she looked fetching in her long, slinky, jersey dress. She smiled at him, as she began chopping lettuce and tomatoes for a salad.

Hubby dished up two plates of the pasta, pouring the red sauce over it. "Dinner is served." He grinned bringing the two plates of pasta with the red sauce into the dining room. He set it down on the table.

Danielle put the bottle of red on the table. She loved her small dining room. It was charming and intimate. In fact, she loved the house. It had the look and feel of a summer cottage.

She had already learned that her new hubby was full of surprises and had hidden agendas. One part of her wanted to slap a restraining order on him and get him out of her life... another part of her wanted to embrace him, hold him, love him and never let him go.

The man was a chameleon and it was causing her to change with his moods. A part of her was fascinated by his unpredictability and undeniable charm. But the other side of her nature warned her that he was a taker, a user and man she could never trust. *Too late for that.*

He'd admitted he thought she was wealthy. He'd

tried to rip her off; but having discovered she was on the verge of bankruptcy, he seemed to bond with her, instead trying to help her. The man was a puzzle. It was time for her to confront him. Living in limbo, not knowing from day to day if he was staying, leaving, suing, divorcing...or God knows what else...was both tiring and trying. She had to smoke him out and find out what his intentions were. Could they go for counselling and try to build a marriage? Did he want to file for divorce and move on? Was there another woman? Sitting on the fence was hardly an option. She had to smoke him out.

After an amazing dinner, they watched the news in the living room. Danielle determined to smoke him out. "Darling, do we have a future together or not?"

Thirty second silence. "Of course we do. What an odd question."

"Is it? Based on your behavior patterns, I'd have to be off my rocker if I asked you any other question."

"Okay, you asked a straight question; you deserve a straight answer. Yes, there is someone else. And before you ask, I'll tell you...she's young, beautiful and rich..."

Danielle saw red. She felt like surely smoke was coming out of her ears. "So what does she want with you? Wouldn't she have her choice of men?"

Her Italian hubby had a massive ego and she'd just stepped on it.

"You're joking, right? I'm a great catch! You don't get that because you're over the hill..." As soon as the words had left his mouth, he regretted them. "I...I didn't mean it...the way it came out..."

Tears sprung to her eyes. She'd just stepped on his

massive ego. "Get out...you Italian stallion. That's all you have to offer anyone. Great sex. Period. Nothing else. No security....no...you don't even bother to work...you don't even pretend to look for a job...you're a taker and you just took your last meal from me. I want you out of the house. Pronto."

"How soon they forget. You have memory loss. You put me on title right after we got hitched. I own half of this house. So...you can either pay me out in cash...and I'm gone, or we can list the house and we'll see if we can make a little more than the appraised value of the property..."

"Get out! Do you hear me? Get out!" She screamed, shrilly.

He ran outside and hopped into his Porche, speeding off.

She knew he'd be back. His stuff was here. As she stood on the porch sobbing, a white Jeep drove up.

Graham and Dana parked in the driveway. Graham stepped out of the jeep. "What's goin' on here?" He'd seen her hubby leave in a huff. *He shouldn't have come here, but Dana kept badgering him about wanting to see her Mom.*

Danielle sputtered. *I've blown any little chance I might have had with Graham. He knows what a desperado I am, now.* "Graham. Dana...how nice to see y' all." She was shaking.

"Is it? Is it nice to see us, Danielle?" Graham had her number. Maybe Dana would have it now, too.

The gloves were off. Her life was transparent. No point in pretending otherwise. "We're getting a divorce. Guess it will be a nasty one."

Her hubby apparently drove around the block and

came back. He hopped out of his red Porsche and strode up the front steps of the house to the porch.

Graham, Dana and Danielle sat on the wicker furniture on the porch.

Danielle's hubby smirked. "Danielle bought herself a husband. She enjoyed the ride; but now she doesn't want to pay. Too bad, she really doesn't have any choice. Maybe she'll think twice before picking up men in bars from now on." He sneered at her, contemptuously.

"Get out! Get yourself packed up and get out of the house." Tears sprung from Danielle's eyes as she fought to stay in control.

"I don't take my orders from you, Miss Snippity! I'm legally half owner of the house, so I shall stay in it until it is convenient for me to move. I'll be happy to sleep on the sofa, since there's no love left between us..."

Graham turned to Dana. "Now do you believe me? Or do you need to hear more?"

Dana felt like crawling under a rug. She had never felt so embarrassed in all her life. *So this was the real Danielle. Not a pretty picture.* "Let's go, Graham. I've seen enough." Tears sprung to her eyes.

Chapter Sixteen

Dana and Graham enjoyed a quiet evening meal. Dana was in a state of shock. She was very quiet...very sad. *How could I have been so deceived?* She couldn't eat. Bitter tears streamed down her face.

"Come on, Dana. Let's watch the news. You need to get your mind off Danielle and her problems."

They sat down in the family room.

Will and Jay bounced into the room. "Hey, Dad...hey, Mom...nice you could join us in the family room." Jay smirked.

"Right. Do you mind if we watch the news here? Could I ask you guys a favor?" Dana peered over at them.

"Speak." Jay smirked.

"We would like to be alone in the family room. Not for long. Give us an hour or less. After the news, we'll head to our room or the living room."

"I guess that would be all right. Just see that you don't make a habit of it, though." Jay smirked.

Violet showed up with buttered popcorn and apple cider drinks. She flashed them a big, warm smile. "Life is meant to be enjoyed, guys. I want you both to kick back, watch TV and hang out. Danielle will come back to her senses. It's a classic case of everything that could go wrong; did. She's been burnt bad... but you know what? She's a tough broad...like me...she'll bounce back."

"Let's not talk about her, Violet. It's emotionally distressing for Dana...and me, too." Graham sighed.

"I get that. But I want to encourage Dana. Danielle will bounce back to what she was..."

Suddenly, Graham twigged. "Wait a minute...maybe she's Bi-polar, did you ever think of that?"

"Graham... Danielle has never acted this way before...I don't ever remember her acting like this..."

"Well, there's no question that this guy pushed her over the edge, after taking her to the cleaners. Add that issue to the embarrassment she feels...along with the anger, etc..."

"And don't forget the jealousy because I married you."

"Somebody's knockin' on the door. Expecting anyone?" Violet peered at them.

Graham stood. "I'll see who it is. But how would they have gotten past the gate? We didn't buzz them in?" He didn't have to wait long to discover who it was.

Billy stood at the door, the usual smirk on his face.

"What can I do for you Billy? Actually, my first question is...how did you get in?"

"None of that is important. I'm here to warn you..."

"Warn me? Of what?"

"Retaliation. Tanner and Troy may be in prison, but they have tentacles that are far-reaching...and they're out to make your life miserable."

"What exactly are you talking about?" He had

Graham's attention.

Billy smirked. "Don't I at least get an invite to come on in..?"

Graham couldn't think of a reason not to ask him in. They had long since forgiven and forgotten the nasty trick he pulled on Dana. "Come on in, Billy. Have a seat."

"Now, that's better." He smirked, plopping down on the sofa.

Dana was initially stunned. She quickly recovered. Graham was here. Billy couldn't and wouldn't try anything stupid. But why *was* he here?

Violet decided not to budge. She didn't offer any refreshments to the intruder. Instead, she stood by gazing at the intruder, like a curious cat.

Billy had his long legs stretched out in front of him as he slumped on the sofa. "I'll be up front with you, Graham. I've got some information that could save you future horse theft. The twins are gunnin' for you and they won't rest until they've caused you some major grief..."

"Tell us something we don't know." Graham's voice was crisp. He did not trust the man. He'd let him in, offered him a seat; though he still hadn't gotten a straight answer as to how he got onto the ranch. He needed one. "Billy, how did you get onto Sugarbush? I need to know for security reasons."

Billy grinned, his eyes twinkling. He chuckled. "Wouldn't you just like to know? Well, I ain't gonna tell you..."

Graham stood. The low life had pushed his luck. "I want you off my property right now. I have no interest in what you want to tell me..."

"Is that so? Just like that! You're gonna throw me out. I don't think so." He pulled out a small handgun, aiming it at Graham.

It was a Beretta. Graham could see that in an instant. He wasn't rattled. If he had this guy's number, he was a coward and a snake. God only knew what his current scheme was.

Violet's mind was always racing. Today was no exception. She threw apple cider in Billy's face.

That gave Graham a chance to wrest the guy away from him. "Dana, call the sheriff." Graham held the Beretta on Billy. "I'll just keep an eye on you until the sheriff gets here. You're tangling with the wrong people. You're out of your league, Kid."

"Oh shut up. It's not you I'm after, anyway. None of this is about you or the horses. My buddy kidnapped Dana. She wasn't supposed to get away. She is mine. Don't you get that?" She was always mine. You may have married her...but that don't mean nothin.' She's white trash just like her old lady. What's that sayin' again? Like Mother, like daughter..."

Graham lost it then. He pushed Billy. Hard.

Billy landed with a loud thud on the floor. During the kafuffle the gun went off.

Willy and Jay raced down the hall from their rooms. They were too smart to come into the living room. Instead, they ran back to their rooms, grabbed baseball bats and hurried toward Graham and Dana. Jay bopped Billy on the head.

Billy screamed and flopped down on the floor.

The shrill sound of a siren pierced the air.

In minutes, the sheriff and deputy sheriff pounded on the door. Soon, they handcuffed Billy and shoved him into the back of the Sheriff's vehicle.

Graham stood by.

"He's a loose cannon, Graham. Probably in line for a big payoff if he can do some damage to you...and maybe the horses... or Dana. That's my best guess." He shook his head and jumped into the Sheriff's marked car. "You might want to hire a security company. Better yet, you might want to rig up cameras in the house and barn. I know you have them at the gate. You've been targeted for some time now. Billy is the front guy...he shows up to test the waters. Maybe case the place. After that, the heavy hitters show up."

Graham soon learned that Billy had undergone a psychiatric evaluation at Lexington University hospital. "Well, Dana...looks like our laid back ranch hand has been up to no good for a long time. Wonder if he'll hire an attorney to get him off... citing mental problems. The guy is a loose cannon. He probably should not be allowed to roam freely about." Graham and Dana sipped iced tea on the veranda, relieved that he'd been picked up.

"Graham, we've had some setbacks, but we need to find a colt to train for the Kentucky Derby. We've gotten side-tracked with the kidnapping and now with another bizarre incident with Billy. But we can't give up. We've seen the images on TV of Holocaust survivors struggling to make ends meet. Wouldn't it be great if we could write a check for a million dollars to help them?"

"You know, Dana. If I wasn't already in love with you...I would fall hard for you now. So many people shut their eyes and ears to hunger and people that are hurting. We've just survived a major crisis with the kidnapping, only to endure another attack...a vicious assault from Billy. But that's good news, honey; because God is greater. *"Greater is he that is in you than he that is in the world."* "An unseen spiritual battle is being waged over us...because God has great and magnificent plans for us. Plans that will show his glory in a mighty way."

Dana was introspective. "Do you think this is the end of the attacks?"

"No. As believers we are engaged daily in a spiritual battle. We must never let up. We must put on the whole armor of God and be prepared to fight this war...and win."

"How, exactly are we supposed to fight a spiritual battle, Graham?"

"I'm glad you asked, honey. Because I'm just learning this stuff myself. And it's the old story...if you can explain what you believe to someone else you solidify your own position on it."

"So we need to stay in the Word and keep praying, right?"

"For starters, yes. We can't ever take our freedom or any other positive aspect of our lives for granted. Instead, we need to seek Him daily, even hourly, with our whole heart..."

"Thanks for the sermon, Graham. Now...may we go searching for a three-year old colt...one that absolutely *will* win the Kentucky Derby this season?"

"Jay is already on it. He's comprised a list of the very finest three-year colts out there and he's organized appointments, leaving plenty of space in between."

"And because today is Saturday, I bet he's leading

the tour."

"You got it, Dana. I'm so proud of him that he's made the honors roll every year. The kid has a good mind and unlimited stamina."

"What is he going to do when he grows up?" Dana peered over at her handsome hunk of a hubby. She flashed him a big smile.

"Brace yourself, honey. His latest goal is to be a journalist. He has visions of being a news anchor. I think he'd be terrific at it."

"He definitely has the brain power and focus to do anything he wants." Dana smiled. *I'm so blessed to be his Step Mom. Thank-you, Lord.*

The door burst open. It was Violet with the two boys. She'd picked them up after school.

Jay and Will followed the smell of fresh peanut butter cookies which Violet had just baked. They found them on the counter and started munching on them.

Graham and Dana followed the scent of the freshly baked cookies in the kitchen.

"Hey Dad.... Hey Dana..." Jay and Will planted kisses on Graham's cheek and then on Dana's.

Violet poured glasses of milk for the boys and served them plates with the peanut butter cookies. "Enjoy!" She smiled. "See you later. I've got work to do."

Graham waited until Jay had finished his snack before questioning him. "Okay. First I want to commend you for your considerable and concentrated efforts regarding the hunt for a potential Derby winner. Secondly, I've been thinking about your desire to be a journalist and/or broadcaster." He grinned, proudly, at his eldest son. "I actually think it's a good fit. Your homework is to watch the news and keep a journal of your observations. Watch FOX, CNN, and the UK channels for starters to give yourself a global perspective..."

"Like...I wouldn't have thought of that? You underestimate me, Dad. I've been studying them for the last couple of years...that's why I've become inspired to be a newscaster. Wolf Blitz is one of my favorites...that might mean I need to travel to Aspen, Colorado to meet him. Maybe he'll become my mentor. You always said if you want to hunt a bear, go where they are. Well, I've heard he hangs out in Aspen. Oh...and speaking of bears, I've been doing some research on them."

"No one could accuse you of being a slacker. What did you find out about bears? I've heard there's quite a few of them hanging out in Aspen."

"There's around twenty that call the area home. Occasionally, they lumber down the main streets of Aspen at night...which I think is very cool...I mean, can you imagine running into a bear at night?"

"Come on, are you serious?" Graham peered at him, skeptically.

Dana was stunned. "Come on, Jay. You can't be serious. You're telling me that bears have been sighted lumbering down the streets of Aspen at night?"

"According to my research...yes. In fact, just last week, a Mother bear and her cub were spotted lumbering down one of the main streets in Aspen."

"Oh my gosh! So what happened? I'm surprised that doesn't make the news."

"Apparently it's commonplace there. It only occasionally makes the local news."

"Well, back to the thoroughbreds. I trust you have a

schedule of the viewing appointments with the colts on the farms."

"How much am I getting paid for this, Dad?" Jay raised his eyebrows, quirky-like.

"Listen, Kid. God gave me a brilliant son...two...actually. I believe we will all work together to train the Kentucky Derby winner. Flaming Bullet was poisoned last year, as you know...and that has been a grave learning experience.

This year I intend to hire an undercover equine expert to watch our new colt 24/7. It's sad that that's how it has to be...but that's the way it is. This time we'll be waitin' for any bad actors that come anywhere near the new colt. We weren't tough enough last year; and we did not anticipate the foul play that transpired. But we've learned from that experience. This year, no one...and I mean...absolutely no one... will come anywhere near our colt, unless they have clearance and we know precisely who we're dealing with."

"And like...don't forget to pray, Dad." Will grinned. "God can do it. God can cause our new colt to win. He has the last word."

Graham reached over and messed up his son's hair, playfully. "Yes, we serve a mighty God. A supernatural God. We do what we can do; and then He steps in and does that...son...so tht everyone gets that it is the mighty hand of God that has performed the miracle. He will do what we cannot do. In retrospect, I see that his timing is always perfect. You see, son...God causes miracles to bring glory to him and to wake people up. Those persons who do not know him are baffled by the miracle and it causes them to believe. Many have been won to Him because of this."

"Cool, Dad. Very cool." Jay grinned.

They drove through the tall, grand gates at Bosley Farms, soon assessing the colt they'd come to view. He was a stately, proud beauty. He reminded Dana vaguely of the world famous Sea Biscuit. Though of course, he was not as many hands high.

Jacob looked him over, scrutinizing him. "I like this one. He's close to eighteen hands high. He has a feisty spirit...probably a wild streak. There is something...special about him." Jacob looked him over closely, assessing him.

The colt reared up, neighing, his nostrils flaring. Like most well-bred colts offered for sale, his sleek body shimmered with radiant health. Sunlight bounced off him making him appear even shinier.

"Thankfully, the rain has stopped." Dana smiled. "And look, Graham... a magnificent rainbow. It's like a wink from God."

After they had spent considerable time assessing the colt, they drove on to the next appointment.

The sprawling ranch soared over the hundred-acre horse farm. A large, ancient house stood far back on the property. There was a massive red barn on the farm. It looked new. Several horses grazed lazily on the rolling bluegrass.

The tall, iron gates swung open. Graham drove onto the farm. They were greeted by an enormous, lone black Shepherd. They stayed in the Jeep, waiting for the owner to approach them. They'd been warned to do that.

A tall gentleman was descending the steps on the

veranda of the massive house. Soon, he moved quickly toward the jeep, soon reaching it. "I'm Donald Bouget. You must be Graham Van Rensellier...and your entourage." He grinned.

"That's right. This is my wife Dana... and my sons, Will and Jay."

"Welcome to Sunny Acres Farm." He shook Graham's hand and then Dana's. He spoke with a heavy French accent. Deeply tanned, he seemed to have a smile pasted on his face. His eyes were not smiling though. They were cold. "We winter in the South of France. I don't actually *live* on this farm though I run it. I have a staff. The ranch hands and caretaker live here."

Jay was a curious lad. "Cool. So...like where *do* you live?"

Donald seemed to take exception to the comment. He was clearly irked. "What does that have to do with anything?"

Woops. We seemed to have rubbed this guy the wrong way. What's his problem? Graham peered at the farmer. "I called you yesterday. You have a three-year old colt you're selling. Is that correct?"

"Yes. The colt is magnificent. Come... I will show you." Graham and his entourage followed the horse farmer to the massive, red barn. "I have some health issues and will not be able to oversee his training; but I am certain he would be a formidable candidate for the Derby. I would not be surprised if he won."

"Well...that's good news." Graham looked over the colt. He was sleek and shiny.

He moved his sinewy body as Dana patted him on the neck and tried to communicate with him to get a sense of him.

The colt reared up

Dana turned to the owner. "What would have caused that reaction?"

Donald shrugged. "There is much that we humans do not know about the horses, despite our best efforts to understand them thoroughly..." He grinned at Dana and Graham.

The man seemed almost human, once his slick veneer was pushed aside and he allowed himself to be vulnerable.

"How much are you asking for him?" Dana peered at the man.

At the price he mentioned, Dana's eyes widened like saucers. "Why so much?"

"I will show you the races he has already won. And...of course... his papers."

"Thank-you."

Dana's gut instinct kicked in. Something was off base here. But what? The horse racing business had an underbelly of rottenness. She wondered how legitimate the horse farmer was and how good the racehorse actually was. She had a check list in her mind. Only if the colt garnered a ten would she even consider it. Will had gone a step further, and doing impressive research, had comprised his own list of requirements for a potential Derby winner.

Graham had learned a lot about horse racing since his arrival almost two years ago. Despite watching the Derby every season for over a decade, he had entered a steep learning curve with Dana as his teacher. "Mind if I take the reins and walk around with him for a bit?"

"Please. Be my guest. I wish I could keep him. I would love to be able to train him and compete for the

Derby, but I must travel to Switzerland in three weeks for some special treatments...my wife is already there." He grinned. "We have a villa in Zurich."

"Nice. I've never been to Switzerland. I'd love to go there sometime." Dana smiled.

"I have never been there, either." Graham said.

"Well...who knows...after you win the Kentucky Derby with Full Moon, oh...that's what I call him...then maybe you will come and be our guest at the Villa Borghese. We will celebrate the winning together. After all, the colt got under my skin...and I hate to sell him. "

"Borghese? But that's Italian, isn't it?" Dana peered skeptically at the farmer.

"You're quite right, Dana. The architect and former owner of the villa were Italian. It is an Italian villa...and sometimes called a Palazzo."

Dana smiled over at Graham. "We'll win the Derby and take you up that generous invitation. Right now...I am more than a little intrigued by the colt you're offering for sale." She peered over at the owner.

Jay grinned, confidently. "I have brought a check list with me. Can we go over it now...together?"

Dana sensed a slight annoyance on the owner's part. She ignored it.

"Of course. Let's go in to my office. It's in the new building." He gestured toward it.

They followed the owner to the new building. His office had a separate entrance. He ushered them in.

The wall was covered with an impressive collection of framed photos of Kentucky Derby winners, as well as several photos of Donald, his wife, and some of their prized thoroughbreds. There were also photos of polo players.

"You have an impressive array of equine photos, Donald." Dana peered at one of them closely. "That polo player...I know him from somewhere..." She moved closer to it, puzzling over it.

"That's my son, Gerald. He's a well known polo player...plays in Aspen, Colorado and Palm Beach. His home base is Buenos Ares. He plays at the Eldorado club there. He's also played in the UK with Prince Charles..."

"How exciting!" Dana gushed. "It is, after all, the sport of Kings."

"I might like to be a polo player someday." Will smirked.

Graham grinned. "Well...that's news. It's the first I've heard of it!"

"Well, like...Dad...I've been keeping it a secret until I get to be a really, *really* good rider..."

Jay jabbed him in the ribs. "Yeah. That's because you don't want people laughing at you."

"That's...well, maybe it's kinda true. Anyway, I didn't want anyone throwing cold water on my dreams...so, like...that's why I haven't said anything before this."

Dana wrapped her arms around her sweet, vulnerable, step-son. "Oh, Will...I've known from the start that you have a passion for horses. It's a magnificent sport to aspire to. You can do that. You can do anything you want! I'm sure your Dad has told you that."

"Yeah, he has." Will grinned from ear to ear, ecstatic. He'd shared his secret dream, and no one had laughed at him.

Dana and Graham perused the thoroughbred's papers

thoroughly. "Thanks for the viewing and showing us his papers. He is a strong candidate, for sure. We would like to discuss it and sleep on it. Assuming he is still here tomorrow, we may put an offer on him. " "As you wish." The man escorted them out of his office.

Dana and Graham drove to the next appointment. Soon, Graham pressed the buzzer on a large, heavy iron gate. Glancing around, he noted the long, white fence and behind that was another fence, an electric one "Mr. Murray?"

"Ah. Mr. and Mrs Van Rensellier?"

"Graham and Dana will do."

He buzzed them in. Graham drove through the gate. Jacob followed behind in his horse trailer.

Soon, they were greeted by a rotund, grandmotherly woman with her hair in braids reminiscent of a Quaker. She smiled at them, lifting her heard from her task of sweeping the front patio.

A tall, wiry gentleman sporting a thin mustache met them at the Jeep. "Graham?" He crooked his head around, peering at Dana. "Dana?...Hans Heinrich. Welcome to Horseshoe Ranch. My groom has Silver Moon ready to show you. Please, follow me."

"Thanks." Graham hopped out of his jeep, his entourage following.

He glanced over at the newly constructed, contemporary house. It had manicured lawns. On the right side of the house there were a cluster of Begonias and Lilac trees interspersed with decorative statues surrounding a circular swimming pool and hot tub.

"Thank-you." Dana smiled, as she hopped out of the jeep.. "Our sons, Will and Jay."

The boys grinned their acknowledgement.

At the barn, Dana was in seventh heaven. She'd never seen so many magnificent horses in one barn. Neither had she ever seen a State-of-the-Art barn as fine as this.

Hans moved toward the sleek Thoroughbred he was selling. The colt reared up and neighed as they approached him. "I call him Leading Man." The farmer grinned.

"Fantastic. Love the name. Were... you ever in the theatre?"

"I was. I am. I keep a place in New York City. My agent is always looking for plumb theatre roles for me. I've done a few over the years...and starred in some prestigious theatres across America."

Dana and Graham exchanged glances. "How interesting." Dana smiled. "What prompted you to get into the horse business?"

"That is a long story. Perhaps another time. At the moment, I am curious to know your reaction to the colt I'm offering for sale."

"Why are you selling him? He looks incredible." *This is the one I want.* Dana was never so sure of anything in her life.

"Why does anyone sell anything?" He shrugged, answering his own question. "The money; of course."

"Of course." Dana flashed the man a smile. *I wonder if he knows Tanner.* She wouldn't get into that now. Still, she couldn't help being curious; particularly since learning of Troy and Tanner's theatre background.

"Well, let's have a gander." Dana was already carefully assessing the sleek colt. So was Graham and the boys.

Dana murmured to the colt, caressing his long, sleek neck. Then she whispered something in his ear. She moved a hand lovingly across his large, shiny body. She smelled him. She peered into his eyes, surveying him with a professional eye. She smiled, nodding to the owner. "He's good. He's real good. Can we take him outside?'

"Of course. His papers are in my mobile unit...whenever you're ready to peruse them."

It was Graham's turn to assess the colt. He went by the numbers. He had a mental list of what to look for. Blessed with a photographic memory, he went through his check list verbally without consulting the paper he carried. He glanced over at Jacob.

Jacob was studying the colt intently. He leaned toward Graham, whispering. "This is the one. I just know this is the one."

Dana smiled. "Yes, Jacob. I agree."

Graham nodded toward Dana and Jacob.

Chapter Seventeen

Graham and Dana put an offer on the colt. They could not risk another buyer beating them out. Time was of the essence. They were several weeks behind the schedule considered ideal for the training of a new colt with the goal of winning the Derby in May.

Negotiations were swift.

Dana whispered to Graham what to offer and what to say.

He followed her instructions. Soon, he shook hands with the former owner. He and Dana were the proud new owners of the colt.

"Congratulations! I will not be surprised if I hear he won the Derby." The former owner grinned.

Dana had been so excited that she'd forgotten to ask the previous owner of the colt, why he was selling. Not that it made any difference. Folks could say whatever they wanted, after all. Still, she decided to throw it out there. "Why did you just sell this amazing colt?"

He grinned, sinisterly. "That is my business...none of yours." His mindset and tone made it clear that it was the end of the conversation.

A chill ran down Dana's spine.

Graham raised his eyebrows.

Jacob peered at him, skeptically. "Do you...mind elaborating on that?"

"Yes, actually I do. It is none of your business, as I just said." His face was set in granite. "Now, then... I take it you can load him into the back of the horse trailer, correct?"

"Yes." Jacob said.

"Thank-you. It was nice doing business with you." The seller shook hands with Graham and then Dana.

Dana noticed for the first time how cold his eyes were. She'd been so focused on the colt and thinking about whether or not he was the best choice out there; that she hadn't taken even a few minutes to assess the owner. She had been on cloud nine, ever since laying eyes on the handsome, sleek colt.

Graham tried to stay cool. They had made the right choice, hadn't they? Whatever hidden agenda the man had, very likely had nothing to do with them or the colt. He probably needed the cash, just like most sellers. After all, paying close to half a million for a colt was a bird in the hand for a horse farmer.

They'd spent over an hour viewing footage of the colt. His papers were impeccable. The farm was very professional. Everything seemed in order. Still, something niggled at Graham.

And something niggled at Dana, too.

Monday morning at the racetrack.

Dana began riding the new colt just to get a sense of him. She and Jacob took turns riding him and orienting him to the racetrack and themselves.

Graham sat in the bleachers. Watching. Praying.

After a long day at the track, Jacob drove Dana, himself and the new colt back to the farm. Jacob let the thoroughbred down the ramp on his trailer, soon leading him to his new paddock.

Dana usually felt exhilarated after a day at the track with one of the colts. Not today. She saw Graham on the porch as Jacob drove up in the horse trailer. He parked and guided the colt out of the back of the trailer.

Graham had been watching for Dana. He hurried down the stairs, throwing his arms around her. "Darling, how did it go?"

"I wish I could say it went amazing but I can't. Something is not quite right with the colt. I don't know what it is, but something is off."

Graham was stunned into silence. He hadn't expected that. After a long pause, he spoke: "Come on in. Dinner is ready. We'll talk about it over a good meal. Whatever it is, it will get sorted out. We prayed diligently, we believed, and Jesus is Lord. We got it right, I'm sure of it. it's just that things don't always go according to our plans, as you well know. Maybe this is a trick of the enemy. Maybe the evil one wants us to lose heart and lose time. That's not going to happen. We made the choice prayerfully, and even though it *looks* like he might be off, it could just be him adjusting to new ownership. But, of course, there might be some inside stuff we don't know about the previous owner and his thoroughbreds."

Violet served roast beef with roasted potatoes and veggies in the formal dining room.

Dana ate heartily

Graham did, also. He turned to her after they'd both finished dinner. "What bothers you, specifically, you about the colt?"

"I wish I knew. It's nothing I can put my finger on. I just had a sense that...I don't know, maybe he had an injury...maybe a bad fall...there's something we haven't been told."

"Let's look over his papers again, together. If we have any questions, we'll call Hans and see what he says."

"I don't know. I don't like it. Something about him bothers me, like I said. I didn't get a sense of that when we spent time with him on Saturday before we made the offer. But I sense it now."

Graham peered into Dana's eyes. "Are you thinking what I'm thinking?"

"I guess that would depend on what you're thinking." Dana chuckled.

"What are you saying? He was fine, but when we went to his office to look over the papers and sign the sales document... and give him our check...could someone have tampered with him during that time?"

"Maybe. I hope I'm wrong. It's just that...the colt was perfect...and now he's...I don't know...something is off...I wish I knew what that was." Dana was so sad she almost started crying.

"Darling. Worrying or crying won't help. We'll get this sorted out." Graham grinned. "Hey, I gave him a check. I could stop payment on it and we could return the colt. What do you think of that?"

"We don't know who we're dealing with. I think we prefer to live, don't you?" Dana peered into Graham's eye

"I thought you said you knew his name and reputation from horsey circles."

"I did. And I do. But that may not mean anything. Unfortunately, people change...and secrets could be well hidden."

"Dana, talk to me. What do you think is going on? What about this colt?"

"Graham...I don't know how to say this...but when I first rode him out at the farm, he was as smooth as silk. A born winner. Awesome...but after we bought him and took him to Sugarbush...and after the initial orientation today... with Jacob and I...the colt just seems...different somehow. I don't know how else to say it. It's like he... changed overnight."

"Dana. Please tell me I'm hearing things...or reading stuff into the situation. We can't...emotionally...go through this thing again..."

Tears sprung to her eyes. "What do you want me to do, Graham? Lie to you? I told you...he was perfect yesterday...and today...something seems off. It's not just my take; Jacob feels the same way."

Graham was at a loss for words. He put his hands on her shoulders. "Dana, darling...my love...we'll get through this one day at a time...sweet Jesus. Maybe it's just a...test...like a hurdle we have to leap over...maybe tomorrow he'll be oriented and cool...and everything will be just fine."

Dana smiled through a mist of tears threatening to spill out. "Maybe." But even as the words sprung from her lips, she had a premonition that things would only get worse. She slept fitfully.

Graham couldn't sleep, either. He couldn't shake the hunch that Dana was right. And when it came to the equines, few were her equal. *But if her instincts were right, had she and Graham just lost over half a million dollars?*

Maybe they should put a stop-payment on the check. But even as the thought crossed his mind, he shuddered. The horse racing business was often sleezy and it was known to bring out the worst in people. Everybody wanted to win the million dollar purse. Everybody wanted the fame, status and money it would bring. Competition was fierce. Who could they trust?

Dana rose shortly after 5:00 a.m. Sleep had eluded her. She glanced over at Graham. He was sleeping soundly. She had work to do. She wasn't sure exactly what that entailed but she definitely did have work to do. She had to find out what was going on with the colt. She kissed him gently on a cheek and slipped noiselessly out of the room.

Violet usually arose around 6:00. She wasn't up yet. She was alone in the massive, old mansion. She made a pot of coffee. Peering in the cupboard, she found some croissants and orange juice. As she bit into the croissant, it hit her. *Maybe Tanner staged this whole thing. Maybe the colt had been poisoned right after they bought him. Somebody wanted them out of the race and out of the industry. And they were dead serious about it. That could only be Tanner and his cohorts.*

As she sat in the prayer room, praying and seeking God for answers, she heard a noise. It seemed to be coming from the back of the house. Soon, she heard barking. The Shepherds barked, at first lazily but soon increasing in their intensity.

Somebody is back there. I better get Graham. Otherwise, why would the dogs suddenly be barking up a storm? She hurried into the bedroom where a sleepy

Graham pulled her hand coaxing her back to bed.

She couldn't resist him. Never could. And couldn't now. It was some time before they emerged. She'd tried to tell him about the intruder but he had his mind on other things. Finally, she sat bolt upright. "Graham. Someone is in the house!"

He chuckled. "Yeah. There's you, me, the boys and Violet."

"Graham. You're not listening. I said *someone...an intruder* is in the house." She whispered to him. "I rose at 5:00 because I couldn't sleep. I made coffee. While I was in the kitchen, I heard noises. Roamer and Rover were barking up a storm. I'm surprised they didn't wake you."

"It's a big house. Maybe they were tearing around it." Graham leaped out of bed, pulled on his terry bathrobe and grabbing his shotgun. "Who would be intruding on our farm? And how would they have gotten in?" He handed Dana another shotgun. "Let's go." He emerged from the master bedroom touting the gun, Dana behind him.

In the kitchen, Violet hummed an upbeat tune as she took fresh muffins out of the oven.

The aroma of gourmet coffee and baked goods assailed Dana's senses. "Muffins, Violet?"

They all spun around as a loud banging noise erupted from the back of the house. Graham turned to Dana. "Let's go, Dana. Violet, call the sheriff."

She did as instructed while Graham and Dana marched toward the noise at the back of the house. Graham yelled "Freeze!" His shotgun was poised and at the ready.

Silence.

"I said freeze. Freeze or I'll shoot."

The back door was being kicked in. Graham slammed a bullet toward it. They heard yelping. The dogs were going nuts.

The commotion awakened the boys who hurried into the kitchen.

Violet motioned for them to be silent.

It was all over in minutes. Billy had managed to find his way onto the farm undetected.

Graham was outraged. He grabbed the scoundrel by the scruff of his neck. "I've had enough of you, Billy. You're goin' to prison this time. They've been lenient on you so far, but we've all had enough of you."

He sneered at them. "You're a couple of dummies. You paid a half a mil for a no-good colt. I told you I was going to ruin you and I meant it..."

The sheriff's siren screeched to a stop in front the mansion. Violet hurried to the front door to let them in.

The Sheriff shook his head. "Okay, Billy...let's go." They handcuffed him.

Danielle had had a rough night. With her new hubby gone and her bank account at zero, she needed a miracle. Fast. *Hadn't the pastor at the little church on the hill she used to attend told her that God was in the miracle business? With nowhere to go and having run out of options, she decided she would give church a shot. What did she have to lose?*

Sunday couldn't come fast enough. It was only Friday morning. She lounged around, barely able to function, watching TV and indulging in too much chocolate ice cream. *What did it matter if she gained a few pounds?*

Finally, it was Sunday morning. Danielle chose a pink jacket and a short charcoal shirt. The matching pink pumps were perfect with the outfit. Not that it mattered. It wasn't about meeting a new man. Today, it was about falling on the mercy of God. She hadn't been following him. And she knew there was a price to pay when you backslid. She'd paid that price and now she had to dust herself off and start over again. *Lord, give me the strength to do it.*

The quaint church on the hillside was an Evangelical church. She hoped God had not forgotten her. She believed he would forgive her. She could start over.

She strode up the front steps and settled onto a pew in the third row. A small choir on the stage warbled out old gospel tunes, while a young man imbued with masses of high energy and much musical talent, enthusiastically plunked out the old time gospel tunes on a piano.

She was worshipping in song when she became aware of a somewhat handsome looking older gentleman. He moved next to her on the pew. She'd left a seat at the edge of the bench, because she always thought it rude when folks took the seat at the edge, forcing newcomers or latecomers to climb over the parishioner to obtain a seat. Though she considered this practise merely good manners; she'd often been surprised and inconvenienced when folks hogged the edge of the bench.

The man settling onto the bench was balding and well built. He appeared to have a jolly disposition. Danielle barely glanced at him.

The minister was young and gave a fire and brimstone inspired service, laced with humor. She heeded the altar call and moved toward the front when it came. It was time to repent and start over.

The tears flowed as she repented. She dried her tears and tried to manufacture a smile. As she was leaving the pew, she noticed the older man standing in the isle. The man ginned at her. "Danielle? Don't I know you?"

She whirled around. *Someone was calling her name.* She did not recognize the gentleman. "I...don't think we've met. I'm Danielle...."

"Oh, I know who you are. I'm a news reporter. The name is Mike Manford." He handed her a card. "I'm with KJRC News, the TV station. May I take you to lunch?"

Danielle was stunned. *What exactly did the man want?* "Sure. Why not?" It's not like she had them lined up. Besides, she'd always been a curious person. She had nothing left to lose, anyway.

"Danielle Girdano." She decided to use her married name. The last thing she wanted was to engage in a conversation about racehorses and her renowned equestrian daughter.

They chatted briefly in the lobby and were soon on their way. "I'll meet you at Il Travantino's. Do you know it?"

"I do. It's one of my favorite restaurants."

At the charming Italian eatery, the man only wanted to talk about Dana and the kidnapping. He'd been unable to contact Dana and Graham since the ordeal and had reason to believe it was not a random event.

She felt like walking out, but she had nowhere to go.

And with slim pickings when it came to friends, she thought it best to bite her tongue and see what the man was about. As he chatted, she warmed up to him. He was humorous and interesting, despite his agenda.

Danielle knew about the kidnapping. She had orchestrated it. Bart had phoned her every day. She was the brains behind the kidnapping. She'd masterminded it. Bart and his new partner were merely puppets on her string. To the outside world, she was wrapped up in her new life and new hubby. And, since becoming estranged from Dana and Graham, she didn't want to talk about them. She was attracted to the man.

It's just a little lie, Lord. I'm sorry, but aren't I entitled to enjoy a man's company after all I've just been through?

She chatted compulsively embellishing her life to make herself sound more interesting than she actually was "Dana was taken from...a parking lot, where she was parked at a mall..." Suddenly Danielle was seized with another persona. She didn't know what was happening to her, she only knew that another personality was taking over. She had a sense that the voice emanating from her was not her own, though she was helpless to stop it. "They grabbed her. Two burly guys grabbed her real quick. It was dusk and there weren't many cars on the lot. They pushed her into the back of their SUV and gagged her. The driver was already in the car. He spun out of the lot, while one of the thugs blindfolded her, tied her hands and feet, grabbed her purse and sped off."

"She told you all this?"

"Of course. The next thing she knew, they took off the blindfold and she was in a warehouse in the

Industrial area of town..."

The reporter peered at her, oddly. "You...you're sure this is how it happened. Lenny at the office has a totally different story."

Danielle laughed. "I'm her Mother. Who are you going to believe?"

The man reddened. "You... of course, Danielle. Maybe that new reporter should be fired. I don't know where he got his information from..."

The fried oysters and salad arrived. They dug in. "The food is wonderful." Danielle smiled at the man.

A faint whiff of a masculine cologne wafted toward her, driven by the balmy breeze wafting over them. "Gorgeous day, isn't it?" Dana smiled at her date.

A smattering of low Palm trees lined the edge of the outdoor patio, giving them privacy from the street. Soft music wafted throughout the area. She peered closely at him. *He's quite attractive.* She'd gotten the impression he was single but she'd better confirm that before she got carried away. "Are you single?" She raised her brows, flirtatiously.

He grinned. "I am. And you?"

"Me, too. Going through a divorce. I had a brief, disastrous marriage."

"Sorry to hear it." He leaned toward her, suddenly. "Are you free tonight? I have tickets to the symphony. My daughter was going to join me, but she cancelled out at the last minute. Said something about the flu coming on."

It was time to play hard-to-get. She couldn't fall all over him anymore than she already had. "I...I'm actually not free tonight. I've made plans." She flashed him a smile. "Perhaps another time."

"Sure. Well, I should get the bill. Thanks for a great interview. I might be able to get it on tonight's news..."

It was a jolt of reality. "Oh. I wouldn't do that if I were you. I have some juicy tidbits to spice it up with. I have a *lot* more to tell you. Maybe we should meet for breakfast tomorrow."

"Sure. Or I could be a No-show and...uh...take you for dinner tonight."

That she could not resist. She'd never enjoyed cooking and wasn't looking forward to another night alone munching on tuna sandwiches. "As I said...I'm not free tonight...but this is important. If I can reach my girlfriend I'll cancel our dinner date and we'll get together."

They traded cell numbers. "I'll see if I can beg off."

Dinner was a hamburger place. This time his questions were precise. Tough. The gloves were off.

Danielle couldn't stand up to the interrogation, she cracked. "I...I don't remember. It's been such a traumatic ordeal...such a nightmare...that I actually think...sometimes I think I'm losing it."

"Relax, Danielle. Just tell me stuff as it comes to you. By Monday morning, I'll push it as breaking news. It would be goo d if you could add some drama we haven't heard about.

Danielle had always been imbued with a vivid imagination. She started talking and couldn't seem to stop. She spun up a mountain of lies and finally burst out laughing. Soon she was hysterical.

The reporter's eyes grew large as saucers. "Dear God, the woman is having a nervous breakdown. That's the story!"

The news of Danielle's compulsive lies, split personality and nervous breakdown hit the front pages of the morning paper.

"Danielle Lockhart, mother of recently kidnapped equestrian, Dana Lockhart, flips out and is hospitalized!"

The reporter didn't relish driving her to the psyche ward of the local hospital but he really had no choice.

During the drive she ranted and raved but when they arrived at the hospital and he took her up the elevator to the psyche ward, she seemed to snap to her senses. She glanced around as though emerging from a dream. "What...why am I here?" Nervously, her eyes darted around the room.

A psyche nurse with a soothing voice smiled warmly at her. "Come with me."

Danielle's eyes darted around the room nervously. "W...why am I here?"

"Let's get you settled in. Come with me, dear." The stocky nurse took control of the situation.

Danielle was in a daze. She peered at the nurse's name tag, saying it aloud. "Sandra Moss."

Chapter Twenty

The next morning, Danielle arose very early. She hadn't slept well. She was disoriented and felt groggy. "What am I doing here?" She spoke the words aloud, despite being in the small room alone.

A young nurse, bright and cheery, clad in a crisp uniform entered the room. "Good morning, Danielle. How did you sleep?"

"Terrible."

"You were..." She glanced at the chart by her bed and then leaned closer into it, reading it carefully.

"Well? What does it say?" Danielle spat the words out.

"Seems you were brought in after considerable rambling and incoherence...coupled with some aggressive behavior."

"I want to go home."

"That's a decision the psychiatrist will make. You are scheduled for some tests and a meeting with him to determine what medication you need to take."

"That's ridiculous. There's nothing wrong me. I want out of here!"

"I'm afraid that's not going to happen. We have

contacted your daughter and her hubby. They will be in this afternoon to visit you."

Danielle stood then. She whacked the nurse with her right hand.

Startled, the nurse quickly recovered. Her face had turned to stone. "Very aggressive behavior, Danielle. Visitation rights are cancelled. I'll give you something to calm you down." She smiled thinly and walked briskly out of the room and, soon returning with a plastic glass filled with water and two pills.

Danielle was slumped down on her cot, her hands over her face, sobbing.

"Take this medication. It will make you will feel better." She handed Danielle two pills with a glass of water.

Danielle threw the water in the nurse's face, heaved the pills on the floor, stomping on them.

The nurse was fuming. Trained not to react and to remain in control regardless of the circumstances, she spoke calmly. "Well, now....that was an unfortunate choice...unfortunate for *you.* You will need to go to the lockup room, given your aggressive and hostile behavior."

Danielle screamed.

The nurse pressed an emergency button. Two male nurses appeared, escorting her to the lock-up room.

Graham received a call from the psyche ward that morning. "This is Janice Hopkins, head nurse in the psyche ward at Lexington University Hospital. I just wanted to inform you that you will not be able to visit Danielle Lockhart until further notice. She is currently in the lock-up room and heavily medicated. Her aggressive behavior has escalated, I'm afraid."

Graham was stunned. He waited until lunch time to break the news to Dana. While they munched on corn beef sandwiches on rye with pickles, Graham spilled the beans. "Dana...I don't know how to say this...but...well...your Mom remains in the psyche ward and has shown signs of aggressive behavior." *I don't have the heart to tell my darling about her being in the lock-up room.*

"Graham, I wonder how she got to this point. I mean...I knew she had issues...the jealousy thing...the compulsion to make more and more money...and her falling away from the faith. It started with her not going to church; then I think she stopped reading the Bible...and it went downhill from there."

"So she stepped out from the supernatural covering of the creator; that gives the devil room to move right in." Graham shook his head.

"Do you think that's what happened?"

"Of course. We must never forget that the adversary surfaces when we are weak and vulnerable. As long as we are actively implementing spiritual warfare, the enemy cannot penetrate our mind or muck up our lives. Remember *Greater is he that is in you than he that is in the world.* Many folks don't get how much power the Word and prayer call down from heaven."

"Well, Graham, she was sure deceived when she fell hook, line and sinker for that loser she married." Dana shook her head. "All this time I thought she was a shrewd businesswoman...but all it took was one good lookin' dude to steal everything she's worked for years..." Tears trickled down Dana's cheeks. "Although it turns out she didn't have much."

"You know, Dana. God always forgives and restores. When she is up to having visitors, we'll drive over to the hospital and bring her some flowers...maybe pray with her and encourage her." Graham peered over at Dana. His heart broke when he saw the tears trickling down Dana's cheeks. "Let's take the Thoroughbreds out for some exercise."

Quickly, she wiped away her tears. "You always know the right thing to say. Let's go, honey."

Mounting Silver Star, one of Dana's favorite thoroughbreds, new joy seeped into her soul like a burst of oxygen. "Come on, Boy...let's go." She didn't wait for Graham, despite knowing he was right behind her riding Midnight Magic, their new, jet black thoroughbred. Instead, she raced down the trail, galloping full out, somehow trying to make sense of everything that had befallen them. She and the thoroughbred soared down the path as though they were on a racetrack.

Graham dug his heels into Midnight Magic goading him to increase his speed. Somehow, he got his left foot crooked onto the horse and it reared up. He managed to stay on top of him, though it slowed him down.

Dana, upset and in her own world, raced ahead, oblivious to Graham's plight. Tears slid down her cheeks as thoughts of her Mother's plight engulfed her, saddening her. "Lord, please heal my Mother... make her well... Lord... as only you can do...you are in control." She fought of more tears threatening to overwhelm her. After the prayer, she glanced over toward Graham. He was galloping away from her. "Graham." She called after him. But he raced toward the barn.

She raced after him, bewildered at his erratic behavior. Soon, she was at the barn. She settled her thoroughbred into his stall and hurried over to Graham.

He appeared to be in pain. "Graham. What is it? You look pale."

It was almost audible. She had a powerful sense of the presence of God. *He needs you.*

Paramedics burst into the barn. Graham had apparently called them. They went to work on him. He'd collapsed onto the floor minutes after Dana had arrived. Paramedics began working on him. "He's had a mild stroke. We got him in time. Hopefully, he'll be okay."

"Darling. You're going to be just fine. Because I'm going to pray and believe for your healing...and never stop praying."

"You can follow the ambulance to Lexington University Hospital where we're taking him."

She could feel the color draining from her face. *Lord, I can't lose him. I can't live without him. Surely you know that.*

Violet had heard the siren and had come out to the barn. She thrust comforting arms around Dana. "The boys are on the school bus. They'll be home soon. You need to be strong for them. And strong for Graham..."

"And strong for Mom." Suddenly the mettle that had been the driving force behind her career as a jumper and trainer kicked in. "Graham will be fine. Because...I'm going to call things that are not as though they are, according to Mark 11:23 & 24."

"You do that, honey. And I will, too." Violet hugged Dana.

Graham sprung back, astounding everyone. He got up. "I'm okay. It's like a miracle...I'm suddenly just fine."

"Darling..." Dana wrapped him in her arms. "Don't you ever scare me like that again." I was praying for a fast, miraculous recovery, and we got it! "They walked hand-in-hand back to the house with Violet.

Dana and Violet held the fort down. Dana threw herself into the care of the horses and supervising the two ranch hands, Wilbur and Joe. She strode over to the barn. Wilbur was diligently grooming the horses. Joe, the new ranch hand was nowhere around. "Wilbur, you're an ace groom and I need you to take Joe under your wing. He's eager to learn and happy to have a room in the bunk house, but you need to work with him on a daily basis to get him up to speed."

"Sure. No problem."

"Also...I need you to keep an eye on him. There's something about him that bothers me, but he sure does know horses and his recommendations were ace. Do you know where he is right now?"

"Not really. He was around about an hour ago but I haven't seen him since then. I should tell you...that I recently discovered he has a girlfriend. He sneaks her onto the farm at night and she stays at the bunk house with him. I was...uh workin' up my nerve to tell you. I warned him that it might cost him his job if you and Graham got wind of it."

Dana saw red. That sort of thing was strictly forbidden. "When did you first learn about it?"

"Just...just last week. I was...workin' up the nerve to tell you, like I said."

"I'll have a talk with him. Is he in the barn now?"

"I think he is."

Dana strode into the barn. Since marrying Graham she had changed her wardrobe. Well, actually, she'd changed a lot of things. She'd taken to wearing men's shirts, but real nice ones. Today, she had a blue striped shirt on, jeans, cowboy hat and of course, her favorite, old boots Her hair cascaded down her back. Graham had told her to keep growing it and forget about cutting it. She usually did what he asked.

She saw red. She'd been busy and preoccupied with Graham and her mom. She hadn't thought about the ranch hands for a couple days. She didn't usually come out to the barn mid-afternoon, because she often picked up the boys from school or helped Violet around the house.

Joe was grooming one of the thoroughbreds, while a very short, cute gal with strawberry blonde hair made goo-goo eyes at him.

"What have we here? I don't believe we've met. And I don't recall inviting you to visit Sugarbush." Dana's gaze was steely. She was uncharacteristically curt.

"Oh, hi. You must be Dana Van Rensellier. I'm Janet Wilcox. Dad owns a farm near here." Then she started yakking, nervously. "I've known Joe for ages...ever since we were young kids..." Her blond braids bounced, saucy brown eyes sparkled with mischief.

"No girlfriends are allowed to sleep in the bunker with the ranch hands. That would be cause to fire Joe. Y'all can consider this a warning. If I see you around here after this afternoon, he's gone."

"Oh, no, Ma'am. Don't fire him. We need this job.

Uh, *he* needs this job."

"Do you need me to drive you somewhere?" She peered at the young girl.

She hesitated a few beats. "Yeah. Sure. That would be good. I don't live far from here. Four Star Ranch is just over ten miles away."

"I know where it is. Come on...let's go."

"Okay." Janet followed Dana to her SUV.

Dana hopped into her white Mercedes SUV.

Janet hopped in next to her. "Nice car."

"Thanks. I enjoy it. So I guess your dad is Allen Wilcox. Am I right?"

"How did you know?"

"Oh, come on. We horse farmers all know each other. It's a pretty small world, actually."

"Did you know that Mom died last year?"

The girl tugged at Dana's heart. She wanted to mother her. "No...no... I didn't."

"Cancer. It was slow." The young woman burst into tears. "I wish I had a Mama. Someone to talk to...someone to hold me...Dad is never around. Since Mom died he's always out...I never know when he's gonna come home...or even *if* he's gonna come home." Tears sprung to her eyes.

"Do you have any siblings?"

"No. I'm an only child."

Dana had a powerful urge to mother the young woman, protect her...teach her the ropes. Maybe she should. Before she'd given it serious thought or prayer, words popped out of her mouth. "Why don't you...uh...come and stay for the week-end. Since it's Friday, you might as well come with me. Lord knows we have plenty of room. Maybe come to church with us on Sunday. Do you go to any church?"

"Never been inside a church in my life."

"The fields are white and ready to harvest, but the laborers are few." The scripture popped into her mind and before she had thought it through, she spoke. "Call him and see what he says. Come for dinner tonight and you can stay over. We have seven bedrooms in the old mansion, there's plenty of room for you."

"Wow! That would be like...so cool. I'd have to go home and get my PJ's though."

"No, you don't. We have PJ's and robes in various sizes for house guests. We're set up that way. The house was designed for guests and a large family...I guess."

Janet was on her cell. "Dad? Like... Dana, the owner of Sugarbush...well, she invited me to stay the weekend and go to church with her. So...like...is that okay?"

Silence. "Ya. Okay. When ya comin' home?"

The young girl peered over at Dana. "When am I comin' home?"

"I can drive you back Sunday night or Monday morning. Your choice."

"Well Dad?"

"Monday morning is fine. I'm busy Sunday, anyway."

"Thanks, Dad."

"Sure, Kid. Stay out of trouble...like I said before."

Dana could hear the conversation. "Maybe I could speak to your Dad for a minute."

The young woman handed her cell to Dana.

"She'll be safe with at Sugarbush. We'll take good care of her." Dana put a smile in her voice as she spoke.

At the house, Dana settled her into a guest room. "Wow! Like this place is so cool. Reminds me of the house in *Gone with the Wind*."

Dana chuckled. "It's pretty nice, all right. God has blessed us real good. We don't deserve it, but yet we're blessed."

"Well...like...how could I get blessed?" Saucy brown eyes peered trustingly at Dana.

Dana smiled. *Was I ever that young?* "Come on down to the living room and we'll talk."

Two hours raced by as Dana started from the beginning and educated the young woman on Bible basics and the power of the Word and reading and studying it.n

"So...like...you're giving me this Bible and I should read it every day?"

Dana smiled. "That's the idea, my dear. You will be amazed at what God will do in your life when you immerse yourself in the word."

"Well...like...do you think I should break it off with Joe?"

"Yes. I think you should focus on your studies and plan to attend college after you graduate from high school."

"Well...like... I think I'm in love with him. And...I think he's in love with me."

"If that's true, and that's God's best for you, then he will work it out for you to have a future with him...provided you follow the right path."

Violet strode into the spacious living room. "Just thought I'd let you know that the boys are home from school, Dana."

"Thanks. Ah...where is Graham?"

"Actually, I don't know. As you know he had some business in the city; but he should be home by now. Maybe one of us should give him a call."

"I will. I've...been doing a little private tutoring." She grinned at the young girl. "But I need to touch base with Graham."

She speed-dialed his number. "Where are you?"

"I...I'll tell you about it when I get home."

"You sound weird. Everything okay?"

"We'll talk after dinner. Are Will and Jay home?"

"They are. And...uh...Jacob is still out at the track. I haven't heard from him. No news is good news. Maybe the colt was just having a bad day yesterday...or has some minor issues."

"From your lips to God's ears."

Graham wore a green floral, short-sleeved shirt. He took her breath away. *He is quite simply one of the most gorgeous men on the planet.* She hurried up to him as he opened the front door to the house. She'd been watching for his Jeep. "Darling." She kissed him, hugging him. "We have a house guest."

"Really? Who might that be?"

She gave him the short version of the ranch hand and Janet.

"Okay. If you think you can help her, go for it."

After dinner, Dana took Graham by the hand leading him into her den. She'd christened it as such, when she'd spotted the built-in book shelves and antique desk, the charming chaise lounge and the embossed gold and burgundy drapes. With the high ceilings and private terrace, it was her private room, the place where she daily communed with God. A private sanctuary. The prayer room was for everyone, but this place was hers alone. Of course Graham was always welcome...as long as he knocked first.

The late afternoon sun shone through the window casting a pale light across his handsome face, as he sat in the wingback chair in her den.

"Darling, what is it? You're upset. I can see it on your face." She moved toward him cradling his face in her arms. "What's goin' on?"

"Dana. I don't know how to say this..."

"What? Spit it out! What's goin' on?"

He lowered his face, his eyes downcast. "It's Danielle. She's had a nervous breakdown. She's in the psyche ward at the University Hospital in Lexington. She exhibited aggressive behavior and...they put her in the lock-up room. Again."

"The lock-up room! Again! Good heavens. How could this have happened?"

"From the chat I had with the psychiatrist, it seems she's been filled with much resentment and jealousy toward you. But it was the brief, rocky marriage and the fact that he wiped her out financially, that seems to have pushed her over the edge..."

"Why did they contact *you*? Why not *me*?"

"Good thing you're sitting down. Danielle insisted they contact me instead of you. Looks like the jealousy and other issues she has with you are very deep seated."

"Oh, Graham. I...I knew she was in trouble...but I had no idea she would slip over the edge..."Tears sprung to Dana's eyes. "I better go visit her."

Graham put his hand on her arm. "No. She doesn't want to see you. She does not want you to visit her."

"What? That's outrageous. What is she thinking?"

"Honey, I don't know. If she was playing with a full deck she wouldn't be there."

"True. Okay, so at least I know there isn't another woman...and now I know what the mystery trip was all about."

"So what's goin' on with the new colt? Did we just drop a lot of cash on a loser, or is he a winner? What do you think?"

She knew the ball was in her court. She was the expert, after all. *Lord, help me out here. Give me wisdom.* "Nothing in life is sure..."

"Except death and taxes." He finished the sentence for her, chuckling derisively.

"Jacob is at the track with him. He'll give us a full report tonight. I refuse to believe that we were deceived into buying the wrong colt. I mean, don't you feel that way?"

"Of course. The colt passed our thirty point check list with flying colors. She got pretty much a 100 on every point and we both felt good about her. Her blood lines are superior. The colt is a great beauty, an amazing animal..." Dana reviewed her thinking. *Could she have led him into making a dreadful mistake? She had been so sure he was the right colt. Lord? Could I have gotten it terribly wrong?*

"Jacob and I decided that I should spend the entire day tomorrow with him. Hopefully, I'll get a sense of what's going down...by the time I return home. Then tomorrow, Jacob will do the same thing. Tomorrow night we'll compare notes."

"This doesn't sound promising." Graham peered over at her. "I think...we already know that we have made a mistake...a very costly mistake...as tragic as that it." He sighed. "I think the key now is to sell the colt quickly and buy another one right away. We have no time to waste. We need to get the colt in the qualifying races as soon as possible."

Later that night Dana knew. A terrible mistake had actually been made. She sat alone in the living room. It was just after dinner. She sipped cinnamon apple tea and meditated on scriptures.

Graham found her there and realized how upset she was. "Dana...darling...what is it? It's the colt, isn't it?"

She nodded, tears welling up in her eyes. "I'm afraid...we...I've made a terrible error in judgement..."

"Ah, honey, stop blaming yourself. I'm a big boy. I thought he was great, too. And so did Jacob. I still think something sinister occurred right after we bought him. We were too trusting. The former owner was alone with the colt for a few minutes...remember...he said he wanted to say a private good-bye to him. And we both identified with that...fools that we were...it must have been then that he slipped the colt something...probably in his food. It's the oldest story in the book...how could we have been foolish enough to fall for it?"

Dana called the vet and was told he would try to get to Sugarbush as soon as he could. He hoped to be there within the hour. He considered it an emergency. He'd told Dana that time was of essence if the colt had ingested something. He would need to do a series of tests and would know after administering some of them at the farm, whether or not he would have to take her to his private equine hospital.

Chapter Twenty-one

The sky teemed with rain. Dark clouds loomed in the skies. A cool chill tempered the air. Dana jumped out of bed and into the shower. Graham had been sound asleep and she knew he needed it. She hadn't known what a deeply compassionate man he was and how he took everything to heart until she'd gotten to know him intimately. Seeing Danielle in the psyche ward had deeply upset him. *"Thank God she's only my step mom; otherwise, I might have inherited her genes. I might have had a proclivity for going off the deep end, myself."*

She toweled off. Humming a tune, she slipped into a western outfit. She would spend her quiet time alone with God in the prayer room. Soon, Graham would rise and they would head to the barn to do the morning chores.

In the prayer room, she began by lifting up praise to the Almighty. *"Jesus is Lord! You are Lord. You are Lord. You have risen from the deal and you are Lord. Every knee shall bow, every tongue confess that Jesus Christ is Lord..."* The song erupted from somewhere deep in her soul. She worshipped and praised God for some time. She'd closed the door for privacy.

There was a gentle tap on the door. "Graham?"

Silence.

"Honey?"

Nothing.

The door was locked. Would it be Violet...or her house guest? "Who is it?" She called out through the door in a loud voice.

"It's me, honey. I just walked away from the door for a few minutes..."

At the sound of his voice, she opened the door.

Graham stood there. White as a ghost.

"Darling? What is it? What happened?"

"Will...he...he's gone missing. He wasn't in his room this morning. When Violet went to wake him...he...he wasn't there!" His voice was rising in hysteria.

"Oh Lord, this can't be happening!"

Graham grabbed her and held her close. They remained locked in the embrace for several minutes. Finally, Graham peered into her eyes and kissed her passionately. "We must pray...fervently...that God will cause a miracle to happen...that he'll come home right away!"

"Let's go out to the barn. Let's see what's going on there. The ranch hands should be on the job by now. Maybe they know something."

Graham took Dana's hand leading her to the kitchen. He grabbed a mug, downed some black coffee and then handed it to Dana. "Take a swig...and then let's go. Time is always of the essence in these things..."

At the barn, everything seemed to be running smoothly. The ranch hands were on the job. Wilbur was whistling a tune and Joe seemed upbeat, too.

"Guys...Will has gone missing. He...he was...apparently... taken from the house... while we slept. We've combed every inch of the house...he's not there."

"Guess you don't know he has a girlfriend." Wilbur smirked.

"A girl...friend? Who would that be?"

"She's ah... stayin...in your house...Janet. She dumped me for Will."

Graham turned to Dana. He was stunned...outraged. "Let's get back to the house. Do you really think that Will is in the guest room with her?"

"Only one way to find out. Let's go."

They found Will in one of the guest rooms. Trying to teach Janet how to play chess.

Graham and Dana breathed a sigh of relief. "Time for school, Will. Janet, we'll drop you at your farm."

Graham hugged Will. "Please...just let us know what you're doing. We just want to make sure you're okay."

Chapter Twenty-two

Danielle was not amused. Graham had shown up but clearly had no interest in her. Anger seethed through her mind and spirit, adversely affecting her body. She shook with it. *Maybe she should...get rid of Dana...oh Lord, forgive me...what was I thinking? But even as the fleeting thought soared through her mind, the compulsion to get rid of Dana grew stronger, more pronounced. That's it. I have the connections. I'll arrange for a hit.* The kidnapping scenario backfired, so I need a new plan.

She shook her head as though coming out of a trance. *"Lord, what was I thinking?"* Still, she couldn't shake the diabolical idea. She had always prided herself on being clever. She could get rid of Dana, insist on more visits from Graham, get better and charm him into marrying her. *He should have done that to begin with. I'm just helping him do what he really wants to do. I can tell he's enamored with me. Might even be secretly in love with me. Yes, this is a perfect plan.*

She had a moment of conscience. But only a moment. She smiled. *I'm so clever. I've always gotten what I wanted. Why should I stop now?"* She walked the short distance to the bathroom used for the few female occupants in the group psyche ward. Closing the door, she peered into the mirror. "I still have it. I'm gorgeous, if I say so myself. And even without make-up. She smiled as she peered into the mirror, staring at her reflection. *"I'm sorry, Lord, but many folks in the Bible murdered and went on to good, productive lives. I know I shouldn't be doing this...but, Lord...sometimes maybe we have to take matters in our own hands..."* She started shaking and then sobbing. Quickly, she stepped out of the bathroom and managed to find her way back to the lounge area where the other patients languished. She flopped down on one of the sofas. A soap opera was on TV. She began watching it. *Maybe it will take my mind off this fixation. I know it's not right, Lord...but it's a compulsion...I feel that I must proceed...* She began sobbing uncontrollably.

Anna, the psyche nurse, seemed to pop up out of nowhere. She handed Danielle a paper cup filled with water and two pills. "Take these, dear. It will calm you down. I know you're under a lot of stress..."

Danielle swallowed the pills gulping down water with it. Soon, she felt sleepy. Again, the nurse appeared, smiling. She took her by the hand. "Come on, I've got a semi-private room for you. Get some sleep. You'll feel better."

Danielle awakened a couple of hours later, feeling somewhat refreshed. Then the compulsion took over. *I must get rid of Dana. My life will be wonderful if I can just get rid of her.* She shook her head. *No, that's crazy thinking. I love Dana...don't I? She's screwed up my life, cost me a lot of money...but I'm her Mom...okay,*

Step Mom, anyway.

Her roommate was watching a soap opera on TV.

She started watching it, becoming diverted from her diabolical plan. *Yes, even she knew it was a diabolical plan.* She continued watching the show until Maggie, her roommate, wacked her on the arm for no apparent reason. Danielle had always been a fighter. She was confrontational by nature. She wouldn't be pushed around by this woman or anyone else. She wacked Maggie on her right arm. Soon, their fighting escalated.

The door to their shared room opened. It was visiting hours. Dana and Graham stood at the entrance door.

Stunned, Danielle ceased fighting instantly. "Graham...Dana...what a surprise...." *Lord, forgive my evil thoughts and plans.*

It was as if Dana knew. She peered at Danielle with a new perspective, increased wisdom and insight. She stood a safe distance away. "How are you, Danielle?" She stared at her mother who had become like a stranger. She only used her Mom's given name when she was disturbed or greatly displeased.

"I'm...feeling better. How soon can I get out of this cage?" She spat the words out.

Dana peered at Graham. Something about Danielle's voice and mannerisms caused her to be leery of her. "You might have to stay here for a while...until you're better."

"Until I'm better? And who makes *that* decision? Not *you*, I hope. You're not a trained psychiatric nurse or doctor." She had raised her voice considerably and was almost shouting.

Dana was not easily provoked; but there was something about the tone and mindset of Danielle's persona that signaled a red flag flashing wildly in front of her. "Come on, Graham...let's go...we'll visit her another time."

Danielle began sulking. "So, you came to visit me...but now you're not staying? Why is that?" Her voice had a sing-song quality to it.

"You seem belligerent and confrontational. I don't know how to deal with that. Sleep it off, Mother. Maybe we'll check back in a few days...or weeks." Deliberately cool and sensing something was seriously amiss, Dana turned to leave.

So did Graham. He glanced back at Danielle after they'd gone a short way.

Danielle was flashing him her version of the Femme Fatale come on.

At that instant, like some finely tuned woman's intuition, Dana turned around just in time to see it. "Let's go Graham. Let's go and we're never coming back." The words were spoken half to herself, to Graham and very much for Danielle's benefit. She was totally disgusted.

Danielle started screaming. In minutes, two burly guards showed up, accompanied by a psyche nurse.

Dana and Graham couldn't leave the hospital fast enough.

Graham was still in shock when he stopped the Jeep at Sugarbush. They hadn't said a word to each other on the drive back. "Darling, how did you ever turn out so great with a Mom like Danielle?"

"She... wasn't always like this. Something...something bizarre must have happened to her."

"Drugs, maybe? Has she ever been on...Coke...or another drug?"

"No way. Well, I don't think so, anyway. Unless her new hubby got her hooked on them."

"Maybe that's exactly what happened. While she was high on coke he cleaned her out."

"I can't imagine Mom taking it. Though...I suppose he might have slipped something into her glass of wine..."

"Absolutely. And that is more common than you can imagine."

"So...you're thinking...that Mom is suffering the after effects of drugs?"

"Maybe. Either that...or losing all her money and her house flipped her over the edge." Graham shook his head.

"That would do it. She's worked hard all her life for what she just lost. I always thought she was smart." Dana shook her head in disbelief.

"Some women are smart except when it comes to men. Then they check their brains at the door."

"Am I one of those women, Graham?" She smiled flirtatiously at him.

"You have a good head on your shoulders, Dana. And obviously, you are nothing like Danielle."

"What's going to happen to her? I mean...she's lost her money, her man and her mind? What else is left?"

They were getting out of the Jeep. She fell in step with him.

He shook his head. "You don't get it, do you, Dana?"

"What do you mean?"

"You don't get the spiritual implications of

Danielle's breakdown, do you?"

"Maybe not. So...tell me."

They had reached the front porch of the house. "I'll ask Violet to serve us some iced tea and some of that amazing cornbread she baked the other day...and then...we will have a little spiritual lesson from Yours Truly, the head of the household." Graham poked his head in the kitchen door, made the request and then parked himself on the comfy, brown wicker furniture on the sweeping front veranda of the house.

Dana sat next to him. She was becoming used to taking orders from Graham. Some days she enjoyed that. Other days...not so much. Today she felt mellow and particularly grateful for him. She praised the Lord for the wonderful hubby he had given her. *Lord, thank you for entrusting him to me. I shall always take good care of him.* It was a promise she'd made to the Lord, because of bestowing the wonderful gift to her of a good man she deeply loved.

Graham reappeared with a pitcher of iced tea and the cornbread. After thanking the Lord for the food, a wave of sadness washed over him.

"What is it, Graham? Your...mood seems to have darkened?"

"I...I'm upset by the condition we found Danielle in...and now that she has no money...don't you go off the deep end, honey...but..."

"Spit it out, Graham! What's on your mind?"

"We have this huge mansion. She's lost everything. The right thing to do is maybe invite her to come and live with us."

Dana's mouth dropped open a mile. She gaped at him like he's suddenly lost his mind. When she finally found her voice, she was blubbering. "You can't possibly be serious, Graham. She would destroy our marriage so fast it would make our heads spin."

"Is that all the confidence you have in me? In our relationship? If it is, our marriage is on shaky ground, anyway."

"No. Not a chance. She's not coming anywhere near Sugarbush. She has designs on you, Graham. That's no longer a secret. If she was living here, God only knows what she might do."

"Dana. As Christians we don't really have a choice. She is homeless, and we own a mansion. She is your Mom. And she was apparently good to you when you were growing up, she gave you the riding lessons...you became an equestrian. She took care of you..."

Dana stood up. Irate. "This is just about the most outrageous idea I've ever heard in my life. No! Absolutely not! That woman *will not* live in my...our house. If she moves in, I'm moving out." The words tumbled out of her mouth. She hadn't meant to say them...but there it was...the ultimatum.

She meant it.

"Dana. You can't turn your back on the woman that raised you...adopted you. Okay, she made some poor choices, but don't we all do that sometimes?"

Dana had remained standing. She'd raised her voice and was almost screaming. She shook. "No! What part of that word don't you get?"

Graham was silent.

Much too long. Dana peered over at him, looking for a sign that he would back down. No such sign was forthcoming. She lowered her voice. "We're at an impasse, Graham. Don't you get that that is what she wants? She wants us to fight and break-up...and she actually deludes herself into believing that she has a chance with you." She shook her head, frustrated.

"Maybe she's right. Maybe she does."

Dana's mouth was agape. Finally she was speechless. It was a full five minutes before she found her voice. "Whatever are you saying, Graham. You can't possibly be serious." She peered over at him. His countenance appeared to be etched in stone.

He waited until the color drained from her face. "Have a seat, Dana. As head of this household, the final decisions are made by me...not you. Of course Danielle doesn't have a chance with me...except as a friend, and as her son-in-law. As I said, we don't have a choice. God would want you to honor your Mother. That's the third commandment. *And* let me remind you of the rest of it. *"Honor your father and mother that it may go well with you."*

Without a word, Dana rose and walked off the front veranda in a huff. She went to her sanctuary, her private den. Once there, she grabbed the first CD on her stack of classical music and put it on. She felt like bawling. Her whole world was falling apart.

Instead, she fell to her knees and wept and prayed. It was as if the Lord reached down and took her hand, raising her up. She heard his voice in a prophetic message. *"My precious, precious daughter, you cannot possibly know the blessings I have in store for you, when you take your Mother into your home. You will enter a new dimension in your relationships; both with her and with the man I have brought into your life. Do not worry about your Mother trying to entice him; you will both rise above that wrong spirit. You will be the teacher. Your Mother will be the student...the child. She has never grown up. You need to pray that the jealous spirit that takes over in her will be healed and that she will be delivered from that compulsion. I will do a mighty work in her. Do not worry, precious daughter. You cannot possibly know how much I love you, or the great and awesome blessings I have in store for you, when you are faithful. Humble yourself. Ask your husband for forgiveness and obey him. It is YOU who will be blessed when you do that."*

And then the supernatural overflowing of the spirit was gone. "Lord...you are a great and awesome and mighty God, and there is none like you." She began dancing around the small room, rejoicing in the Lord.

Graham was in the massive living room reading his well-worn Bible. He glanced up as he saw her approaching, but did not speak.

Dana smiled, certain her countenance reflected her change of heart. She hurried over to him. Reaching the large, comfy sofa, she moved onto it with him. "Honey, I'm sorry. I was wrong. Yes, of course, we must invite Danielle to live with us. I'm sorry I did not obey you when you first said it."

Graham wasn't sure he trusted her. He wanted to, of course; but this was a huge and fast turnaround. His voice was mellow. "What made you change your mind?"

Her eyes twinkled with merriment. "God! The Holy Spirit moved upon me like the mighty waves of the sea! The Lord spoke to me! I heard his voice. It was supernatural! Prophetic words fell upon me. I danced in the spirit. I repented..." She overflowed with joy.

Then Graham knew that she was telling the truth. She really *did* have a change of heart. God had shown up. He had heard Graham's prayer for Dana to see the light, to be compassionate, to honor her mother. He took her in his arms then and wept. "Oh, Dana...I was crushed...I didn't know what to do...I feared losing you...thought you might walk out...I was... beside myself...I went down on my knees and wept and prayed. I prayed for a miracle and God gave me one. Oh sweetheart. I love you so much; and I know we both have compassion for Danielle and all the bad stuff that has happened to her. I just know that we can help turn her life around. And if she really wants to hook up with a new man, we'll get her immersed in the scripture and remind her of Psalms 37:4 *"If you delight yourself in Me, I will give you the desire of your heart."* Maybe she can find a singles group at one of the churches. Bars can be potentially dangerous."

Chapter Twenty-three

Dana and Graham had a business meeting in his office. The issue of training a new colt was hanging over their heads. "What are we going to do, Dana? What does Jacob think?"

"He doesn't like it. Something about the new colt bothers him, too. He can't quite put his finger on it. When I pressed him...he said, "I don't know how to say this...but I have a sense that the colt has been tampered with...it's just a gut feeling I have." He was so upset I thought he was going to cry."

"Okay. We'll contact the vet, of course. But do you also know a horse expert? Graham peered at her, his heart sinking.

"Do you think maybe we should start with the Insurance company? Let's peruse all his papers and see if we can find some sort of clue there..." Dana felt like crying. Then she remembered. It came to her like a flash of understanding. "Graham. Why should we be surprised? This is spiritual warfare. A battle is raging over our goal to win the Derby and donate the money to Israel. The enemy wants us to fail, so he dispatches his minions to cause heaps of trouble with the colt, our personal life...etc., etc. He actively works to derail us."

"I know you're right, Graham. I don't know what planet I was on thinking we were going to sail through this. Whenever a child of the most high God tries to do something wonderful for the kingdom...that old serpent is on the job. We delude ourselves if we think he's going to roll over and play dead while we have a great victory and then bless Israel." Dana sighed. "Where are the boys?"

"Probably in the family room watching TV. By the way, Jay has started writing short stories. Isn't that exciting?" Graham grinned, proudly.

"It sure is. I'd love to read them."

"He says he doesn't want anyone reading them until his teacher checks them out. He's very fond of Mrs. Murcher. She's the teacher that has been encouraging him to go for his dream of becoming a reporter...TV newscaster...and that sort of thing."

Dana and Graham perused the colt's papers very carefully. Then they called the insurance company as well as the former owner. No new information or light was shed on the situation. Graham sat on the leather chair behind his large, walnut desk.

Dana was nestled onto the leather couch in his office, notebook in hand. She set down the phone on the side table. "We've come to a dead end, Graham. What do we do now?"

"Good question, Dana. Really good question." He shook his head. "Pray. That's all we can do." Graham bowed his head at the desk. Dana joined him. "Lord, we praise you that you hear and answer prayer. We praise you for all the blessings you have bestowed upon us...and now, Lord, we ask you...where do we go from here?"

She strolled to the bank of office windows. Gentle rain drizzled. As she peered at it, silently praying for wisdom, it increased in intensity. After a few minutes, she turned to Graham. "Well, I'm going to let you make this decision. Do we invest time and money training a colt we no longer believe in?" She peered at him. "Or do we swiftly move on?"

"Selling him is a problem. I mean...how can we do that in good conscience? The prospective buyer may be looking to train the colt for the Derby..." Graham was in deep thought.

"Is there a way that we can sell him...and fess up about the downside of the colt? Then, look for another one?" Dana peered over at him.

"Maybe I can write the loss off on my income tax. I think the Lord is showing me not to give up..." Graham peered at Dana. "We need to go into much prayer and then ask God to lead us to the finest colt out there. Time is of the essence."

"Good thing you have deep pockets, honey."

"True. I just never thought I'd have to tap into them as much as I have. But like you, I am driven to succeed, driven to make a difference and despite these current setbacks, we're going to plow right through."

"Okay, honey. Let's do it.

TWO WEEKS LATER

A miracle happened. Dana and Graham located a colt that was so amazing, so beautiful, so glorious that they fell madly in love with her. And so did Jacob.

A mottled grey Thoroughbred, he stood 17 hands

high. Imbued with impeccable bloodlines, regal, stately and bearing a track record rarely seen by a three-year-old colt. It was an answer to prayer. The opportunity of a lifetime. "Why are you selling him?" Graham fired the question at the farmer, while Dana, Graham and Jacob carefully scrutinized him.

"I'm comin' into retirement...got no time or interest in trainin' a colt. My son bought him just under a year ago...with that in mind...but...the kid died in a car crash...you may have heard about it..." Tears sprung to the old man's eyes.

"I did, in fact." Graham remembered the fatal crash. It was local.

They both had that good gut feeling. They peered at each other. They spoke in unison. "This is the one."

Chapter Twenty-four

Danielle awakened with an agenda. The compulsion to win Graham for herself had elbowed its' way into the front of her mind. She had to get him. No way was she going to go through life living in a small house or a rented apartment. Then the thought hit her. "I'll move onto Sugarbush. She thought better of it. *Nah. That would never fly.* Dana is fed up with me and my flirting with Graham. No way would she trust me to live in the house. She would have to cook up another plan. But what?

She had always prided herself on being clever, on dreaming up good, sound plans. Today was no different. Considering the trauma she'd just endured, she could feel herself quickly moving back to normalcy. She could easily outsmart Dana...and Graham, too, for that matter.

In her small room, sitting on her cot, she took out pad and pen from her purse. Yes, she was already feeling stronger emotionally. She would pretend to be nutty to ensure a free place to live until she could master mind a solid plan for living accommodations, preferably at Sugarbush.

The next morning after breakfast, Danielle poured another cup of coffee from the group living room and sat down at the small wooden table. Another patient sat across from her staring at her, a bizarre expression playing over her features.

Danielle focused on her plan. Her mind had bounced back swiftly and now she began forming a game plan. *I've always had acting talent. I used to do amateur theatre. I played leads and got rave reviews. She would have to find a way to get Violet fired...if that didn't work, maybe she would just disappear. Then, she would be mistress of Sugarbush. She hated to rehire the thugs she'd used to kidnap Dana. That plan had backfired. What were the odds of a stupid pizza guy spotting Dana peering through the dirty, cracked window at the warehouse? Slim and none. But it had happened, causing her scheme to be mucked up.*

If Violet disappeared and she lived at Sugarbush, she could volunteer to do the cooking and cleaning and run Sugarbush. Then, she could easily spy on Dana and Graham without them ever suspecting anything. Then, one day, she would simply poison Dana, wait through the grieving period and then it will be just Graham and her. It was a perfect plan.

They would bond during the grieving period. Then, it would be just a matter of time before the two of them would get hitched. "I'm sorry, Lord. I know you're disappointed in me. But I'll make it up, somehow..."

But even as she cooked up the wicked scheme, the spirit of God fell heavily upon her. She resisted. She had done enough evil deeds that her conscience was becoming seared. Evil no longer bothered her like it once had. She deserved to have a good life. A big life. Just like she'd always envisioned. Maybe she was wiped out financially; but darn it...she would pick herself up, dust herself off and start over again. God would give her the strength; provided, of course, that he was still talking to her.

Danielle's mind seemed to have snapped back. But had it? If her thinking was rational, why would murder be on her agenda? Were the anti-psychotic pills she'd been taking causing her to spin out and think irrationally? She didn't know. All she knew for sure is that she intended to live a grand lifestyle, regardless of what or who got in her way.

After dinner, Danielle stayed in her shared room watching T.V. A Hallmark Movie was on. She munched on popcorn and gazed half-heartedly at the screen, oblivious to her dozy roommate, Lizzy. *Her name is probably short for Lizard. She looks kind of slithery to me.*

Lizzy stared at her for a few minutes. Then she sat on her bed flipping her legs upward as though doing the bicycle. Surprisingly, "The lizard" was actually an acrobat.

"What the heck are you doing?" The woman was weird. But then again, this *was* a psyche ward.

"None o' yer business, Dummy."

Dummy? Nobody calls me dummy. Danielle grabbed the nearest object she could find. It was a lamp. She threw it at Lizzy. It missed.

Lizzy started screaming and in minutes the psyche nurse accompanied by two burley guards, grabbed both of them and stuck them into the dreaded lock-up room.

The next morning they were released and both women were interrogated by the psyche nurse and informed that they would be seeing the psychiatrist as soon as appointments could be arranged.

Danielle had alienated all her friends. She was alone in the world. She had nothing to lose. *Didn't God forgive David when he had an affair with Bathsheba and arranged for her hubby to be on the front lines in the war zone and predictably died? God would forgive her, too.*

Three months later.

Danielle was released from the psyche ward into a group home temporarily. That was okay, because she still had to flesh out her plan and she might need an accomplice. Her goal was clear. Dana would have to be eliminated in order for her to have a clear path to hook Graham.

Every night, she wrote notes in a little book she kept hidden in her purse. The purse was with her everywhere she went. At night, she slept with the black notebook under her pillow, placing it back into her large, black purse every morning. *No one must ever find out. No one must ever learn of her plan. And, of course, no one ever would.*

Every day Danielle gained more emotional strength and control. Every day she walked for twenty minutes or more, building up her stamina. Her goal was to power walk three miles a day. Between that and swimming and working out in the gym, her figure would be just about perfect. She would look so amazing with Graham. They were meant for each other. He just didn't know it yet. Oh, he would grieve Dana. But then he'd get over it. Men always did. Most of them hated being alone. Some guys even got married just so they wouldn't have to be. She would hook Graham. She knew exactly how she would do it. Getting rid of Dana would be a challenge, because unfortunately she no longer trusted her. *I wonder why that is?*

She loved having a room to herself, though she knew it was only temporary. Until someone else...another recovering patient would share her room. It usually took about a week to get rid of them. The fake snake trick did wonders. And the ones that didn't go for that got wicked surprises in the dead of night. She prided herself on cooking up unique ones.

Danielle didn't know when she'd become so demented; or why. All she knew is that she was obsessed with winning Graham and she'd morphed into a ruthless woman with an obsession to win him at all costs. She really wasn't sure how she got to this place; only that she had.

Chapter Twenty-five

Dana hadn't slept well. She'd had a terrible nightmare. In the dream, she'd seen Danielle coming after her with a kitchen knife. She'd been jolted awake. "Darling!" She shook Graham. "I...I had a horrible nightmare..." She told him about it.

"Oh sweetheart. Your fears are understandable. Danielle has been pretty weird lately, and maybe some of the meds she's taking aren't conducive to good mental health. Maybe she's over-medicated or allergic to some of them..."

He held her so close she thought she would break. He took her in his arms and kissed her fervently....

The next morning Dana felt great and very relaxed. During her morning shower though, the nightmare came back to haunt her. It had been so real. So very, very real. She had to talk to Graham. Maybe it was warning from God. But would he listen?

Over breakfast and after the boys had been picked up for school, Violet usually disappeared giving them some private time together. "Graham, maybe you won't believe me...but I feel the dream was significant...I feel like it was a warning dream...Maybe we should...put our plans on hold for now."

"Dana, God has not given us a spirit of fear but of power and love and a sound mind..." He grinned, giving her a peck on the cheek. "So...you won't even consider that it could have been a warning from God?"

"Dana. Of course I'll consider it. And we'll pray about it. But Danielle is going to need a place to live...real soon...and there are enough people in the house that she couldn't do such a thing even if she was inclined to. She would have to go through me, first. And she won't be able to. We'll keep our bedroom door locked at night. If she tries to get in, we'll hear her..." He stood then. "Honey, come here. You're just...scared. I've never known anyone that has been in the psyche ward. I'm sure you haven't, either. It's scary stuff. You've always had an over-active imagination..."

Dana had always leaned toward hysteria. Ever since enduring the trauma of losing her younger brother, Stephan, in the jumping accident...she'd been tender and maybe too sensitive. She sighed. "Let's get on with the day, honey. It was probably...just a bad dream. I know sometimes I have an over-active imagination."

But that night, she had the recurring dream again. She awakened, hysterical. "Graham...the dream...the nightmare...I had it again."

He soothed her, kissed her, made love to her and calmed her down. *"Lord, what is happening with Dana? I hope she's not losing it, too."*

The next morning, neither of them mentioned the dream.

Dana gave Janet a crash course in salvation, in

preparation for the Sunday morning service.

Janet was thrilled to accept Jesus as Lord. "Like...nobody ever told me this...this is like... so cool...to know that Jesus loved us so much that he...like...let himself be tortured...and then died and rose again. Wow! Mom was a believer...I know she prayed for me...but I don't ever remember her explaining...like...the salvation plan..."

Dana hugged her. "You'll be okay in jeans and that nice sweater. Our congregation cuts the young people a lot of slack. Many of them come to church in jeans."

"Cool. Maybe I'll see someone there I know."

"I'm sure you will. It's a great place to meet new friends, also."

Dana hugged her. She could feel the tenderness and delicacy of the young woman. She sensed that for some reason, the teenager had been largely ignored. "How...long was your Mother ill...before she passed?"

Tears sprung to Janet's eyes. "A...long, long time. For as long as I can remember."

Then Dana knew the deep sorrow Janet had gone through. *No wonder you prompted me to befriend her, Lord.*

Graham and Dana had work to do and no time to lose. They needed the vet report on Soaring Eagle, the new colt/

Eduardo Lopez spent about two hours putting their new colt through a series of tests.

Dana and Graham observed the process.

Finally, when all the tests had been concluded, Eduardo made his assessment. "The vials will go to the lab and we'll have answers in about two days. I must tell you, though...I am not optimistic. Something *is* wrong with this...great beauty...this incredibly regal creature...I can sure see why you chose her..." He shook his head. "I only hope that I am wrong. But I fear that I am not."

Two days later the tests came back. Graham got the call late morning. It was Thursday. "We need to meet. I have several concerns. The colt has ingested something...we have our suspicions what that is. I would like to see you both in person. Then we can go over everything. I suggest you move forward with selecting another colt, if you intend to compete for the Kentucky Derby in May. Some of the damage done to the colt is fairly serious."

Graham and Dana found another colt. It wasn't easy, but God led them to a beautiful, feisty three-year old. They bought him. This one had spunk and personality. Jacob drove the horse trailer to Sugarbush and popped down the ramp. Dana named him Fury.

Dana and Graham parked next to the trailer and helped Jacob with the new colt.

There was no time to waste. So much time had already been lost. Right after Violet served Jacob, Graham and Dana a delicious lunch complete with chocolate milkshakes, which were Graham's personal favorite, the work began.

Out on the track, Jacob rode the dark grey bay with great verve. After taking him around the track a few times, he gave Dana and Graham the report. "He's a winner! Fantastic! You know...as much as I liked the last colt, this one is vastly superior.

THREE MONTHS LATER

188

Jacob had been working with Fury diligently day after day and watching him like a hawk. Jacob had moved into the mansion so he could keep a close watch on the colt. He would stay here until after the Kentucky Derby. And this time they would win. That had to happen. He would trust God for the victory.

It was Monday morning. Graham had hired a security guard, coverage was 24/7. No way were Graham and Dana going to lose this colt or have him tampered with. "Never, never, never give up. Victory at all costs." Churchill's motto became theirs.

Day after day, the grueling training process continued. At the end of each week, Jacob and Dana along with Graham had a meeting and assessed where they believed they were in the process.

They entered their colt in the Kentucky Oaks race. He took first place! They were ecstatic. Greatly encouraged. Nothing would stand in their way now. As long as God was on their side, they would work diligently to steadily groom and train the colt to run for the roses and win!

Graham had gone into the city on some business. Dana and Violet kept the home fires burning. The boys were at school.

It was late fall. Most days tended to be chilly.

Dana decided to ride solo out on the rolling Bluegrass. She loved to gallop across the peaceful meadows reveling in the smell of fresh country air and the sweet scent of bluegrass, even the earthy scent of her colt. She galloped at a steadily increasing speed. A rock flew up toward her and her horse, barely missing her eye.

It spooked the colt. He reared up and then started

backing up. *Not another snake?* She stayed calm, barely managing to keep the colt under control. Soon, they cantered smoothly along, joyously listening to birds chirping, flitting from the tree branches of the lone, huge Hanging Moss tree near the edge of their property.

On the way back to the barn, her cell chirped. She waited until she reached the barn. She heard loud noises. It sounded like men's voices. An argument? Adroitly, she dismounted, walking the colt inside the barn.

The ranch hands were engaged in a nasty fist fight.

Dana saw red. She had little patience for this sort of thing. "You're both fired! I want you off the property...by the weekend! Pack your stuff and be gone!"

The ranch hands were stunned. And suddenly mellow.

Dana realized she'd acted hastily. "Shake hands and say you're sorry and you can both stay. This is a warning. If I see you two engaged in a fist fight just one more time, you're both gone permanently. So...if you value your job here; try to get along."

"Easy for you to say. You live in a palace...we're squeezed together in a bunk house with barely enough room to turn around..." Hank peered over at her, scowling.

"Why didn't you say something sooner? The guest house is vacant. The two of you can live there if you like. It has two bedrooms. I've been meaning to mention it..." She put her hand up. "I would have to check with Graham, though. He makes all the decisions."

"Wow. That would be amazing. If I'm livin there...I might even take you up on your invite to go to church...Janet seems to like that church...and I sure do like *her*..." He put his hand up. "I know...I gotta respect her and treat her like a lady. And...I'll do that if I get another chance with her...you see, Ma'am...I'm in love with her..."

Dana was impressed and surprised. She'd inadvertently smoked him out and learned that he was actually a gentleman. He just needed someone to bring it out in him. "Tell you what, Hank...if Graham says okay, the two of you are invited to join us for Sunday lunch. And of course, I'd have to check with Violet first, since she'll be doin' all the cookin'..."

Hank grinned and for the first time Dana realized he was not a bad looking kid. Sandy haired with freckles, he had green eyes. She chided herself for treating him as though he was just a ranch hand not really a man with dreams and hopes and ambitions like everybody else. *Lord, help me to see people as they actually are. Help me to look past their words and their faces and their jobs and see their hearts. Help me to contribute to their lives and make a difference. I know we're put on this earth to help others and fulfill the purpose you have for us. I know I have a mission, but Hank and Wilbur have missions, too. And so does Janet. Maybe we're supposed to lead all of them to the saving knowledge of the truth.*

Chapter Twenty-Six

Sunlight peaked through the cool, overcast day. It was a mild winter so far.

Violet puttered in the kitchen. She'd worked hard all morning and had overseen the monthly heavy cleaning done by the service Dana had arranged when Graham first took over the house. She took a break, propping her feet up on the ottoman in the family room, and turned on the local news.

"Danielle Lockhart has escaped from the psyche ward at the University Hospital. She is believed to be in Bluegrass country where she has family. She is an attractive, shapely blonde. Her age is listed as fifty-six, though she looks considerably younger. She was last seeing wearing a brown knit sweater and beige slacks. She is probably carrying a large black tote bag."

Violet was riveted to the screen. *So Danielle was on the loose.* She hurried to the phone to call Graham. Her call went directly to voice mail.

A few minutes later, the ground line rang. "Graham here. What's up, Violet?"

"Danielle has escaped from the psyche ward at the University hospital. It was on the TV news."

"What? You...you're joking...tell me you're joking..." Graham was on overload. With everything that had happened with the colts and Dana's kidnapping...now this. *Lord, when does this end? I didn't sign up to be another Job...* But even as the murmuring left his lips, he began repenting. *"I'm sorry, Lord, you have blessed me. You have given me so much. I have so much to be grateful for. Lord...give me the strength to deal with this...help me to be a tower of strength for Dana...I have no solutions, Lord. Only problems and questions. I acknowledge that I can do nothing without you. But I can do all things through Christ who strengthens me."*

Graham had gone into town for horse feed and other sundry supplies. He'd taken Hank with him. He wanted to familiarize him with the various food options at the feed store. If he was travelling or busy with the colt and Dana, Hank would be familiar with the feed store the way Wilbur was.

Graham dropped Hank off and climbed the stairs of the old mansion. Entering the kitchen, he spotted Violet. "Hey, Violet...any coffee?"

"Just made a fresh pot. I'll pour you a cup." She poured him a cup.

Graham flopped down on a kitchen chair and began drinking the coffee

"Could use a cup myself." She plunked down at the table opposite him, knowing Graham would want to hear the full report. "So, I guess Dana won't be home from the track until around 5:00..."

"Right. And...maybe by then...they will have found Danielle..." He frowned. "What exactly did they say on the news about her?" Graham peered over at Violet, upset.

"They said Danielle Lockhart...I guess she's already reverted back to using her original name instead of her recently divorced hubby's name...they said Danielle Lockhart has been reported missing from the psyche ward at the University Hospital as of early this morning. She'd asked for permission to go outside for a cigarette...though it was later determined she doesn't smoke...anyway... she disappeared from the outdoor smoking area...early this morning, right after breakfast...about 7:45 to 8:15."

"Do they have any idea where she is?" Graham's mind was spinning. *What is the woman up to? Is she going to show up here? Is she dangerous? Maybe I shouldn't take her onto the ranch. She might be a negative...even destructive influence on our happy, little family. And if she did have anything to do with Dana's disappearance...well, having her here would be like asking for trouble.* Graham took a deep breath, drank some of the ice water set before him and then gulped down some coffee. "I...I just don't know what to think...other than the fact that it appears that everything Danielle is doing is bizarre. Nothing she's been doing lately has any rationale...to it."

The doorbell rang. Violet peaked through the peep hole, spotting Danielle.

She turned to Graham. "It's Danielle. Should I let her in?"

Graham took a deep breath. "Sure, we'll see what she has to say for herself."

Violet opened the door. "Good morning, Danielle." Violet prided herself on being able to assess and handle any situation. "What a...surprise. We just heard the news report...that you're a missing a person. I guess I'd better call the police."

"I wouldn't do that if I were you." Danielle sneered sinisterly at both of them. "I just...need to use the bathroom."

Graham stood. He didn't trust anything about her. He'd felt sorry for her, but after this latest caper, his compassion was wearing thin. *What is it with this broad? Can't she just leave us alone?"*

Danielle returned from the bathroom. She'd been in there for a bit too long. She wore a Cheshire cat smile, like she had something up her sleeve.

Graham decided to take the bull by the horns. "What is it Danielle? What do you want?"

She flashed the weird half-smile again. She raised her eyebrows for accent. "Silly... silly... boy. May I whisper it into your ear?"

Violet was all but taking notes. Blessed with an excellent memory, she remained silent but watched their guest like a hawk, computing everything. "Coffee, Danielle?"

Danielle did not respond immediately. She appeared to be mulling this simple request over and sifting through the possible ramifications of accepting coffee...or was she thinking about what mischief she could get into once she took the coffee. "Yes, coffee would be good. Thanks" She plopped down at the large, round table where Graham and Violet sat, drinking coffee.

Graham was leery of every word that sprouted from her lips. "Danielle, why are you here? The news reported you as missing. You need to tell the psyche ward that you've taken a taxi here. I'll call the police and have you taken back. I don't know who buzzed you in at the gate...but I'll find out. Let's cut to the chase. What do you want, Danielle?"

"Silly boy. A place to live, of course. It's not rocket science. Oh...just for a couple months, of course...the guest house will do nicely. I'm sure you don't want the embarrassment of having a Mother-in-law on the street, now...do you?" She smirked, flashing her sea green eyes from Violet and then to Graham. "Or in the psyche ward, for that matter..." The half smirk was there again. "It would be better for your image if you invited me to stay here."

"I will need to consult Dana...and my attorney. There could be legal implications...as well as potential complications...I cannot give you an answer right away."

Danielle stood then. Irate. Her eyes narrowed. "Think you're so clever, don't you? Marrying my daughter...taking her away from me...and now, you don't have the time of day for me, do you? Well...we shall see about that..." *She hadn't meant to berate Graham. But he was a big boy. He'd get over it.* She flashed him her femme fatale smile to smooth things over.

Graham stood then. He'd had enough. He should have called the authorities the moment she walked in. But he'd been stunned and was curious to hear what she would say. "This meeting is over. I was going to invite you to be our house guest until you found a suitable place to live...but given your nastiness and considering how ungrateful you are...I...don't think I want you anywhere near us." You're bad news, Danielle. I have no idea how or why you've sunk this low...and I have to wonder if you merely pretended to be whacko for the bad publicity it would bring to Sugarbush and our noble quest to win the Derby and give the winnings to charity."

He took a deep breath. "My assessment... dear Mother-in-Law; is that you are a spoiled brat. Used to having your own way...used to calling the shots...used to controlling everyone....like puppets on a string. Well, it's over, Danielle. Your little games are over. The most I shall do is rent you a room in a boarding house in town. I'll take you there now. I'll ask Wilbur to go with us. I don't want to be alone with you. Also, you are persona non grata at Sugarbush. In fact... I've been thinking of having a guard gate built and installing a twenty-four-hour security guard at the gate. I think I'll implement that plan immediately."

Danielle stood then, erupting into gales of laughter. "All because of *me*, darling? I didn't know you cared." She winked at him, smiling broadly.

Graham burst into laughter. Her behavior was so outrageous, so bizarre, that he was baffled and hardly knew where to turn. His laughter broke the tension. "What exactly do you want from me, Danielle? Why don't you cut to the chase and save us both a lot of aggravation?"

"I thought you knew, Graham. Have I under-estimated you, somehow? The simple fact is, dear...you've married the wrong woman. It's *me* you want. Don't you get that? I'm the...cunning...I...I mean stunning...brilliant woman you need to help you run Sugarbush! Not Dana..." She chuckled "That little airhead doesn't have a clue. She never did finish college...you know...she just didn't have the focus...or the marks to do it. Not like me. I was a straight A student. An honor student, actually. I graduated Summa Cum Laude. Oh, don't take my word for it...do your own research...I attended Kentucky University and majored in business. I'm the perfect match for you..."

Graham had heard enough. He had the urge to throw her out. "You've had your chance. I offered to drive you to town and help you rent a room or an apartment. You seem to be living in some sort of self-manufactured fantasy world; so I can't help you. I don't trust anything about you. I don't even trust you to ride with me in my Jeep...God only knows what you might do." He pushed 911 on his cell. "Police? This is Graham Van Rensellier. I'm calling from Sugarbush Farm. Please pick up Danielle Lockhart. She's the woman on the news that escaped from the psyche ward earlier today. I'll watch for you at the gate."

He was glad he'd ordered work immediately to set up cameras up at the gate for added security. Now he had to hire a 24/7 security guard. Danielle was a loose cannon. God only knew what she would do next.

Danielle got up and stomped out of the kitchen in a huff.

Graham went after her, grabbing her by the arm. "What do you think you're doing, Danielle? You heard my call. You need to return to the psyche ward. You need help. You're in deep trouble. You cannot live here at Sugarbush. I don't trust you or your motives. I wouldn't be able to sleep at night, wondering what you're up to."

She stood then, sneering. "Think you're so smart, don't you? Well...if you're so smart...how come Dana got kidnapped...on your watch? How did that happen?"

Graham did not respond. He refused to react to her wild accusations and bizarre tactics. "Finish your coffee, Danielle. You are persona non grata at Sugarbush. My new gate guard will enforce my wishes. You are banned from visiting Sugarbush. Understood?"

"No. I only speak French. I didn't understand a word you said." Danielle smirked.

Graham grabbed her arm. He was afraid she might run away and escape the police. She'd escaped from the psyche ward; God only knew what the next item on her agenda was. *And he'd always had suspicions that she was involved with Dana's kidnapping. He had a private investigator checking into some details, but the kidnappers hadn't left a trail and they weren't talking. He had to wonder if that was where a lot of Danielle's money had disappeared to. He'd never quite bought the story that the new hubby married her and quickly depleted her bank account. Danielle was too smart for that. It made much more sense that Danielle, through jealousy and frustration and...maybe a destructive spirit, had wanted to take Dana out of the picture so she would have a clear path to victory with him. What a laugh. If she were the last woman on earth, he seriously doubted he would give her the time of day...especially now that he'd gotten to know her.*

He buzzed the sheriff in.

He was glad he'd moved fast to install a security system with the cameras. The electric fence surrounding the acreage had been there since he bought the farm. It would not be easy to gain access to Sugarbush without an invitation.

Sheriff Brady knocked briskly, announcing his arrival and entering the house.

Graham met him at the door. "Welcome sheriff. Nice to see you. You know Danielle Lockhart, of course. I'm sure you know she escaped from the psyche ward...she's ah... right here..." But as he looked around he didn't see her. *In the bathroom?* A weird feeling swept over him. *She better be in the bathroom.* He checked the main floor bathroom door. It was open. And empty. In the next instant, he knew she'd run off. *She won't get very far. We're a long way from everything. She wouldn't be able to walk to her destination, even if she had one. Could she be hiding somewhere in the house? Why would she do that?* "Ah...Sheriff...how about giving me hand...finding her...she was right here...but she...she's gone somewhere."

"Did she drive here?" The sheriff was puzzled.

"No...she came by taxi, I guess. Violet must have buzzed her in. Probably thought it was one of the ranch hands, or..."

"Well, I guess we haven't gotten used to screening folks before they gain entry. And with two regular ranch hands...and the pest control guys...well, it's a busy place."

"So she slipped through our fingers. Could she be hiding in the house?"

"Could be, I guess."

"All right. Let's do a sweep." The sheriff and deputy sheriff began their search.

Graham and Violet assisted them.

"It's nice to live in this old mansion, except when someone hides in it...there are doubtless a lot of nooks and crannies to hide in." The sheriff and deputy sheriff began their intensive search.

AN HOUR LATER

"She's not here. Someone must have picked her up while we were combing the place...I can't believe we let her slip through our fingers..." The sheriff shook his head in dismay.

Chapter Twenty-Seven

Danielle couldn't believe her luck. It had been so simple to get lost in the old edifice. Being petite had some advantages. She'd curled up under the bed in Will's room on the main floor. While they were on a wild goose chase checking out all the bedrooms and nooks and crannies, Will sat in his room doing his homework. The deputy sheriff popped his head in the door. "Seen Danielle anywhere?"

"Well...like wouldn't she be staying in a guest room? Why check my room?"

"Oh. Guess you didn't know, Will. She escaped from the psyche ward...and she's at large right now."

"No kidding. Well if I see her, I'll let you know."

Danielle felt like twittering. *If he only knew. She had no intentions of remaining under the bed the entire night. No...she'd wait until he was asleep and then she would sneak into one of the guest rooms upstairs. She knew every detail of every room, thanks to her photographic memory. And when she had visited Graham and Dana and had dinner here, she'd been given the grand tour. She knew the design of the house. It would be a cinch to hang out here until she could figure out what to do or where to go. But how would she eat? Well, she would have to take a chance and in the wee hours of the morning, sneak into the kitchen pantry or fridge and take small amounts of food, very carefully sealing packages and always leaving everything just as she found it.*

She knew she wasn't playing with a full deck, but, still, it was a lot more exciting to be an escapee from the psyche ward and hanging out in the old mansion, than renting a room somewhere, or an apartment. Neither had any appeal to her.

Quickly, she formed a game plan. She would have to be extra careful. She absolutely could not get caught. Or it would be game over. She would be hauled back to the psyche ward and doubtless relegated to the lock-up room. She was glad she chose to wear the tan slacks and brown knit sweater. She'd dumped the grey outfit she'd worn earlier that morning, since she knew the newscaster would report what she was last seen wearing. The slip-on canvas shoes were good, too.

As long as she stayed with the program of only visiting the pantry in the wee hours, no one would be the wiser. Once she was sure Will was sound asleep, she would stealthily sneak out of her hiding place under his bed, exit the room and sleep in one of the lovely guest rooms. She knew she was taking a big risk. What if someone decided to recheck the room on a hunch, or what if Violet decided to clean that particular room bright and early the next day? Still, life was a chance game and she would have to take her chances. "I've made my bed and I shall lie in it." She smiled. She loved that old British expression.

It was well after 11:00 by the time Will turned out

the light. Seemed like he was reading something, though, of course he might have been on his computer. She glanced at her watch which lit up at night. When it was almost midnight, she was sure he would be asleep, so she noiselessly slithered out from under his bed. Then, on her tippy toes she started toward the door. A board in the floor of the ancient house squeaked. *What are the chances of that happening?*

Will stirred, then sat bolt upright in bed. "Hey, anyone here?"

The room was pitch black. She would remain motionless.

After a few minutes, Will snuggled under the covers. She heard his muffled voice. "I must have been dreaming..."

Danielle waited a half hour. She wanted to make certain he would have drifted off to sleep. Quietly, noiselessly, she crept to the door of Will's room and opened it, letting herself out. She heard the "meow" of a cat. *"I must get to another room and get some sleep." There was no light in the hallway, Just a dim night light at the other end of the hall. It was by the staircase she intended to climb, which led to the upstairs guest rooms.*

She hurried up one flight of stairs to the second floor and glanced around. All was clear. Then, she headed up to the third floor. The best rooms were up here. They were larger and they all had en suites. "I will be very comfortable here." She mouthed the words. "Thank-you for your hospitality, Dana and Graham." She smirked. *If they only knew she was behind the kidnapping, they would never speak to her again. But then, again, they weren't speaking to her now. But she had the last laugh. She always had the last laugh; because she was smarter and more devious than anyone she had ever met. She prided herself on being able to outsmart everyone. She would find a way to be a permanent house guest in the mansion, if she so chose. Maybe she would retire and be the gardener here. They sure could use one.*

Danielle slept soundly. The deep, luxurious mattress was conducive to a good nights' rest. She was pleased with herself. Pleased she'd cooked up this devious scheme. No one would find her. It would start to get old, though...hunting for food in the wee hours...while praying her stomach wouldn't growl. She gave herself kudos for being such a convincing actress. She'd always had talent. She'd played the leads in a number of plays in her youth, always receiving good reviews. But amateur theatre didn't pay, and she didn't want to devote herself to the tough, competitive world of professional show business; even if she could get into it. She'd chosen business, instead. This little scheme was sort of like playing a role. It gave her a certain thrill to outsmart and outwit Dana and Graham. She wished she could be a nicer person, but nobody had everything, so she would just roll with the punches.

Sunday couldn't get here fast enough. She wondered if she'd taken the plan too far, pretending to be nuts so she would be taken to a psyche ward and then escaping. *Maybe she really was nuts.* After all, what normal person would live this way? Still, she wouldn't dwell on negatives. Her goal hadn't changed. She had to get rid of Dana, so she could have Graham for herself. And living in the house was the surest and easiest way to eliminate her. She didn't know when she'd morphed into a ruthless killer. Must have happened incrementally. Either that...or maybe she really *had* lost it. Still, she had her goal; which had morphed into an obsession. She admitted that freely. But no matter, she was determined to achieve it. Danielle had never set her sights on a goal she did not achieve.

She awakened early. She'd always been an early riser. She only slept five or six hours. That was a distinct advantage. She could do her ablutions and select her hiding place for the day before anyone in the house stirred. She had already learned that Violet arose around 6:00 or 6:30; so she figured she'd be safe to steal food around 5:00. Oh she knew she was taking a chance. What if Violet or someone else in the house couldn't sleep and arose early and decided to get a snack or some water in the kitchen? It would be game over. But if the truth be known, she thrived on danger.

Maybe it would be safer to rise in the wee hours of the morning, around 3:00. But what if someone in the house...for whatever reason...happened to get up and go in the kitchen? Well, life didn't come with any guarantees. She would take her chances. She could pray. *But God probably wouldn't hear her prayers.* A scripture flashed into her mind. It went something like this. *"...if I regard any inequity in my heart...God does not hear my prayers." "I'll repent later, God. Right now, I need to survive this ordeal.*

She checked her watch. 4:47 a.m. Now or never. She had to get some food. She would have to pinch small amounts of food so no one would notice or become suspicious that food had gone missing.

She moved stealthily down the staircase. She heard a noise. She stopped. *Must have imagined it.* She continued down the staircase. She heard the noise again. It was coming from the direction of the kitchen. She'd better head back up the stairs. Fast. She turned, noiselessly and briskly moving to the upper landing.

"Who's there?"

She knew the voice was Violet's. She apparently didn't require much sleep, either. Maybe she sometimes got up in the night for whatever reason. She would have to be more careful. She managed to duck into the nearest room upstairs, because she had a sense that whoever it was could be following the noise to check it out.

Her stomach was rumbling but she couldn't chance it again. She would somehow have to get enough food to last for a couple of days. The emergency chocolate bars she'd bought at the hospital vending machine kept her from starving, but she craved real food. *Sunday. When they go to church on Sunday, I'll be able to eat some leftovers and pinch some real food.* Sunday couldn't come fast enough.

She remembered that Violet had a cleaning schedule for the house and had professional cleaners come once a month for a thorough cleaning. She realized then that she might have to leave Sugarbush...on foot...then call a taxi and give the driver some lame story...and get into town and buy some food. Then, sneak back onto Sugarbush. If Violet or anyone had become suspicious, she might be wise to get out of the line of fire right now.

Violet was as sharp as a tack. And she had highly developed instincts. Danielle could tell. She made a fast decision. She would rent a room somewhere or check into a cheap motel. She was glad she'd put her belongings in storage, this way she was free to go wherever she chose. She smiled. She enjoyed the challenge and danger of staying secretly at Sugarbush. *Graham was so near and yet so far. But that was about to change.*

She would wait until they were all at church and then she'd slip out the back door and call a taxi from her cell. In her large purse, she pulled out the red, curly wig, stuck it on and the false lashes. She was a missing person so she needed the disguise so the taxi driver wouldn't recognize her. She changed tops to throw off anyone looking for her. "Last seen wearing..." would no longer apply.

Maybe she could get rid of Dana at the track. But how? *Way too many people around.* No, she would have to do the dirty deed right here at Sugarbush. She had cooked up a few ways to take Dana out, but she hadn't hit on the perfect plan...yet. But she would.

She had recurring bad dreams that her murder scheme had backfired. In the dream, she was handcuffed and sent to prison. *I swore when I finally got out of prison last time that I would never go back.* Still, her obsession to win Graham superseded all logic. One look at him, and she knew it didn't matter what she had to do, as long as she could snag him for herself.

The taxi dropped her at a house about half a mile away from her buddy's house. She'd pretended not to have the exact address. "I know the house. Just don't remember the address." She walked the half mile to Pete's house where she'd parked her car. Her white

Toyota Camry was there, right where she'd left it. She rang the bell at the house but no one answered. Too bad, she wanted to brainstorm with Pete about getting rid of Dana. Kidnapping hadn't worked. She'd paid him the big bucks in advance but Dana had been rescued. He had no motivation to make Dana disappear. Unless she made it worth the risk of doing the evil deed. Maybe she would just do it herself. That way she'd know it was done properly.

She wasn't sure when she'd slipped over the edge. It was probably when the bank foreclosed on her house. She'd given most of her existing cash to the thugs, but since the kidnapping had failed, she'd received no cash from the scheme.

She stepped into her car and drove into town. It was still early, the sun was just rising. She finally found a thrift shop open on a Sunday. She rustled through a lot of merchandise, finally finding some tailored, plain clothes; the polar opposite of how she usually dressed. She found a royal blue jersey top with black, white and gold on it and matching solid blue jersey pants. She grabbed a pair of plain black slacks that would go with the top, as well. She missed her sexy, slinky jersey tops and pants and designer shoes. She would have plenty of time to enjoy them once she was married to Graham.

She would have to commit the murder without leaving a trace. There was no other way. That's why her original plan of having Dana kidnapped and having her disappear was the cleanest and simplest plan. But that plan had failed.

Chapter Twenty-Eight

Dana and Graham arose early. It was Sunday, their favorite day of the week. "Good morning, darling." Graham's voice was husky and mellow. He leaned toward her, kissing her on the cheek.

"Good morning, darling." Dana's soft, sexy voice purred.

Their voices overlapped. With buoyant, thankful hearts, they hugged each other, ecstatic to be together and deeply grateful for their beautiful, blessed union.

Over coffee, Graham brought up the dreaded subject. "So...no word from Danielle. Weird. She can't just disappear."

"You don't know my mother. She can disappear. She's a master at pulling rabbits out of hats. I've seen her do some remarkably creative and imaginative stuff over the years."

"Really, like what?" Graham's curiosity was peaked.

"Honey, let's get dressed. And I need to put on some make-up. Let's talk over breakfast. The boys won't be up until later. I think they stayed up late and watched a movie last night."

Over breakfast and great coffee, Dana shed some light on the subject of Danielle. "Look, the women is brilliant. She may have lost everything. But that won't keep her down. Trust me. She will rise again. You know...sometimes I think maybe she just cooked up this nervous breakdown drama to get attention..."

"No kidding. Okay. So...where do you think she is she now? She's a missing person. Where would she go? Does she have any close girlfriends or buddies in other states? Maybe another town in Kentucky?"

"Mom has some friends I don't know much about. And...I hate to say it...but she also knows some shady characters..."

"Where would she have met them?" Graham stared at her skeptically. "Was...she ever... in prison?"

Lord, I didn't want Graham to know about Mom's background. We've done such a good job hiding it from the world. But we're safely married. And I shouldn't keep any secrets from my hubby. Dana toyed with her fruit. It was chopped up fresh pineapple. She suddenly lost her appetite. "Mom... was in prison. She spent six months at ......"

"Really? For what?"

Dana couldn't breathe. She remembered the day the sheriff had come to the house. And her Mom being hauled off in handcuffs. Remembered watching the sheriff push her down into the back of his marked car. It had been traumatic for her.

"Dana. Tell me. You must tell me what she did. We're married...we have no secrets...remember?"

"She was charged with attempted murder." Dana lowered her head as the tears began to trickle down her cheeks.

"Attempted murder! Who was the...target?"

"Some guy she met who did her wrong. His name was Bob Jansen."

"What happened?"

"She tried to push him off a cliff, but denied doing it. There was a witness that testified to the deed. Problem was that the witness had a record. Anyway, she wound up serving two years...that time in prison changed her forever. She was never the same after that. Something happened to her in there...something she would never talk about."

"So...that's why she has these problems now."

"Pretty much. She was real solid before she served time. After that...she did some really strange stuff..." She put her hand up. "Stuff...I don't want to talk about."

"Okay, honey." Graham rose from his chair. "Darling...I love you. You've made me a very happy man. I never dreamed I would be happy again. Never could have imagined that I would develop a powerful love for you...for anyone. I really believed after Myrna died, that there would never be another woman." He grinned. "But God has a wonderful way of surprising us...a fabulous way of showing up and causing great and wonderful things to happen in our lives." He kissed her lightly on the cheek before sitting down to finish breakfast.

"Yes, God is a God of miracles. Sometimes I wonder...well I'm surprised that folks who claim to be believers deny the power of God..."

"What do you mean?"

"I mean that humans limit God. They believe him for small things but they don't give him credit for being the great, Almighty, powerful God that he is. And by their own words of unbelief they thwart the miracles and answers to prayer that could be theirs."

"Since when did you become so smart, Dana?"

"If that's a hint that I should get back to teaching Sunday school, I'll take it. I know I'm supposed to be doing that. It is part of my gifting...and I have not been using it for the glory of God."

"I never told you that I used to teach Sunday school, also. We should both do it. God often puts folks together that have a similar gifting. Maybe he let us enjoy each other with the honeymoon period...and perhaps now he wants us to give back. We've both been given so much." Graham finished his coffee, a somber look playing over his features.

Sunday service was excellent as always. Graham and Dana were both inspired to trust in the Lord with all their hearts and lean not on their own understanding.

Graham drove the family to Villa De Vinci for lunch.

Just as they were finishing lunch, Dana glanced over at a woman that had an air of familiarity about her. The woman had red, curly hair and was heavily made up. She wore large, dark sunglasses, despite being indoors. She was clad in a print top in royal blue jersey and blue jersey slacks. The outfit looked dated. *I've seen this woman somewhere before. She has an air of familiarity about her.*

Graham was grinning at Dana. "Darling...I'm

thinking of having fried oysters on the half shell to start. Join me?"

Dana snapped back to reality. What did it matter if she'd seen the woman before? So what? She could not help noticing that the odd woman was dining with a much younger man. The man had caught her eye a couple times and grinned. *Very irksome. I'm with my dream man. Can't he see that?*

His eyes had quickly averted once she'd locked eyes with him and turned away. *So the guy is a flirt...so what?* She moved her chair slightly, which put her out of the eye line of the man.

Graham drove them back to Sugarbush. Sunday was spent in worship, praise and relaxation. The ranch hands took care of the horses. They always took Sunday off. "I found a great Hallmark Movie. We haven't seen this one. It called *Prince Charming.*"

The movie was a delight. Violet made popcorn and served it with apple cider. "Hey, come on and join us Violet..."

"Oh, don't be silly. I'm gonna let you two lovebirds have your privacy. I'll watch it my room. Three is a crowd." Her eyes twinkled with merriment. And laced with a hint of mischief, as usual.

The next morning, Violet had the cleaning crew arrive for their monthly cleaning. By mid-afternoon they were done and on their way. Violet paid them out of the budget Graham had set up for her as head housekeeper at Sugarbush.

As Zena, the sweet Spanish girl, was taking the cash, she frowned, peering at Violet. "You said you've had no house guests this month, except for the lime green room. You told us not to change the sheets in the other guest rooms upstairs. Well...I have something odd to report. It appears as though someone has slept on the sheets in the second bedroom on the third floor...in the Pink Room. Also, the towels are not the way we left them last time we were here...not even close. Also, the bed was not the way we made it. I flipped off the comforter...well...the sheets have definitely been slept in. We changed them, of course, but I wanted to report this... oddity to you."

"Oh, my dear. Thanks, but Dana invited a young gal to stay a couple nights..."

"Yes, I know. You told me that. She stayed in bedroom number two, the lime green room, correct?"

"Well...yes. That is the room she stayed in." Dana sighed.

"Someone definitely slept in the pink room!"

Violet shook her head, no. But then the shrewd side of her surfaced. "You are...absolutely sure that someone slept on those sheets?"

"Absolutely, Ma'am. Thought we'd better let you know. Hope one of the ranch hands hasn't sneaked into the house and decided to try one of your comfortable beds."

Dana's mind was reeling. *Danielle?* She had an over-active imagination. What had she been thinking? Why on earth would *she* want to sleep in a guest room? Anyway, how would she have gotten into the house, undetected? Dana couldn't believe she was considering the possibility, even for a moment. "Well...uh...thanks for letting me know. I'll tell Graham...and I guess we'll have to watch the ranch hands more closely. Can't imagine anyone sneaking into the house..." *But even as the words sprung from her lips, she knew she could imagine Danielle sneaking into the house. Though she'd played it down with Graham, Dana knew that Danielle had done plenty of odd things over the years. She was so glad she wasn't her real Mom. No one could accuse her of inheriting the same odd tendencies and bizarre behavior that Danielle displayed.*

That night sleep eluded Dana. She tossed and turned, her mind racing and reeling. She lay in bed, fully awake. Somehow, her restlessness caused Graham to awaken.

"Honey...what's wrong? Why aren't you sleeping?"

"I don't know....I sense that... Danielle is up to no good. I don't know what. But she has something on her mind. She's going to do something...extreme. I don't know what that is going to be...but she's cooking up mischief...I can smell it..."

"Let's talk about it tomorrow." He cuddled up to her, kissing her passionately. Soon, they were both sound asleep.

Chapter Twenty-Nine

AT THE TRACK

Graham accompanied Dana to the track. He was determined to learn everything he could about the process of training their colt to run for the roses. "So...the workouts are timed by the official clocker. We'll start doing that as soon as I think he's ready."

"Whenever Myrna and I placed wagers on a race, we checked the industry papers and track programs to see how the horse has been performing up to the race." Graham glanced at Dana.

"Of course. It's like being in a fishbowl. Horse enthusiasts from all over the world come to the Derby. Typically, the keen betters come in a couple months before the Derby and watch the last bit of training, especially the competition between the colts, when they race against each other. How they perform with that, near the deadline, is a sure indicator of victory or defeat." Dana smiled over at Graham and locked eyes with him. *You're a gorgeous hunk and you're all mine.*

He held the gaze. "I love you, gorgeous." He grinned at her, appreciatively.

Dana worked with Jacob and their new colt, day after day. The challenge intensifying as she worked the colt up to the one and a quarter of a mile long race.

Danielle hated herself. She wasn't sure when that scenario had begun, but she actually despised herself. She tried to pray, but felt blocked. She was pretty sure her mind had become warped when she'd been behind bars. That was all the more reason why she deserved to have a wonderful man in her life. And the only man that met that criteria was Graham Van Rensellier. How dare Dana capture him? She was much smarter than Dana and just as beautiful. Okay, she was a tad older; but significantly smarter. She'd been the mastermind behind Dana's rise in the equestrian world. She'd created her and she could destroy her.

Danielle toyed with the idea of repenting but her heart wasn't in it. She would get back to God once she took Dana out. *But could she get away with it? She couldn't go back to prison. It was dreadful there. She had to be very, very careful. She got a thrill out of staying at Sugarbush secretly. She might go there one more time just to prove how stupid Dana and Graham were. Maybe she would head to Sugarbush next Sunday when they were at church. She could hide under the bed until everyone was asleep. She would pick another room, of course. Still, she would have the problem of the dogs and breaking into the house. Plus, Graham had mentioned he intended to hire a 24/7 guard at the gate. Maybe it was in place now.*

Still, she was smart as a whip and thrived on challenges and danger. If she decided to do it; she would find a way.

Chapter Thirty

Pete Jansen drove Danielle to his shack after lunch. He chided her for stepping onto Graham Van Rensellier's private club, Villa De Vinci. Taunting them and causing them to be suspicious was a bad idea.

"I like to have my fun. And I did. I got a big kick of watching Dana peer at me. Seemed she felt like she knew me from somewhere. She had this puzzled expression on her face. She didn't figure it out though. I knew she wouldn't. She's not all that bright."

Danielle lounged on a wicker chair on the back porch of Pete's shack.

Pete occupied a chair next to her. "I want to know how I'm getting paid. I thought you said you lost all your money...or... your ex stole it...or whatever..."

Danielle had always been a master at bluffing. "You're joking, right?" She let out a harsh chuckle. "I have some cash salted away...cash he knew nothing about. What do they call it...an emergency fund? You'll get paid. Just as long as you don't get too greedy."

"So what's the plan?" His long legs were sprawled out in front of his lean frame, as he slouched on the chair.

Danielle watched a humming bird flit from a small tree nearby. "I don't want to do this. I admit I'm conflicted. If I'm caught, I'll plead insanity. You must admit it was pretty smart of me to pretend to be nuts, so they would drop me off at the psyche ward. With my history of *mental illness,s* I should easily be able to find an attorney who will get me off, if it ever comes to that."

"What about *me?* I don't give a rat's ass about *you.*"

"Relax, Pete. So...do you want to hear my plan, or not?"

"Of course I wanna hear it. But I'm not sayin' I'm gonna do it. I'm a free man right now, after serving six...and I ain't never goin' back to that hell hole."

"If you're a scardy cat, Pete...maybe I should just find somebody else."

"So...let's hear the plan..." He scowled.

The sunlight peaked through a smattering of white birch trees on his one-acre property. It was a cloudless, clear, blue day. A soft breeze rustled the leaves.

Pete started shaking even before she told him the plan.

Danielle smirked, her eyes dancing with mischief. "

"I like it. I wish I didn't. Easy cash for me." He scowled and was silent for a few minutes, computing a few things. "Sure, count me in. It's the last job I'll pull. I want ten G's up front."

"Thought you'd feel that way." She shook his hands, smirking.

"What if you finally nail this dude and marry him, and he ain't all he's cracked up to be?"

"That won't happen. He's the best thing to hit this area in decades. Way too good for Dana." Danielle turned to go. "I'm staying up the street at the Sleep Easy Motel. They've foreclosed on my house. It's doesn't matter. I'll be moving onto Sugarbush soon."

He watched her from his deck as she drove off. Suddenly, he was stuck with a queasy feeling, a hunch of sorts... a premonition. "Somethin' could go wrong...jest like it went wrong with the kidnapping. My buddy is doing time. I don't wanna be next." *Maybe I should get out of it. Maybe I'll get the up-front cash and disappear for a while. Problem is...this broad has a long memory. I better not double cross her. Who knows what she might do if I did that. She's whacky.*

Still, after she'd sped off, he mulled over the plan. He didn't like it. Plain and simple. He just didn't like it. He wouldn't discuss it on his cell. He drove over to the motel. She'd given him the room number. He knocked on the door. "Danielle? Open up. It's Pete."

She peered through the peep hole. *Is he wimping out on me? After I've confided my plan to him? I don't think so.* She opened the door in a fury. "Well?"

He pushed his way inside and plunked down on the chair next to the small desk. "Why don't you...ah...give this plan...some breathing time..."

"Do I look like I have breathing time? I'm hangin' out in a motel...while that...step daughter of mine is living in the lap of luxury..."

"So rent a nice house and find your own guy. Live and let live."

"Oh, I see. You're here to wimp out on me. Or are you planning to double cross me?" Her voice was ice. Her glare lethal.

"I just think you should give your plan some

breathin' time... like I said."

"Oh, so you think you know better than me. Really? Fine. Why don't you mastermind the hit, then? Let me know what you come up with. Take...24 hours...and tell me your plan."

"Danielle. I don't think you should do it. It could backfire. Why do you want another murder on your hands?"

"*Another* murder? Is that what you just said. *Another murder?* You don't think it was an accident...that guy falling off the cliff?"

"What planet are you on, Danielle? You were convicted and imprisoned for murder. Your attorney pleaded insanity and that's how this whole vicious cycle occurred. It's not like we just met...we have some history...remember?" Pete scowled.

"Well, fine. Sleep on it." Danielle saw him to the door. *Wimp. And after she'd told him her plans. But he wouldn't dare double cross her. Or would he?*

That night sleep eluded her. She tossed and turned, struck with an acute attack of conscience. *What if the murder plan failed? What if she was charged with attempted murder and sent back to prison? Was it really worth it?*

But as she began drifting off to sleep, she knew she would proceed. She had nothing to lose. Her girlfriends had bid her farewell, not that they mattered much. But Graham and Dana had taken a walk from her...and that mattered a whole lot. In fact, she was in constant, emotional pain because of them turning their backs on her. She had nothing to lose. She might as well proceed. She didn't need Pete. She would be better off alone and it would be cheaper. She would get the ten grand back from him, immediately.

It was after 10:00 p.m. She didn't call him. Just drove to his house and pounded on the door. No answer. His old black Nissan was gone. A strange premonition seeped through her. Did he pack up his belongings and drive off with her cash?   Did he abandon the rental house, leaving behind the few sticks of furniture he'd put in it? Danielle was seething. She would get him for this. And she would have no mercy. She tried calling and texting. No response.

Pete had fled with her cash. That night, she was at the end of her rope. With her money gone and no family or friends to turn to, she fell on her face before God and repented. With great sorrow and travail, she confessed her sin and her evil, wicked scheme. Then, she denounced it. *What had she been thinking?*

God forgave her and took her back. As Danielle lounged on her bed watching some evangelist she'd never heard of preach the gospel, she was convicted of the sin she intended to commit. After repenting, she fell asleep feeling better about herself than she had in a long time, despite losing the ten grand.

But it was the last of her cash. Her emergency fund was now depleted. She checked her money belt. She counted out less than nine hundred dollars. That wouldn't go very far. She would have to get a job real quick. Plus, she had to track Pete down and get the ten grand back.

Pete couldn't sleep. He awakened in the middle of the night, sweating. He'd had a nightmare about the wicked Danielle. *The woman was capable of anything. She would track him down like a Bloodhound. He'd better give her back the down payment and wash his hands of her. He would tell her the truth. He'd planned to go straight. She'd tempted him and he wasn't thinking clearly when he'd agreed to do the hit. He shouldn't have left town with her cash.*

Pete drove through the night, pounding on Danielle's motel door early the next morning. He spoke through the door. "Can I buy the gorgeous Danielle breakfast? I hate to eat alone."

Pete was up to something. She knew that for sure. The only time he'd ever flattered her was when he wanted something. Still, he had her ten grand and he'd shown up. Must have had an attack of conscience. Either that or he feared repercussion from her.

She had always been into clothes...and wardrobe...make-up and hair. She wore a sleek, black Cleopatra-style wig and a foxy, red outfit, more of the thrift store purchases. She swung the door open, flashing him a welcoming smile and batting her long, fake lashes. "Couldn't stay away from me, could you?"

"Well, you're looking fetching, Danielle." He'd always fancied her, despite knowing it was a one-way street. It was why she was able to manipulate him into doing her dirty deeds. He'd been alone too long. Didn't have much to offer a woman, so he'd stuck to himself mostly. But when a beautiful, sexy woman like Danielle was right under his nose, he couldn't and wouldn't turn the other way. "Aren't you going to invite me in?"

She was caught off guard. *What was he up to? She never trusted ex jailbirds.* "Coffee?" There was a mini kitchenette in her small hotel room, just enough room for a mini fridge and coffee maker. Plus a small desk and chair.

"Sounds real good."

She let him in and started the coffee.

He took a seat opposite the small desk. "Danielle... I've already spent some of the advance you gave me...and...I wanna go ahead with the hit. Flesh out the plan for me, would you? When do you want to do this?"

She didn't know how she could tell him all bets were off. She had come to her senses and now she could hardly believe she had entertained the idea of taking Dana out. "Honey, she's my daughter...I've got to kiss and make up with her. I don't want to proceed."

"Come on, Danielle. You can't be serious. What made you change your mind? You were adamant about taking her out." He stared at her, stunned. "What about Graham? And your obsession with him? And what about the ten grand you gave me? That was an up-front promise."

Danielle peered directly into Pete's eyes. "Well, Pete...I guess my promises aren't worth much. But you knew that anyway. So, don't sweat it. Give me what you've got. And make darn sure you get the rest of it to me, pronto."

"I can't believe what I'm hearing." Pete stared at her.

"Last night I met the Lord. I mean...really met him. And he made it clear that murder is not an option. I guess...Satan had blinded my eyes and I allowed myself to become obsessed with getting Graham. I can't believe how depraved I was...cookin' up that weird plan. Just give me the upfront cash I gave you. Give me what you have left...and get the rest of it to me as soon as you can. I want to forget we ever had a murder plan."

"Just like that! I don't think so, Danielle." He slapped her against the wall with his strength. "The cash is gone. All of it." He smirked. "Secondly, you're not dealing with amateurs, here. Your conversation was taped. It's game over, Danielle...and this time *I* outsmarted you. I'm workin' for the cops. I'm undercover." He smirked.

"On no you don't!" She slapped him. Hard. She tried to wriggle out from his grasp, but couldn't. He overpowered her. She was boxed in. Outfoxed. Overpowered. She had nowhere to run. Nowhere to hide. *Help me, God...what do I do now?* It was a desperate, silent plea for mercy and help from Almighty God.

My precious, precious daughter. You cannot sit on the fence. You are either for me or against me. There is no middle ground. You have been given a free will. I love you more than you could possibly imagine. You need to give up everything for Me. If you seek Me with all your heart and mind and soul you will find me."

"I get it, Lord." She did an about turn. The lights had been turned on and she wanted to live for the Lord. Really live for him. Still, she was in big trouble and had to find her way out of it.

Danielle had to think fast. "Pete, I'm going straight. We're both going straight." She put her arms around him and kissed him. She begged him to throw out the tape, whispering to him. She leaned in whispering to him. "Let's forget the whole thing. God has been dealing with me and I need to repent."

He glared at her, but she could tell he was softening. "Yeah. He's been dealing with me, too."

She shook his hand and kissed him goodbye.

Chapter Thirty-One

Dana awakened with the sniffles. A chill hung in the air. She didn't feel up to training today. She would tell Jacob to proceed without her. Over black tea and honey, along with a slice of well done rye bread, fresh garlic and a hot drink of lemon and honey, she padded back to the bedroom. Settling onto the bed, she turned on the TV. It was good timing that Graham had gone into town early to take care of some business. Danielle was on her mind; and despite the rocky relationship they had, she felt led to call her. "Hey, Mom. What's goin' on? Did you go back to the hospital?"

Danielle was ecstatic. *This truly was an answer to prayer. She tried to keep the desperation out of her voice.* "I've recovered. It was...a temporary thing." She avoided answering the question for now.

"What's goin' on? You sound okay."

Danielle didn't want to tell a fib. Not so soon after repenting. But what choice did she have? *Didn't Rahab in the Bible, lie to the spies, telling them that the men they sought were not in the house? When, in fact, they were on the roof, hidden by tall stalks of wheat?*

Maybe she was too smart for her own good. "Yeah, I returned to the hospital, but they discharged me. Said I was okay. Told me to take it easy." *Lord, forgive me for lying. But the problem with lying, she'd discovered... was that it had no end. And it became easier to embellish a situation than to admit what deep trouble she was actually in.*

Dana thought for a moment. It didn't ring true. Danielle had changed...and not for the better. She no longer trusted anything she said or did. "So...what's goin' on? You're buying another house? Or renting an apartment? Where are you living now?"

Danielle chuckled, trying to emulate her old self. "What is this? Twenty questions? I've...got a lot goin' on right now. Next time I see you, I'll get you up to speed."

"Sure. Of course." Dana was used to her Mom being in control. It was one of things she liked and admired about her. Or *used* to like and admire about her.

Danielle knew she had to keep a positive spin on things, if she was ever going to repair the damage done to their relationship. *I don't pry into her personal life; and she shouldn't pry into mine, either.* "Gotta fly. Talk to you soon." She ended the phone call before Dana could fire more questions at her.

Dana knew instantly that something was wrong. What was Danielle hiding? After a few brief phone calls, she learned that to her shock and chagrin Danielle was still missing, as far as the authorities were concerned. She had not been formally discharged. She'd lied to Dana. She phoned Graham immediately. It went straight to voice mail.

Dana started feeling worse instead of better. That's

when she knew she was coming down with the flu. *I'd better stay in one of the guest rooms. I don't want Graham to be sick."*

She found Violet polishing the furniture in the living room. Standing a safe distance from her, she spoke. "I'm coming down with the flu; so I guess I'll hang out in the lime green guest room, if that's okay." Bundled up in a white terry robe, she sniffled, shuffling up to the second landing and making herself comfortable in the guest room.

Violet followed her. "Drink as much liquid as you can. Lots of lemon and honey drinks. Maybe an apple or two. We have pineapple. That will be good for you." She continued polishing the wood railing on the staircase as she spoke. Fifties music wafted throughout the house. It was Violet's favorite, though she never played it when Graham was home, because he disliked it. "I'll bring you up some hot drinks. You just get yourself comfortable, honey."

Dana settled into the comfy bed, snuggling under the fluffy, white comforter and admiring the quaint, ancient white iron design of the bed frame. She drifted off.

She awakened after what seemed like about an hour. Danielle was powerfully on her mind and heart. She prayed fervently. Something was going on with her, but she had no idea what that was. *She's gone off the rails. Where do we go from here?*

Violet appeared with a mug of steaming, hot lemon, handing it to Dana. "How are you feeling, honey?"

"Not so good. Frankly, though, I'm real concerned about Mom."

"So, what's the latest?"

"She said she was discharged. I called the hospital

and they denied it. Said she was still missing. Danielle won't tell me where she is."

"Maybe you should stop worrying about her. The woman is a survivor. She's tough. And she's smart. She'll find away to get a loan for a new house. Before you know it, she'll be back on her feet."

"I dunno. I have a bad gut feeling about her. Just not sure what she's up to."

"What do you want for dinner, honey?"

"No appetite. Ask Graham. I'm goin' back to sleep." She sneezed and coughed, used some Kleenex and snuggled back under the comforter. "Please tell Graham not to visit me. The last thing we need is for him to get sick, too."

"But I don't matter, right?" Violet smirked.

"You said you never got sick, when you took the job here. I believed you then and I still believe you."

"Okay. Then do you mind if I give you some advice?"

"Go ahead."

"Stay away from Danielle for a while. She has some...questionable friends."

"How would you know that?"

"Saw her when I drove into town the other day to do the shopping."

"You didn't mention it."

"I didn't want to alarm you. The guy I saw her with is an ex jailbird. I remember an artist's rending of him in the newspaper. He looks suspiciously similar to one of the thugs that kidnapped you. That's why I'm tellin' you to stay clear of her...at least, for now."

"The guy likely just resembles the kidnapper. Anyway, I'm over that trauma, thank God. And the nightmares have finally ended."

"I'm sorry to say this; but I don't trust Danielle. Something has happened to her; maybe something she doesn't want anyone to know about."

Dana waited until after 5:00 to phone Jacob. "So...how did it go today?"

"Silver Star is doing remarkably well. He's a quick study and very focused. Absolutely the best colt I've ever worked with."

"Great. We're on target. I'll be back in a day or two, to take him through his paces. Have your lined up any other colts to do a practice run with?"

"Not yet. It's still early days, don't you think?"

"Yeah. But let's get all our ducks in a row." Dana grinned, happy to hear the good report. Have you been praying before every session?"

"With a name like Jacob. What do *you* think?"

"God will see to it that we win." Dana sniffled.

Dana got worse.

Graham figured she had pneumonia. He moved her down to the guest bedroom on the main floor; which was adjacent to the master bedroom. "If you don't improve significantly by the morning, I'm admitting you to hospital, Dana."

She was barely cognizant of what he was saying. In a hazy, dream-like trance, she sighed and turned in the bed.

Graham tried to cheer her up. He even did his clown act, followed by his puppet act. Nothing.

Dana took a turn for the worse that night.

Graham knew what he had to do. She was pale and shaking. "I've called an ambulance, Dana. You're going into hospital." He peered over at her.

Dana was in a daze. Totally out of it. Not cognizant of anything that was going on.

The ambulance picked her up and transported her to Lexington University hospital.

Graham got her checked into the hospital.

Soon she was resting comfortably in a private room. "Honey, you look so pale..." An icy chill ran through him. *Lord, she's got to get better. H*e could see that she was delirious. "Dana...Dana..." He called her name over and over.

She was sweating, her eyes blurry, unfocused. She lay too still. She was deathly pale.

Suddenly, it hit Graham. *She's been drugged. Just like the horse.*He called Violet on his cell. "She had lunch with Jacob at the track every day. Could one of our enemies or competitors like Tanner... or someone else, have paid off someone to poison her food?"

"Maybe." Violet was suddenly very alert.

Graham leaned toward Dana.

She lay still as a corpse.

"Honey...you have to get better. You have to..." He was fighting panic and hysteria. *What was happening to him? Lord, no...not after all I've been through...I couldn't take losing Dana, too. Please Lord...."* Graham put his hands over his face and sobbed bitterly.

Three hours later, Dana awakened.

The doctor had informed Graham that she'd been heavily drugged.

Her skin remained stark white. Her eyes dull. She gazed at him, vacantly. She seemed to get weaker...smaller right before his eyes."

He leaned toward her. "Honey, I love you. I love you...so...so much. We've been through a lot together. Don't...don't leave me now. Get better. Get well! You have to." Graham erupted in hysterical sobs. Seeing Dana like this was like a replay of watching his first wife, Myrna, slowly ebb away.

The head nurse rushed into the room. Her voice was calm and even. "I'll get you something, Sir. Sudden...acute illness in a loved one...often brings on powerful emotions..."

Graham covered his face with his hands, sobbing. Shaking. Out of control.

Dana looked over at the strange, emotional man in her room. But her mind was blur and she felt deathly ill.

Swiftly, the nurse returned with a couple of pills and a glass of water, handing them to Graham.

The young lady doctor was a petite Indonesian woman, Violet observed. She was glad she'd gone with Graham to the hospital. It had just been an instinct. No one should be alone in a crisis. Thankfully, Wilbur had agreed to stay in the house until she returned. He would keep an eye on the boys.

"Dana. I'm Dr. Rancine. How do you feel?" She smiled over at Dana.

Dana peered at her, a glazed look filling her countenance. She did not respond.

Doctor Rancine smiled. "You'll be fine. You've ingested a miniscule amount of poison. Folks can react in a variety of ways to it." She stuck a thermometer into Dana's mouth, shook it and read it. "You need to get well. And you will. Your husband needs you."

Dana lay on the cot. Unresponsive. Groggy.

Doctor Rancine wrote out a prescription, handing it to Graham. "This should do the trick."

"May I speak to you privately, doctor?" Graham peered at the doctor. He was gradually getting his equilibrium back.

She glanced at her watch. "Yes, but I have less than five minutes. Perhaps we can step out into the hallway."

"Seems like she's been poisoned. I'll check on her later tonight. Meanwhile, you need to get some rest. You can come back later and stay next to her bed, if you like. We'll wheel in a cot for you."

"Thanks. I'll do that."

"We won't draw any hasty conclusions. She's not in a life-threatening situation. And I've prescribed some medication that should get her condition under control, quite rapidly."

Chapter Thirty-Two

Danielle turned on the TV in her motel while she munched on Kentucky Fried chicken and chips. The news was on. "Famous equestrian, Dana Van Rensellier, who recently survived kidnapping, is embroiled in yet another drama. She was rushed into emergency last night. It is unclear what has transpired. But the former Show Jumper is gravely ill..."

Danielle knew then what she had to do. It had been a wicked, plan poisoning her food. And she regretted it, now that she'd given her life to Jesus. She had to visit Dana. Graham would try to thwart it; so she would slip into one of her many disguises and head over to the hospital tomorrow. *Won't I look adorable as a nurse?* Having just spent time in the hospital, she knew exactly what they wore. With any luck, one of the thrift stores would have one or more uniforms in her size. She spoke aloud, for emphasis. "If someone says they don't recognize me as being staff, I'll smile at them and whisper "I'm an angel." She smirked, speaking aloud. "Hospital staff usually embraced the supernatural world of angels. If a patient was gravely ill with no hope for recovery, family and hospital staff hoped for a miracle.

Lord, I'm so sorry I drugged Dana. I want to make up with her. And if she won't see me...I'll just keep praying for her.

She regretted paying the server at the track to poison Dana's food. Still, too many wonderful things had been happening to her; in contrast to her own life, which had been ripped apart. The only way to keep Dana humble was to cause hardship to beset her. The poison would make her sick. But it wouldn't be fatal. It was just enough to take her off her high horse and let her have a little humility. Besides, Dana still owed her for the many years of riding lessons and steep equine expenses over decades. Not to mention all the work and money involved in raising her.

Yes, it was her turn. And if God didn't see fit to give her an abundant life, she would move forward and make it happen herself. She threw off the disguises. Maybe this would be her best opportunity to become friends with Dana again. She ripped off the wig and silly outfit. Next, she dressed fairly close to the old Danielle. She was glad she'd hired an attorney to write a strong letter to the hospital, stating that she was in top form when she left the hospital and had no reason to return; despite not being formally discharged. *Letters from a respected attorney with a good office and impressive letterhead always contained power and smoothed things over.*

"Dana! Honey...oh you look...pale. You poor darling. What happened?" Danielle had managed to get onto Dana's floor.

Dana had always been blessed with fine instincts. She wasn't sure why she didn't trust her Mom; but she knew for sure that she didn't. "I...I don't want any visitors right now." She peered at her Mom, nervously; and then remembered the buzzer on the wall. She pressed it.

Danelle saw her do it. "Oh, okay. I'll come back another time, darling." She hurried out of the room, down the elevator and into the hospital parking. As she was about to step into her car, she almost bumped smack into Graham.

His eyes were steel. "What are you doing here, Danielle? Haven't you caused enough trouble, already?"

"What could you possibly be talking about?" She flashed him a big smile. She knew her bright green eyes widened when her face was lit with a smile. Then, on an impulse, she was helpless to stop, she moved onto her tiptoes, planting a peck on his right cheek. "A little display of affection from your beloved Mother-in-Law." She flashed him a cheeky smile.

"There should be a law against women like you!" His tone was icy. He turned on his heel and hurried to the front door of the hospital.

Danielle stood rooted to the spot, watching him go.

Strangely, he turned and peered at her, just before opening the door to the hospital.

Danielle's smile was huge. Encouraged, she threw caution to the wind. "You haven't seen the last of me, yet!" She flashed him a big, happy grin and then stepped into her Toyota Camry which was only a few feet away. Soon she was racing down the freeway, heady with success, the music blaring. "He's intrigued by me. I have a chance. All I have to do is get the competition out of the way. Too bad she's my step-daughter. But it's it a tough world out there." She smiled big. "The man is intrigued by me. *I have a chance with him. Not a big chance. But it is a chance. Somehow she would parlay that crack in the door into a wide open door of opportunity. Yes, it was all going to happen. And she was so close to success, she could almost touch it. I'm sorry, Lord. I'm so, so sorry.*

But something was bothering her. Oh, the God thing. *Yes, Lord, I repented. Well, what was she going to do? She couldn't have it both ways. So the Bible said. She was greatly conflicted but she'd finally seen a glimmer of hope with Graham. She couldn't quit now.*

It was time to use the excellent brain God had given her. First, she would sharpen up her image. Somehow, she would have to buy another house. But with no down-payment and no job, it would take a miracle. But wasn't God in the miracle business? Okay, then.

From her seedy motel room, Danielle called the most successful agent in the area. She'd heard glowing reports about him and knew he was making a ton of money. John Wilcox. Folks said he had a heart of gold. Well, she was about to find out if that were true. His name came to her right away. Of course, she'd often noticed his ads on billboards, and in the local real estate papers. He was the number one producer at Re Max. She phoned his number and reached his assistant. "Hi, I'm Joan Barnes, one of John's assistants. How may I help you?"

"My name is...She'd better give a fake name for now. In case the woman watched the news. She would come clean with the heart of gold agent, just before he was about to write the offer. "Joan Barnes is the name. I want to buy a house. As soon as possible. I'm not fussy.

I want the cheapest house in the area."

"Hi, I'm Lacey, one of John's assistants. May I ask you a few questions?"

She opened a new file on the computer. "How soon do you need to be in?"

"Right away. As fast as possible."

"Do you have a house to sell first?"

"No. Its...sold." Little white lies came too easy for her. She would come clean with the heart of gold agent. But right now, she knew she had to get past the gatekeeper.

"So, you want an appointment to view houses as soon as possible. Correct?"

"That's right."

Danielle, posing at Joanne received a quick phone call late that night from the hot shot agent, John Wilcox. "One of my assistants has lined up houses for tomorrow starting at 2:00 P.M. Does that work for you?"

"It does. Oh...and I'm not fussy. It's all about price. I just need a house...somewhere to live. The cheaper the better. I lost my other house in an ugly divorce."

"I'm sorry to hear it. Don't worry, we'll find you a new home."

She took a deep breath. She felt much better already. She sensed his genuine concern.

Danielle wasn't sure how she was going to break the news about her lack of a down payment to the agent; but she trusted God to lead the way.

The agent showed her the two cheapest houses he could find. "I'm sorry...I don't have any more inexpensive homes to show you. It's a tight market. I was lucky to find two...and that's only because there was a collapsed sale on one of them. There are more buyers out there than properties available."

Danielle chose one of the tiny houses. The smallest and cheapest of the two. It would do. The one-bedroom cottage sat on a teeny lot on the outskirts of town. The area was quite rundown. "Thanks for finding me this house. Wait until you see what I'm going to do with it. You won't recognize it." She smiled confidently at her agent.

He took her for a steak sandwich at a nearby cafe. "How much down do you have?"

"I told your assistant. Guess she didn't pass the info along." She paused, giving him a heads-up that the news she was about to depart, wasn't the greatest. "I don't have a down payment. And...I have a favor to ask you."

"Let's hear it."

"Look, I know this is an outrageous request, John. But frankly, I've heard you have a heart of gold and love helping folks get settled into a home. Is there any chance you would consider...using your commission as the down payment? And hold a second mortgage on the property yourself? I'll have huge monthly payments...I know that. But I'll be in a house and I'll be forever grateful to God and you."

"Do you have *anything* down?" The agent was stunned.

"No. Just the money for the notary. Closing costs." She knew she risked the chance that he might be outraged.

He was very quiet for a while. Suddenly, her broke into a wide grin. "You know something. With the kind of courage you have to cook up this deal and ask a big favor from a total stranger...well, I give you a lot of credit. So...you know what? I'm going to do it. Assuming your offer is accepted, we'll deal through my favorite mortgage broker; and she'll put the deal together."

Money was no big deal to him. He made more than he could spend. Give and it shall be given unto you. He'd always lived by that motto. "Your payment will be real high." He grinned. "Of course I'll give you the best break I can on the mortgage. I need some write-offs, anyway. This will be a loser for me."

She jumped up from her seat. "Fantastic! Praise the Lord! You know...I just became a Christian...and I asked God for a miracle house. First, he gave me the *idea*. Then, he gave me *you*. Now, I'm getting a house!" She was ecstatic.

He grinned. "Don't tell anybody, but actually...I'm going to enjoy putting this deal together way more than all the pricey houses with hefty down payments. I went into this business to help people like you...folks who lost their home to a misfortune or folks who thought they would never be able to get into the market. I help them find a way to own property. I have great joy in putting this kind of deal together. But remember, I still have to present the offer. Hopefully, I'll be able to do it tonight."

It was easy to see why the man was so successful. God had blessed and prospered him; just like he'd done with King Solomon. The King had asked God for wisdom to help the people he would rule over; but because he was not greedy for himself, God gave him wisdom *and* prosperity.

Late that evening, her agent phoned her. "You just bought yourself a house, Danielle. Congratulations!"

She screamed in delight. "Fantastic! Praise the Lord!"

The agent chuckled. "My assistant will be calling you. We need to go over the details of the financing and the private mortgage, etc."

"Sounds wonderful." She ginned. "Lord, thank-you. I know that this is a wonderful blessing from your hand. I praise and worship you. I never would have dreamed it was possible...but I felt you nudging me...goading me forward...you said in your word that you wish above all things that we would prosper and be in good health. So, Lord, I know this is God Wink, if there ever was one."

She'd managed to overcome some hurdles. She had to convince him she wasn't wacko. She'd told him that her attorney had arranged for a legal discharge from the hospital. She was glad she'd finally pulled that off. Just in time. Plus there was the fiasco of losing her house.

Danielle settled into her new, one-bedroom house. Thrilled, she hung up curtains and repainted the rooms in turquoise and pink. She did the bathroom in tangerine. Thanks to a good credit rating, she was able to charge up a few, great contemporary pieces of furniture. She added huge throw pillows in turquoise, peach and other bright shades. Oversized plants, fake and real lent a tropical air to the place. And so did the bright, cheery pictures of Arizona and California landscapes.

She stepped back to survey her new home. Walla! The place had sprung to life. "Well, if I say so myself, this place looks incredible! It's Inviting and... quite marvelous." She spoke to the walls, as though they might reply.

Putting on some music, using her portable CD player she kicked back, poured herself a glass of Chardonnay and admired her handiwork. "Back on my feet again. Thank-you, Lord." Somehow a scripture came to her mind. *"I will restore the years that the locusts have eaten."* She wanted that with all her heart. Having this new home was the beginning of great and wonderful things. She just knew it.

She hated herself for the scheme that kept elbowing its' way into her psyche Sinister forces were at work. A part of her wanted to proceed with her goal and obsession of snaring Graham; another part of her wanted to turn her back on evil, repent, make up with Dana and Graham and be a wonderful Mother-in-law.

Chapter Thirty-Three

Danielle had managed to charm her way out of the bad situation with her double-crossing, former buddy, Pete, and she'd spent considerable time repenting. But when she'd awakened the next morning, she still had the obsession to win Graham's love.

Of course she would have to get rid of Dana before anything could happen between them. The poison she'd arranged for her had caused her to be in the hospital. She was vulnerable. It was sad that it had to end this way. But really, Dana had had quite a dazzling life, considering the show jumping and marrying the fabulous Graham Van Rensellier. All she had to do was show up late at night when she was sure Dana would be asleep. Prick her arm with a needle. One little pinprick and it was curtains for her.

Maybe she had a split personality. She felt driven to take Dana out. Maybe losing Stefan to the jumping accident had pushed her over the edge. He'd always been her favorite. He was the light and love of her life. Dana had been adopted. But she had given birth to Stefan. She would never recover from the loss of her only son.

Danielle slipped into a disguise. Wearing a nurse's uniform and a dark, curly wig and glasses, she would pose as a brand-new nurse. No, that wouldn't work; because the head nurse would quickly realize she didn't work there if she happened to show up. The night shift was often quiet. She would be noticed. *What to do? Just like that, a flash of lightning struck her. She would slip into the disguise of a visiting chaplain. She would go during the daytime. She would wear a disguise and hang out in the coffee shop, which was right near the door that led to the parking lot. Graham would likely visit sometime between 2:00 and 4:00 in the afternoon. Visiting hours. Once she spotted him leaving, she would make her move.*

Finding the appropriate garb for a chaplain would be a bit tricky, but she was up to the task.

Once Dana was out of the way, she would wait an appropriate length of time before putting the moves on Graham. She would re-invent herself. First, there would be Botox and an eyelift. Next, she would have a neck lift. She wouldn't go for a full face lift. She didn't need it. She joined Curves and started working out every morning. Her body had to be perfect. She had to look really gorgeous for Graham. She plunked down the big bucks for color and styling. She chose a sporty, slightly longer, sexier hair-do.

Just like that; she dropped ten years.

A new house.

A new image.

A new man.

Her obsession to be mistress of Sugarbush was looming closer and closer to her.

Danielle visited all the thrift shops in town, finally

landing on the perfect outfit. She tried it on, peered in the mirror and knew she'd struck gold. Hurrying to the cashier, a smug grin plastered on her face, she nearly fainted with shock as she spotted Graham milling around. "G...Graham! What are you doing here?" She could feel her mouth gaping as she stood in a short lineup, waiting for the cashier.

"Funny...I was about to ask you the same thing, Danielle."

"Oh....well....I...." She started laughing, nervously. Even to her own ears she knew it was laced with hysteria. "I...I..." No words would come.

Graham peered closely at the garment Danielle held. "What...on earth is *that*?"

"This? Why...it's...it's. Well it's...a..."

"Yes, Danielle. It's a... what?" Graham's countenance was stern. His voice reflected distrust and disgust. Uncharacteristically, he grabbed the garment from her. "Let's see what we have here." He peered at the garment, holding it up. He realized what it was. "Planning on becoming a chaplain, Danielle? I hardly think you're suited for that profession. Maybe a prison garment would be more appropriate."

"Give me that back! Who do you think you are? I'm in the theatre; in case you didn't know. I've...gotten back to amateur theatre; and this...is for an audition...if you don't mind!"

"Really? What is the name of the play? And the name of the theatre? Dana and I might like to come and see you perform in it."

"You are just too boring for words, Graham. Like you have time for theatre with everything going on in your life."

Graham peered closely at the chaplain garb. "A chaplain's outfit?" His mind raced. He'd been on to her for some time. Didn't trust a word out of her mouth. "What could you possibly be planning to do with that? The local playhouse...I just happen to know... is doing Gypsy and there are no chaplain roles in the musical. I know the show. You probably don't know that I'm a theatre buff. Have been since my youth." He grinned, softening slightly. "Believe it or not; I actually wanted to be an actor at one point..."

"I knew it! Takes one to know one." It was time to flirt. Her only hope of diverting him or restoring his humor...of getting him off this dark mood he was in...was to lighten it and divert him. She was a master at that sort of thing. She turned on the charm. She was glad she'd had veneers done. She looked amazing. Folks often thought she and Dana were sisters. None of that mattered; except maybe if Graham concurred.

"Hey. Wanna see my new house? You can't keep a winner down! I lost one and bought a new one! Real cute, too. Fixed it all up. Come on over, I'll show you."

Like I'm going to be alone with this devious woman? Does she think I was born yesterday? Graham's steely gaze said it all. No words were needed.

"Suit yourself. Maybe if Dana gets better, the two of you will come and visit." She smirked.

"*If* she gets better. What's that supposed to mean? Of course, she'll get better! We're praying. Folks at church are praying. We're believing God for a total healing..."

He knew how to press her button. *Dana. Dana. Dana. And God. That's all he ever talked about it. He had a nice, cozy little world. Two sons, a housekeeper, a wife and Sugarbush Farm. She had no one. A tiny little house and a car. Things had to change. She was meant for a bigger life than the one she currently had. But while Graham was around, she would play it sweet and cozy.* "What a nice surprise seeing you. If I get the role of the chaplain in the play...I'll be sure to let you know, so that the two of you can come and see me in it..." She flashed him a big, sexy smile. "They're doing it after Gypsy."

"Sure, Danielle. That play doesn't exist. And we both know it. You're a phoney and a fake. Dana gets that, too. I'm sorry it has to be this way...but please do not contact us or try to see us." He glared at her. "You are persona non grata in our lives and at Sugarbush."

Danielle didn't bat an eyelash. "Oh Graham. Silly boy. Family is forever. Dana is my daughter! We'll kiss and make up; it's just a matter of time." She smiled at him, despite the fact that her heart was crumbling into a million pieces and she was fighting fearful thoughts that he might be dead serious. Something had happened to her. Something to turn her into the ruthless, self-seeking cobra she'd become. She didn't like herself. And no one else did, either, for that matter. Still, she felt helpless to move in any direction; other than the one she was moving in. She was stuck. Still, she'd found God. So then maybe she really *was* a split personality.

Graham had gone. She stood on the street, frozen, watching him roar off in his white Jeep. Tears streamed down her face. *What is wrong with me, God? What happened to me? What happened to turn me into the witch I've become?*

That night Danielle went home and repented. She fell to her knees, weeping uncontrollably. *"Lord, you have blessed me with this wonderful house. You have restored me time and time again. And yet...I have failed you over and over. Help me to be all that you have created me to be."* Tears streamed down her cheeks. She was bewildered and confused. She could never harm her own daughter. What had she been thinking? She found herself praying that Dana would be okay.

She flipped open a spiritual book she'd picked up from the thrift store. It talked about spiritual warfare. As she read the book, she understood what had been happening to her. An unseen spiritual battle had been waging over her. It told her that Ephesians 6:10 needed to be prayed over her life daily, in order to combat the spiritual war raging over her. Now, at last, she was beginning to understand what was really happening to her.

Chapter Thirty-Four

Danielle awakened the next morning with a new attitude. She really had repented. She didn't know much about spiritual warfare, until she'd read the book she found at the thrift store. It was by Derek Prince, a renowned Bible scholar from the UK. Now, she was beginning to have a glimmer of what was happening to her in the spiritual realm.

The book told her that a spiritual battle is being fought over every soul. She realized, now, that she needed to stay in the word and bind the forces of evil on a daily basis.

Sunday morning, Danielle got up early, dressed carefully and slipped into the new outfit she'd recently bought. She drove to church.

Praise and Glory church was a quaint, old white church, set off from the main road and perched on a hill. *It looks like a picture post card.* She parked her car and stepped out confidently, knowing that her new outfit; a pink jacket and short grey skirt; and pink pumps, looked fetching. She had checked her image in the mirror. The face work she'd had done looked remarkably effective.

She walked purposefully toward the front door, her confidence rising with each step. *I look amazing! My new sassy blond layer cut looks youthful and terrific. Maybe I'll meet a new man at church, Lord. I have truly repented of my obsession of winning Graham and harming Dana. Now, I just want to follow you!*

"From your lips to God's ears" rang from her heart and mind and soul, as she almost bumped into an interesting-looking, older man.

He was alone as he stepped out of a blue T-Bird sports car. "Good morning, Ma'am. Lovely morning." He nodded graciously, not seeming to notice her as an individual, despite almost bumping into her.

So much for cosmetic surgery.

After the service, she almost bumped into him again. "We've got to stop meeting like this!" Danielle smiled at him, noticing for the time, how handsome the man was. *No way this guy is single.* Still, by nature, she was aggressive. "Excellent sermon, wasn't it?"

"I've heard better. I'm not a believer. I'm a skeptic. I hit a different church every Sunday, with a view to seeing how the other half lives. *"He is risen.* Seems to be the Easter message. "I haven't decided if I believe it or not."

He had her attention. "So then you don't believe in eternity. You think we die and that's the end of everything?"

"Maybe. Probably." He shrugged. "Well, I have a lunch date. See you around."

"Wait a minute, Sir. I want to see you in heaven when I get there." Danielle peered at him.

His laugh was caustic. "Sure lady. Church folks bin

tryin' to win me over for years. None of 'em succeed, though."

"Sounds like you're proud of that fact. I wouldn't be...if I were you. None of us ever knows how long we have..."

He cut her off. "Give it a rest, lady. I've heard it all before." He turned and marched toward his car.

She watched the sleek Robin's egg blue T-Bird speed off. "I tried, Lord. I really did."

"*Go after him.*"

"Did I hear you right, God?"

"*Go after him.*"

She had heard God's voice correctly. Hopping into her Toyota Camry, she wheeled out of the parking lot.

The man in the sports car was not far ahead of her.

She stepped on the gas. Soon, she was right behind him. *So now I'm literally chasing a man. God has a sense of humour. He works in mysterious ways.*

He stopped at a hamburger joint. *Funny, I had you pegged for hitting gourmet restaurants. As the thought raced through her mind, another thought settled there .Invite him to Villa de Vinci.* God didn't have to tell her twice. He was just settling into a seat with the menu when she approached him. "Hey, handsome. How about being my lunch guest at Villa De Vinci? I assure you the food is amazing there." She turned on the charm, flashing him a sly smile.

For a moment it seemed as though he were going to decline. Then he grinned. "Why would you want to do that? Let me guess...you're on a mission to convert me..."

God was surely leading her. She was out of her depth. "We don't have to talk religion. I don't want to dine alone. And looks like God put you right under my nose. Don't read anything into it."

"Where is that place? I've heard of it. I hear it's amazing. How far a drive is it?'

"Almost an hour. But it's well worth the drive. Your car or mine?"

"Oh no you don't. I take my car; you take yours. We both have our independence. I'm warning you, if you start pushing religion down my throat, I'm gone..."

"My dear, I haven't been inside of a church for years. I just happened to show up this morning. I do need some male company and you fit the bill. Do me a favor? Don't read too much into this."

Lunch was amazing and to Danielle's delight and surprise, her new friend bombarded her with spiritual questions. However, she was unable to answer most of them. She realized she'd better get in a Bible study and become more knowledgeable. Otherwise, how could God use her? Danielle had always been smart. She knew it. Dana knew it. Her former girlfriends knew it. And God knew it. He'd given her a good mind. She had a list of spiritual books she would buy as soon as she got settled. She'd been given the list by a professor friend of hers, who had moved away. Doubtless, those books would shed light on the quest of getting close to God. She wanted to hear that still, small voice and be led by the Holy Spirit.

She glanced at the notebook in her purse, scribbled a few titles on a pad and handed him her card. Maybe he would call her for dinner. Stranger things had happened.

When lunch was over, her companion called for the

bill.

"No...no...no. Lunch is on me. I invited you."
Danielle was adamant.

"Nonsense. A gentleman always pays. And I am
most certainly a gentleman." He grinned, glancing at
his watch. "And now I must go. I promised my
daughter that I would watch her in the Round Robin at
the club this afternoon. She's a pretty decent tennis
player."

"What club does she belong to?

"Fairview Tennis Club. Do you know it?"

"I do. I used to play there. I haven't played in ages,
though. I know they renovated the club last year."

"Yeah, they did a great job. The club looks amazing.
You're welcome to join me, if you like."

"Sounds like fun."

The Fairview Tennis Club was a ritzy place. She
peered around, duly impressed. "Wow! They have
seriously upgraded this place."

"Yeah. The renovation caused a bundle. Membership
fees have skyrocketed. Still, the club is at capacity.
Closed to new members. It's a busy place."

*Danielle thrived on being in the middle of the action.
Why hadn't she thought of joining the club sooner? It
was a perfect hunting ground for hubby number three.*
"What are the fees to join? I know the owners;
assuming it's still Harry and Alice Truber."

"Yep. They're actually friends of mine."

"Well then...you can put in a word for me if I decide
to join." Danielle flashed him a smile.

"Like I said...membership is closed. And there's is a
long waiting list. Guess you missed your chance."

I never miss my chance. And I never give up. I'm going to join this club. I was too busy with Dana and Graham and all the stuff that's been happening; but now that I've decided to circulate socially, I really must join this club; I'm not sure how I can skip the line; but where there is a will; there's a way. And God help anyone that stood in her way.

The outdoor brown wicker furniture was large and luxurious. Outdoor seating in the restaurant overlooked the courts. The place bustled with high energy.

After the games were finished, a well-tanned, athletic gal with auburn hair in a pony tail came over to their table. "Daddy. You made it. I'm impressed." She smiled, slyly. "So, who is your lady friend?"

"Danielle Lockhart, meet my one and only daughter. My precious angel; Sophie"

"Hey, Sophie. Real nice to meet you. You looked pretty good out there. You're a fine player."

"Nice to meet you, too. Thanks for the vote of confidence." She peered at Danielle. "I feel like I may have seen you here...maybe a while back..."

"You probably did. I used to belong to this club." *Now is my chance. Maybe she has some clout."* "I hear they have upped the fees..."

"Big bucks. Ten grand to join...and a long waiting list, at that. Sure glad I joined when the fees were in the hundreds..."

"Who is head of membership?" Danielle's mind was racing. She *had* to join, now that she realized what a challenge it would be to do that. And bonus, there seemed to be a fair number of men around. More than she had seen in any one group other than on the golf course. And golfing wasn't her thing.

"That would be me." Sophie smiled.

Danielle was stunned. *Lord, are you orchestrating this? She'd never believed in coincidences. Maybe, somehow, her future was wrapped up in joining this club, maybe meeting a new man here; or maybe even the agnostic she was sitting with could figure into her future. Maybe he would find the truth.*

Danielle peered directly into the sea green eyes of the young athlete. "Look...I started playing tennis when I was around fourteen. At that time, the tennis pro told me...this is the God-honest truth...he said I should seriously consider becoming a pro. Told me I was a natural; and if I trained seriously, I could probably play professionally..."

"So we need to have you at the club...is that what you're saying?" Sophie flashed Danielle a look of thinly veiled disdain.

"I'm just sharing my tennis story with you."

"Sure you are. Well, let me tell you something, Danielle. I know who you are. I know all about you. As it happens, I'm a friend of Dana's. When I'm not on the tennis courts; you can probably find me riding one of my thoroughbreds. Maybe riding with Dana."

Danielle felt like slamming her head against a wall in frustration. *Dana, Dana, Dana.* When is something in this life going to be about *her?* A cold wall of steel settled around her heart. *Oh, she would join this club all right; she just wasn't sure how.* A thought flashed through her mind. She had always prided herself on being able to outsmart everyone. A plan began to form in her mind.

Simple. She would get a job here...work herself up to

management. In no time, she would have the clout and contacts to become a member. It was a no-brainer. "I'm going to the powder room; see you in a bit." She flashed Sophie a smile, turned and headed down the corridor to the ladies' room. Inside the powder room, she glanced in the mirror, reapplied her pink lipstick and headed out of the powder room, directly to the front desk. She flashed a bright smile at the young woman standing behind the desk. "Do you have any jobs coming up here at the club? Anything at all?"

The cute, pert brunette manning the desk, didn't even bother to look up from her computer. "Nothing, Ma'am. And we have a long waiting list of applicants."

"Thank you so much." She smiled at the receptionist, waiting for her to lift her eyes off her computer, so she could make eye contact with her. Danielle handed her a card, which contained a flattering photo of herself. "Here's my card. I live nearby." She leaned forward, speaking conspiratorially. "I pride myself on being able to do absolutely anything. And I'm a real fast learner. I adapt at the speed of lightening."

The sleek woman had her hair pulled back in a chignon. One of those perfectly turned out, well educated types. The type she actually couldn't bear. *Grew up with a silver spoon in her mouth, no doubt.*

"Well...you're certainly not lacking in confidence, are you?" The brunette finally looked at her, although it was dismissively. "Thanks for thinking of us; but frankly, you would be wasting your time to apply. We hire *young* people when we do hire new people." She smiled. "Look around you. Do you see anyone over...25...30... tops?"

Danielle saw red. She forced herself to remain cool.

She took a deep breath and flashed the woman a smile. "Sometimes companies change their policies. Perhaps this is one of those times."

The woman at the front desk raised her eyebrows, but did not comment.

It was time to look up an old friend. Hilbert Travenstock lived in Dallas, though he travelled to Kentucky every season in May for the Kentucky Derby. He'd proposed to her many years ago. She'd been thrilled about the prospect of becoming his wife; but they had gotten into a tiff. Somehow, the rift had never really healed and they'd gone their separate ways. And, of course, given they resided in different cities, they naturally drifted apart. He hadn't remarried to her knowledge. They spoke on the phone every now and then, remaining friends over the years. He was one of the owners of the club. He could get her a job here, if he wanted to.

She returned to the table to find Sophie gone. Her new friend was sitting alone. They enjoyed a glass of white wine, along with guacamole and chips. "Why have you suddenly decided you simply *must* work at this club?" Her date peered at her, waiting for the reply.

"I don't have much of a social life. Maybe working here will change all that."

"You've met me. Who else do you need to know?"

It took her a minute to digest this news. She smiled big. "You like me that much?"

"Matter of fact, I do. I thought you got that."

She hadn't, in fact. "So...where do we go from here? You're sitting on the fence as far as your faith is concerned. I've just repented and committed to following God with my whole heart, mind and soul."

"Maybe that's what I want, too."

She stared at him. Stunned. Silent. "Well...is it? Is that what you want?"

"I don't know. Maybe."

"Then again, maybe not?" she peered into penetrating, hazel eyes. "The Bible says God will spit you out of his mouth if you are lukewarm. That is a very serious warning." Danielle was amazed this stuff was tumbling out of her mouth. She really *had* *repented.*

Chapter Thirty-Five

Dana awakened with a splitting headache. Despite that malady, she felt somewhat better. *What had happened to her?* She found her Bible on the night table and began to read. Somehow, inexplicably, she was led to Ephesians six. As she read about the spiritual battle being fought over every soul, she knew that she was in that battle, and for reasons she did not understand, the enemy was seriously targeting her.

She didn't want to think the worst of Danielle. But too many weird things had gone down with her; coupled with the negative reports from Graham. *Was Danielle evil? Did she want to harm her? Was she actually obsessed with winning Graham for herself, as he'd speculated? She had no idea. Right now she needed to rest. She'd overheard the doctor saying that someone might have attempted to poison her; but she'd been admitted to hospital quickly enough that the potential damage had been aborted. Modern medicine was a remarkable blessing to mankind. She felt much better. Whatever the doctor had given her had worked.*

The nurse popped her head in the door, handing her a couple of pills and a glass of water. She took them and soon began to feel drowsy.

When she awakened a few hours later, her ruggedly handsome husband, Graham, was peering at her. His penetrating blue eyes locked with hers. Standing by her bed, he grinned and leaned over, planting a kiss on her cheek.

"Hey Handsome...when can I get out of here and come home?" She was married to the sexiest and best-looking guy on the planet. He had a fast, sharp mind and was enlightened. He was, quite simply, one of the most amazing men God ever created. It was humbling to realize that she had been chosen to be his mate. God was a God of miracles. He lived in the supernatural, thrived in the miraculous. She was beginning to understand that *she* really *could* move mountains if she believed she could. In fact, moving a mountain was no big deal for God. After all, he created them! Silently, she reflected on Mark 11:23 & 24. *"If you say unto this mountain, be thou removed and be thou cast into the sea, and shall not doubt, but shall believe that that which he saith shall come to pass, he shall have whatsoever he saith."*

A flash of fresh insight soared through her. Comments Danielle had made over the years. Remarks that proved she was competitive with her. She wanted to trust her Step Mom with all her heart. Still, she could not ignore Graham's repeated warning not to trust her. "She has a ruthless side to her, honey. I'm sorry to have to say it, but she would sacrifice you in a minute to get what she wanted. She has an obsession to get rid of you and win my love, as bizarre as that is, Dana. In her deluded mind, she views you as the competition; the woman that stands in the way of her achieving that goal."

Reluctantly, Dana knew she had to close the door on her relationship with Danielle and keep is closed. She was so blessed to have Graham. Hanging out with her Mom could destroy or contaminate the rare, precious closeness they enjoyed. It would be just a matter of time. She knew what she had to do. Cut Danielle off once and for all. It would be the hardest thing she would ever have to do. "Darling...I...I'm going to cut Danielle off...at least for now. I think you're right about that."

"You may already be too late." Graham's tone was somber.

"Whatever do you mean?"

His demeanor was somber. He pointed to the newspaper. Unfolding it, he laid it across her lap, since she was sitting up.

Dana glimpsed the paper. There, on the second page in the second section, was a photo of Danielle trying on nurses' uniforms in a thrift store. The article read as follows:

Local businesswoman, Danielle Lockhart has filed for bankruptcy, following her brief marriage to a man who absconded with her money and illegally gained title of her property.

Danielle Lockhart now claims she is a thespian and will be playing the role of a chaplain in an amateur theatre production, locally. However, our research shows that no such production is being mounted locally. Further, if she were to be cast in any of the theatre's upcoming productions, she would typically obtain her costumes through the wardrobe department at the theatre.

Dana has recently been poisoned and is presently recovering at the Kentucky University hospital. Well known to the horsey set, Ms. Lockhart recently married Count Graham Van Rensellier. The newlyweds reside at Sugarbush Farms, locally. Their previous colt Flaming Bullet was the subject of much controversy, given the discovery of his poisoning, during the Kentucky Derby."

"You're coming home with me tonight, darling. The doctor is discharging you into my care. Unfortunately, Danielle is cunning. It's tricky to anticipate her next move."

Dana cried the entire way home. "What happened to the wonderful woman that raised me? How did she go off the rails like this, Graham?"

"I don't know, Dana. And it's purely speculation, but I have a hunch she's been hobnobbing with the wrong people. And once you get mixed up with them, it's hard to get out. I still say she masterminded the kidnapping..."

"Let's not talk about it anymore, darling."

Chapter Thirty-Six

Training was intense. Dana's fierce discipline, focus and unwavering ambition kicked into place. "Go, go, go...Jacob...Come on... Big Boy... move, move, move...you're a winner ...let's see the chips fly! Show us your stuff..." Sometimes Dana just acted as a cheerleader egging the jockey and colt on. She was a coach and that task varied depending on what was required. This one was as smooth as silk.

Lord, is this colt really going to win? I praise you and glorify you for helping us find this amazing racehorse. Please strengthen Jacob and me and the colt so that he will thrive and win the Kentucky Derby! We can do nothing without you, Lord. But we can do all things through Christ who strengthens us."

The time flew. Suddenly it was 4:00 and the day's work was done. She hurried over to the colt. He was sweating and tired and seemed unsettled. He moved his large, muscular body around restlessly. *That's understandable. He's worked hard. He's worked long hours. I think he thrives on it, but there's a fine line between ruthlessly driving a colt to achieve and spurring him, exciting and inspiring him to become a champion by winning the Derby. Only God himself knew where that fine line was.*

Jacob drove the horse trailer. Dana sat in the front seat with him. As usual, they talked about the day's training and the colt's progress. The prized colt was in the back of the horse trailer.

Three more months and it would be time to race in the world-famous Kentucky Derby. She knew that Graham was counting on her to coach Jacob and the colt and win the purse. He had a farm to run.

Graham wasn't in the house when Dana arrived home.

Will and Jay bounced out of the family room greeting her. "Hey, Dana...how's it going?"

She grinned at the boys. "Hey, guys. Nice to see you." She glanced around the family room. "So, where's your Dad?"

"Like...isn't he with you? I thought he went out to the racetrack." Jay looked surprised.

"No. I didn't see him there. You must have misunderstood him."

"Maybe. I'm starving. When can we eat?" Jay moved toward the kitchen.

"Come on... let's see what we can find. Violet probably has something amazing cooked up."

"Think so?" Jay looked hopeful.

Ah. Growing boys. Violet had made lasagna with a salad. "You go ahead and have dinner. I'll wait for Graham. I don't know where he could have gotten to." She glanced at Violet.

"He went to the bank. Said something about doing some business and a couple of errands. He said if he wasn't back by dinner, to go ahead and eat without him...guess he didn't want to bother you while you were training the colt..."

"Excuse me, Violet. I'll try his cell again." Dana began wandering around the house and redialing Graham on her cell. She finally reached him.

"Hey, Dana." Graham's husky voice always excited her.

"Hey to you. Where are you?" Dana was relieved, but still curious.

"Uh.uh.uh. It's a little mystery."

"Really. There better not be another woman, if you know what's good for you."

"Dana. It's our anniversary. I thought *you* would be the one to remind *me*. Instead, it's the other way around. It's tomorrow and I'm out doing some last minute shopping for a gift for you."

"You rascal. Get home for dinner. Violet made her famous lasagna."

"I just drove up, actually. Look outside and you'll see me in the jeep."

Dana hurried to the front porch, bounding down the stairs, Rover and Roamer hot on her heels, barking up a storm. Running up to him, she threw her arms around his neck. "Darling, I missed you..."

They went to the Villa Medici for a private dinner, complete with musicians. After dinner he presented her with a gift; a cocktail ring with emeralds and diamonds.

"Darling, you shouldn't have..." But she didn't mean it. She loved it and loved being spoiled. She slipped it on. The light caught the diamonds and emeralds causing them to sparkle brilliantly.

As they were finishing their salmon dish, a gentleman strolled by their table.

As Dana glanced up, it struck her that the gentleman looked vaguely like photos she'd seen of Tennessee Williams. She'd seen the man somewhere before. He was tall, lean and looked every inch the Southern gentleman. He stopped at their table. He caught Dana eyeing him. He smirked, pulling out a gun and aiming it at her.

Graham had seen it coming. His arms were around the man's neck, forcing him backwards, forcing him to drop the pistol.

The server was on his cell. "Sheriff..."

"What have we got here? One of Tanner's boys?"

The elegant looking gentleman was aghast. He did not answer.

"You will find that we are formidable opponents, Sir. And we do not scare easily." Graham peered into the man's harried face.

"I was forced into making this move." The stranger was breathing heavily, discombobulated and disheveled. He brushed himself off, and struggling, scrambled to his feet.

"What was your mission?" Graham studied the harried gentleman, not amused.

"I...I...oh what the heck...I don't want to work for him anymore...I...was supposed to disable one or both of you...throw a damper on things so you wouldn't enter the Derby race..."

"Have a seat. You've disrupted our romantic anniversary dinner. You might as well join us. A glass of champagne?"

The man flashed a tentative grin. "That would be

nice. I...I'm sorry about all this." He brushed himself off, straightening himself up a bit as he sat down.

"Bring our guest a champagne glass, waiter. He'll be joining us for some champagne." Graham addressed a male server, hovering nearby.

The server raised his eyebrows but refrained from commenting. Soon, he returned with a champagne glass.

"To our health!" The three of them clinked glasses.

Graham waited until their guest had downed a glass of champagne. "Tanner is in jail, as I'm sure you are aware. He won't be getting out for a very long time. He'll probably die there. So why does he care who wins the next Kentucky Derby?"

The man was silent for a while. He appeared to be mulling that statement over, though somehow Graham knew he was merely preparing his retort and how it would be worded.

"He hates your guts. And Dana's, too. Mostly because the two of you are relentless in your pursuit of learning the truth. And of course, he'll never forgive y' all for discovering the secret ranch. And he's irked that you're continuing to pursue wining the Derby."

"What are you going to tell him about this fiasco?" Graham raised his eyebrows.

"Don't know yet. Maybe I won't take his calls. He hasn't paid me yet. Maybe that's a blessing. I might just disappear off his radar..."

"That might not be as easy as you think. He has far reaching tentacles. He's been a scammer for a long time." Graham peered over at the man, assessing him.

"Yeah. True enough."

The man stood. He snapped photos of Graham and

Dana on his cell.

The sheriff suddenly appeared. His timing was superb. He handcuffed the intruder.

"Oh, so that's what the glass of champagne was all about." He shook his head. Like *dumb... dumb... dumb.*

When Dana was undressing for bed that evening, Graham came up behind her. "I'm afraid it's not over yet. Tanner is a game player, as we're both aware. Obviously, his latest game it to try to intimidate us to give up. And Lord knows who else he's targeting. He's going to try to disable as much of the serious competition as he can."

"He must have a few thugs on the outside implementing everything. No way could he be running things from inside prison." Dana looked, questioningly at Graham.

"It's been done before. Sheriff told me he's been in and out of prison since he was a teenager."

"So he's like a master puppeteer...and works with guys on the outside?"

"Maybe so. The key word with him is *Game.* He's a game player. As long as we're always thinking in terms of games, we have a shot at heading him off at the pass."

"Well, that's nice to know. Maybe I'll take a stab at learning chess after all, Graham."
"You should. You'd be good at it once you got into the swing of it. It takes a little time. When do you want to start?"

"Tomorrow would be good...after training and after dinner."

"You're on."

Dana and Graham sat across from each other in the games room. It was just after dinner. Violet appeared with cool whip, strawberries and some exotic fruit drink. "Have fun." She smiled and walked out of the games room. "Ring the buzzer if you need anything. I'll be up until 9:00...9:30."

Dana had had enough. "Graham. This is not my thing. I...just don't...I just can't seem to get into it..."

"You'll be great at it. It just takes some time and focus. It's not something you learn overnight."

"Well how did Jay and Will manage to get the hang of it? They're just kids."

"It's in their genes. They both took to it like ducks on the water."

Dana stood up in frustration. "Well, I don't seem to take to it."

"Sit back down, honey. We both agreed that to beat Tanner and the competition, we have to become adept at games. This is good practice for us."

Dana did as she was told. "Okay, okay. I guess you're right."

Three hours later. 11:30 P.M.

"Honey. I think I'm getting it! It...it's all falling into place. I can do this."

"What did I tell you?" He wrapped her in strong, protective arms. He was momentarily distracted. "What was that?"

"What was what?"

"That thud. That loud noise."

"Sounded like...it was coming from upstairs. Like someone fell out of bed or something."

"Hope Violet is okay."

"Violet!" Graham called out her name.

"Come on, let's go on upstairs to her room and make sure she's okay."

She wasn't. She'd had an accident. Graham turned to Dana. "This was not an accident. She's unconscious."

The loud wail of an ambulance cut into the still night.

"Somebody is in the house, Dana. Stay with me while I check the boys' room"

He opened the front door. "Come on Rover and Roamer...let's see what the two of you come up with."

The Shepherds barked ferociously as they raced around the house on their mission.

Jay and Will had hurried out of their rooms when the commotion began. They followed the action and moved toward Graham, who was at the front door. "Hey, Dad. What's goin' on?"

"The sheriff...and ambulance are on the way. We'll have some answers soon."

Rover and Roamer raced gleefully around the old edifice, barking up a storm.

"We've checked every room, every nook and cranny in the house. There's no one here. How did she fall?" the deputy sheriff peered at Graham.

"You got me on that one. How could she possibly fall out of her bed? She's as spry as a spring chicken."

"If she was pushed... why was she pushed? And how did the intruder get in? And how did he escape?" The sheriff shook his head in bewilderment.

"That's what I want to know." Graham was deeply disturbed by this new event. *Who was next?*

The roar of an ambulance screamed, stopping

outside. Two men carried Violet on a stretcher, moving her into the back of the ambulance and roaring off to the hospital.

"Are you thinking what I'm thinking?" Dana peered at Graham.

"If you mean do I think Tanner's playing us like puppets and trying to throw a monkey wrench into our lives, you'll be right. If he can get our lives to be chaotic, we'll lose our focus and the main chance."

"He is a destructive force. Quintessential evil, lurking around, determined to disrupt our lives. It's a battle we have to win."

The sheriff was still going from room to room, looking for clues. Finding none, he shook hands with Graham. "Sorry, buddy, we have another call. Gotta go. Wish I could help you more." He hesitated for a bit and then peered at Graham. "I'm glad you're seriously considering hiring 24/7 security. Between the training of the colt and last season's fiasco, you can't leave anything to chance."

Graham sighed. "Yeah. That's what I'm thinking. Good thing I have deep pockets. Huge dints in them are taking place, though."

"I don't know what else I can suggest, Graham. I'm sorry you and Dana have been targeted for all this foul play."

"Thanks for taking the time to stop by, Sheriff."

"Anytime."

"The pattern with stuff like this is that they leave you alone for a while; and just when you think they've forgotten about you, they resurface..."

"I'll be interviewing for 24/7 security. Between Dana's kidnapping, Will's kidnapping and now this mysterious incident with Violet, I can't just stand by and wait for the next attack."

"No, of course you can't. It's really the only option that makes sense. It will be interesting to see if it all goes away after the Derby."

"If we win, they could target us viciously. If we lose, they might lose interest. No way am I going to roll over and play dead. They'll keep trying to bully us; but if we stand up to them, eventually, they're going to back down."

"Sounds about right to me." The sheriff nodded his head, thoughtfully. "Well, good-night. Y'all get some sleep now."

"That *is* what we need. There's been a lot of trauma going on." Dana gave Graham a peck on the cheek.

Graham awakened in the wee hours with a premonition. *Something very bad was about to occur. But what?* He didn't want to awaken Dana, so he tiptoed out of their room and down the hall to his study.

In the privacy and solace of his den, he reflected on God, Dana, his sons and his life. Soon, he was on his knees praising God for all the blessings that had been bestowed upon him. *And then he knew. God was calling him into repentance and fervent prayer. He needed to repent because he had begun to take Dana for granted. She did her thing. He did his. But they had grown apart.* "How did I allow this to happen, Lord? I thought I was a master at the institution of marriage. I thought I was an ace hubby. *But the Lord was showing him that he had a long way to go to earn that title.*

It had started...the growing apart thing...when he was preparing his rather complex income tax. At that time, he'd told Dana not to bother him. Though she'd tried on many occasions to pop her head into his office; serve him a cold drink or some other refreshment, after several rejections, she'd finally given up and stopped bothering him.

That's when she'd started going to bed very early. She was usually asleep by the time he came into their room. "Lord, I always thought I was a model husband. I...I thought I was doing everything right."

"*My precious, precious son, you are doing everything right. But she needs to spend more time with you. She needs you. Ever since the kidnapping, she's been uneasy; and with all the drama going on with Danielle, it has upset her deeply. She needs you.*"

"Lord, thank-you for showing me the truth." He prayed fervently for the wisdom to handle Dana and for restoration of their fractured relationship. It wasn't too late. They had both invested a lot into this marriage and he wasn't a quitter. Dana wasn't either.

He rose from his knees and his precious time with the Lord, renewed. "This is the day that the Lord has made, I will rejoice and be glad in it!" God was a God of miracles and he knew what was wrong. He hadn't been seeking Him with a whole heart the way he had when he'd been desperate during his late wife's long illness. Life was good, and he was busy. *I'm sorry Lord, I realize that I have not been putting you first, the way I did when I desperately needed you. Still, you have always been there for me. Lord, thank-you for this wake-up call.*

Chapter Thirty-Seven

He hurried into the bedroom just in time to see Dana reaching for him. "Darling? Darling...where are you?"

He moved quickly to their bed and wrapped strong arms around her. "My darling, I love you so much..."

She was half asleep and peered strangely at him. "Graham...where were you? I called for you...over and over...I was scared...alone in the bedroom...with everything that's been happening..."

"Of course you were, darling." He kissed her passionately moving into the bed. "Ssh. We'll talk about it later."

Vivid morning sunlight streamed through the shutters. Dana leaped out of bed. All was right with the world. "It's going to be an amazing training session today. I just feel it in my bones."

At the end of the training session, Jacob and Dana felt good. "We're going to make it. I feel it in my bones. God is going to grant us victory." Jacob grinned.

"Is that a word from the Lord, Jacob?"

"I believe it is."

"Okay, then." She gave him a high five. A goofy gesture she'd picked up from the boys. "From your lips to God's ears."

"You're full of clichés today, aren't you?" Jacob grinned. "You know, Dana, I've been around horses all my life...and because of it, I've developed a sixth sense about them...the way you have...and I'm absolutely sure we're going to soar through to the finish line and win the purse with this colt. Won't that be something? We'll be the toast of the town!"

"I hope you're right, Jacob. Something tells me it's not going to be quite that easy, though."

"Who said anything about easy? I'm just sayin'... as long as we keep up the grueling training schedule and keep praying for favor with God... and wisdom with training the colt, we'll triumph."

"I'm afraid I'm taking a different approach, Jacob."

"And what's that?"

"I'm leaving it *all* in God's hands. I'm not going to get obsessed with winning, the way I did last year. I'm not going to live and breathe the dream of winning the Kentucky Derby. I'm not going to be fixated on anything other than God...ever again."

"Okay." He stopped and stared at her. "You have a good point."

"I think so. Last year, I was unwittingly coveting that prize above and beyond God. God is a jealous God; and I will not bow down to any other gods; including and especially the god of the Big Win. The Kentucky Derby purse. None of that matters." She smiled, "It's the sport, my dear...always the sport. "She laughed, joyfully. "It's the sport I fell in love with when I became a show jumper; it's the sport I fell in love with when I knew I wanted to train colts to win major races, including the Derby. But despite our shared passion to win the purse and give it away...it's still akin to an obsession; that elusive goal of winning the big prize, isn't it?

"Yeah, I guess it is."

" It's the pursuit, the passion to win...but we need to die to our flesh...to properly serve Jesus; and we also need to die to any passion and pursuit that tries to edge itself before God Almighty. God is a jealous God. We should never forget that."

"I think you missed your calling, Dana. You should have been an evangelist." Jacob grinned, as he led the colt onto the ramp at the back of his horse trailer. "You know, Dana...working with you has been a remarkable experience. I have learned so much...not just about horses, but about life...and God. . You are a woman of considerable wisdom."

"I like to think so. But if that's true, why doesn't Danielle even speak to me?"

"She has problems. And...sorry to say...but my take is that she's green with envy over your life with Graham at Sugarbush."

"Well I'm praying that God will heal the rift between us. I believe he will. He desires the restoration of families. It's Satan's bait if we allow disruption and separation of family members. At the risk of sounding preachy, Jacob; *"All have sinned and fallen short of the glory of God."*

"So we should all kiss and make up?"

Dana laughed. "Pretty much."

"You should watch her, though. If I read her right, she's a complex person. Doesn't take well to not getting what she wants."

Chapter Thirty-Eight

Danielle was livid. She was out in the cold again. Starting over was never easy or fun. Sometimes, she thought she had an evil spirit because she felt compelled to throw a monkey wrench into Dana's perfect life. *Why should she have everything while I have nothing? The kidnapping ploy had backfired. It was time to cook up a little more mischief. Maybe just derail Dana. Or maybe she'll have an accident with one of the horses.* She gave her head a shake. "Oh, Lord...what am I thinking?"

That night Danielle tossed and turned, torn between good and evil. She knew she should read the Bible and seek God, but her fleshly desires won out. She wound up watching a movie. Oddly, it was about an equestrian who travelled to a remote area known to have wild horses roaming the area. With the help of a wrangler, she managed to corner one of the horses. In an attempt to break the horse in, she is thrown and dies.

Danielle wrestled with herself. She was a new believer and she'd been told to read the Bible and pray daily and especially read Ephesians 6:10 putting on the whole armor of God. She would do it tomorrow.

The next morning, Danielle arose with a new plan to put a monkey wrench into Dana's "Perfect life." The life *she* should be living. She knew there was a rodeo coming up in the area. If she could get Dana sidetracked into watching the show, she could get close enough to her to invite her for lunch including a glass of wine. Then, she would slip something into it. Just like that. So...so simple. With Dana back in the hospital, she could visit her and slip something fatal into her coffee. Dana loved coffee and would never turn down a cup.

Dana believed in forgiving and starting over. It was her mindset. And she always believed in thinking the best of people. She agreed to attend the rodeo with Danielle. She would come for the last half hour, so they could have lunch together. It was time to make up. She missed her mother so much.

"I'm really glad you called, Danielle. Graham gave me permission to hook up with you and check out the rodeo. He knows how much I love it. I can't stay long, though. I need to get back to training."

"Sounds good." Danielle smiled. *What a fool her step daughter was.* They agreed on a meeting point.

Danielle and Dana sat together, both of them cheering and jumping out of their seats in excitement, as they watched a cowboy lasso one of the calves.

Danielle knew she had to distract Dana, in order to slip the drug into the coffee. She had already decided she would pretend Graham had shown up unexpectedly. While Dana peered in the direction she indicated, Danielle would make her move and quickly drop the lethal drug into the coffee.

"Where? I don't see him?" Dana fell for the trick.

"Oh...you know...maybe it's not him." She shrugged. "Guess it's just someone who looks like him."

Soon, Dana was drowsy and could hardly stay awake. "What's...happening? I feel...strange." Some instinct told her Danielle had slipped something into her drink. Her head kept drooping. *I must get help. I must call Graham...I have to stay awake...keep fighting..."* She struggled valiantly, all to no avail. Her head slumped down.

Danielle leaned toward her, smiling. "You'll be fine," she whispered. Of course she didn't believe that for a minute. She hated the fact that she had morphed into a ruthless woman.

She spun out of the parking lot to the sound of wailing sirens. Someone had already called them. With Dana out of circulation, she could contact Tanner and get on a retainer like her buddy. She had the ability to get close to "the enemy." She would use their Christian, "goody-two shoes" attitude to her advantage.

Dana was in the hospital for tests. She didn't want to believe that Danielle had maybe slipped something into her coffee...but no matter how many times she replayed the scene in her mind; it always turned up the same. There were just the two of them having coffee together. No one else was around. Suddenly she'd become drowsy and then conked out. It all pointed to Danielle. How had her Step-Mom sunk so low?

Dana was discharged three days later. At home, chatting with Graham in the living room, she felt bitter, betrayed and confused. "Darling, we're losing valuable training time. I need to get back to work."

"Yes you do. We need to win some races. We need

to believe God for great and mighty things, such as winning the Derby. After all, it is *He* who gives us favor and the skill to train a winner. It is *He* who leads, guides and directs our every move." He shook his head. "I warned you about Danielle, honey, though I hoped I was wrong. Dana...I'm sorry... but you need to write her off. There's not much else you can do. We'll pray for her."

"Maybe you're right. What do you think pushed her to go off the rails?"

"Jealousy, honey. It's probably always been there. But when you married me, she couldn't stand it. She's always comparing your life to hers. She shouldn't do that." He sighed. "Then... the betrayal of her new hobby...and finally... losing her house and her money. I guess she just didn't have the mettle required to move forward after that." Graham shook his head, taking a healthy sip of the gourmet brew.

Dana took a sip of coffee. "Well, she did buy another house. That's something."

"True. But if I read Danielle right, she wants a whole lot more out of life than just a little cottage."

They sat at the large, circular table in the enormous country kitchen, chatting and drinking apple cider. The sun streamed through the East facing windows.

Violet made waffles with maple syrup, topped with blackberries the boys had picked. "By the way, Danielle called." She shrugged. "I wonder why she didn't call your cell?" She peered at Dana.

"Because I wouldn't have answered, that's why." Dana could hardly believe she had the nerve to call after all that had happened. Still, there was no concrete evidence that she had slipped something into Dana's coffee. And, theoretically, it *could* have been someone else.

"Call her back on the ground line, honey. I'll listen in on the extension." Graham smirked.

"What are you up to, darling? You just said I should take a walk from her."

"It's just a hunch. But I think we can set a trap for her. She should be convicted. She's a danger to society and should be rehabilitated."

"Okay, I'll call her back. I'm safe here with you, honey. What should I say? What should I ask her?"

"Let her do the talking. We'll learn more that way."

"Keep your enemies close to you?"

"Exactly."

Together they strolled to the long bank of windows in the massive kitchen. One of the mansion's phones sat on an antique Roll Top desk. Dana plunked down on the chair next to it and called Danielle's cell number. It rang several times. She got a recorder and hung up. "Weird. She just phoned and now she's not answering."

"I'm going with you to the training session today, Dana."

"What about the farm?"

"I'll get Wilbur to take care of everything. I'm not leaving your side. Come on, let's get what we need and head off to the racetrack. It's just a hunch; but I think Danielle is going to strike again."

"No kidding?"

"Yeah. She seems to be on a mission to destroy you. It's got to be a satanically inspired agenda. It must be confronted head-on and stopped. Plus we need to do spiritual warfare daily."

AT THE RACETRACK

It was the end of a long, grueling day of training. Jacob was pleased with the progress their new colt was making.

Dana was overjoyed. She was beginning to see the light at the end of the tunnel...beginning to have a sense that this colt truly was destined for the big win. Oh she knew, of course, that every trainer, every jockey, every Thoroughbred owner training a colt to compete for the roses, felt the same way. But competition inspired her and challenged her. It was in her blood. It made her tick. When she'd been a show jumper, she'd always had the secret dream of training a colt to win the purse at the Kentucky Derby. It would happen. It had to happen.

Jacob drove the trailer with their colt back to Sugarbush. After settling the colt into his stall at the barn, he hugged Dana. "It's going to work out. Have a great evening. See you tomorrow." Jacob headed off.

Dana decided to take a ride and just commiserate with the Almighty.

God makes no mistakes. His thoughts are not our thoughts. We cannot comprehend his mind or fathom his vast depths of mystery. Sometimes, when Dana needed solace and was struck with a burning desire to contemplate the greatness of God and His Majesty, she galloped along the Bluegrass, singing songs of praise and worship. *"Lord, you are a great and mighty God. There is none like you. There is none like you. No, there is none like you. You are great. You are true. No matter what I do. You are always there. Always there for me. How can I...comprehend your greatness? How can I... tap into the vast sea of mystery? How can I? How can I? How can I?"* Her voice soared to new and glorious heights. She'd been gifted with a beautiful voice and she loved to use it to worship the creator.

"Every step I take, I check with You. Every move I make, I seek Your face. Every song I sing, I plead for grace. Grace takes me back to You. Back to You. Right back to You.

How can I? How can I see your face? How can I? How can I know your grace? How can I? How can I know? How can I? How can I show? The world. The world that needs you so. Needs you so...Needs you so." How can I? How can I know? How can I grow? How can I know you more?

"If there should be. A mystery. If there should be a song to sing. If there should be eternity. If there will be a place for me. A place for all eternity. A place so sweet. That at earth's feet, I seek to know. I seek to grow. I seek to show... what joys you have for those who seek to know.

"Wow, Lord. You weren't kidding when you said you would pour your spirit out on all men in the last days! It's amazing that you gave me a song, Lord. I'm so thrilled! Thank-you, Lord! I wish I had my tape recorder with me."

One of the many joys of owning Sugarbush was the freedom of doing what she wanted. She'd always reveled in solitude. She raised her hands in worship to the Almighty. "Thank you, Lord, for that amazing song! Praise Your Holy Name!" She'd been given several songs in the past and had been dilatory in not taking a tape recorder with her wherever she went. The Almighty didn't wait until we were ready for an increased anointing or an outpouring of a worship song, the spirit moved in mysterious ways. No one can fathom the mind of God. Considering his voice is like the sound of many waters, it boggled her mind. She could not imagine that sound. *Ah, I am but a mere mortal, Lord.*

Dana galloped speedily back to the barn. Graham was waiting for her. He was actually standing outside the barn watching her as she galloped in from the rolling bluegrass. The vivid sunshine lit his face. His countenance was sad, strained.

She dismounted expertly. "Hey, what's goin' on?" She'd barely finished the greeting as she met his lips.

He kissed her fiercely, lingering.

She tied the reigns of her thoroughbred to the outdoor post and turned her attention to Graham. "He's restless. I need to give him some water and sustenance."

Pulling apart from the embrace, he peered at her, his countenance sad and concerned. "Danielle is back in prison."

"What? Dana was stunned. Her emotions rising, her voice louder, she peered at Graham. "Who told you that?"

Graham sighed. "Let's get your thoroughbred watered and into his stall. The boys are being picked up by Violet. Come on, I'll walk you into the barn. We won't talk about it until we get to the house. We don't want to share this stuff with the ranch hands; and we never know when they might show up."

"Yeah. Of course."

Graham opened the front door on the porch for Dana. Neither of them spoke as they moved into the house. "We'll go to my den in case the boys come home...we need privacy."

Dana had a sense of foreboding. *Why do I not like what he is about to say? Why is it making me nervous before I ever hear the scenario?* "Spit it out, please, Graham."

"Danielle was in a terrible accident. She's in critical condition at St. Mary's Hospital."

Dana went into shock. She was dumbstruck.

Graham stood and held her close for a very long time. "Darling...I'm so...so sorry this happened to your Mom."

Dana's breathing was labored, she struggled to speak. "Wh...what happened?"

"Have a seat, darling." He pulled apart from the embrace, helping her onto the leather sofa in his den. He moved next to her."She...got into an altercation with some young dude. Their words got nasty."

"So, what happened?"

"She sped away, upset...the car crashed. The vehicle is totaled. She...she's in real bad shape. She's been asking for you..."

"And probably you, too."

"She's only asking for you. I'll drive you there...but you go ahead and visit her on your own..." Graham was sad.

Dana and Graham drove to Kentucky University hospital. Soon, they were in the emergency area. A doctor was monitoring Danielle. He motioned for them to take chairs but remain silent. Danielle languished on a cot, her head bandaged.

"Mother..."   Dana was stunned. Danielle was unrecognizable...and yet Dana knew it was her. Tears rushed down Dana's cheeks as she went into shock.

"Mother? What happened?"

Danielle lay very still.

Dana felt like a little girl again. She remembered the way things had been when she grew up, when they'd been close. The years... the jealousies... the traumas in both their lives had torn them apart. But now her heart brimmed with compassion and love for the woman who had brought her up, indulging her dream of becoming an equestrian. Danielle had stood by her through all her childhood trials and tribulations, encouraging her to follow her dreams during her teenage years, right on to womanhood. *How had they grown so far apart? What had caused Danielle to plunge on a downward spiral, finally ending up here? This woman she peered over at was like a stranger to her.*

The doctor continued to monitor the machines that were hooked up to her. He motioned to Graham and Dana, taking them aside. "Don't try to talk to her. Don't attempt to find out what happened. Just be there for her. Let her sense your presence...feel the warmth of your touch...know that you care. That's all you need to do. The fact that you showed up is all that matters."

Dana breathed a sigh of relief. She peered over at Graham. A silent understanding united their hearts. She managed a half-smile, her eyes brimming with tears. "Mother...I love you. I've always loved you. I don't know what happened between us... but all is forgiven. Just get well...please get well...we have so much making up to do..." She leaned over to Danielle and lovingly brushed aside some of her platinum locks, flashing a warm smile. *Faith, hope, and charity...but the greatest of these is charity* rang through her heart and mind. *She was called to love fervently and forgive regardless of what had gone down.*

THREE MONTHS LATER

It had been a long road to recovery. The head-on car crash had left the other driver dead, both cars totaled and Danielle, by the grace of God had survived and was on the road to recovery.

SIX MONTHS LATER

Finally, the day for Daniele's release had arrived. Graham and Dana picked her up at the University hospital and brought her to Sugarbush Farm to rest and recuperate. They helped her get settled into the pink bedroom. "Get some rest, make yourself comfortable. Violet is making roast beef and baked veggies for dinner. Dinner will be served in the dining room at 6:00."

Ironically, it was the very room she had dreamed of occupying as a house guest, and had, in fact, secretly hung out there for a few days, reveling in the mischief.

The formal dinner was a celebration of Danielle's survival and recovery. It was a time to praise the creator and give thanks for all that he had given them. Everyone sat at the long dining table, enjoying the wonderful meal Violet had cooked.

"You're lookin' good, Grandma," Jay teased. "You'll do anything to get attention. Even get in a car accident and flip out." He smirked.

"Yeah. I think you get better lookin' as you age." Will raised his brows and grinned, saucily.

After dinner, the boys headed off to the family room to watch a movie.

Graham, Dana and Danielle hung out in the living room. Graced with two long banks of windows, the room looked out onto a pair of Hanging Moss trees set off about hundred feet away. A Palm tree graced the area near the bottom of the stairs.

Graham, Dana and Danielle settled onto the wraparound sundeck. It was a blissful, warm day. The sun streamed through the long bank of windows.

Violet served iced tea. Then she peaked at the tall cage where her red Cockatiel was kept. He began chattering gaily, as she approached him. She chatted to him, fussing over him for a while, before carefully and skillfully plucking him from his cage and letting him hook himself onto her arm. She chatted with him and fussed over him, soon disappearing into the house with him.

Graham opened the conversation. He was determined to find out how Danielle had morphed from a nice, attractive gal into a monster. "I know you've only been under the psychiatrist's care for a few months...have you made any headway? Any new revelations?"

"Actually I have."

"Well?"

"I have a split personality. In the spiritual realm, some believe I have an evil spirit...a spirit that may have jumped onto me through some wrong associations. You see...the bad stuff I did was...uncontrollable. And the more evil I did, the more I wanted to do. It became a viscous cycle. A cycle I felt helpless to control or stop."

"I see." And Graham did see. A voracious reader, he'd read extensively on split personalities, multiple personalities and people afflicted with demon spirits. "That's a scary but very real scenario. So...you just felt *compelled* to do evil?"

"Pretty much. I look around me now...and I can't believe how low I sunk..."

"How did you get off the treadmill?"

"Interesting question. I'm not sure I'm off it. I crashed my car as you know..."

"The enemy wanted to kill you. He comes to kill, steal and destroy. God was watching over you, though. The angels were protecting you...because it is nothing short of a miracle that you survived the crash."

"That's pretty much what the paramedics and cops said. Were y'all praying for me?"

"Oh yeah." Dana sighed. "You have no idea how much we prayed."

"I'm beginning to. Well...maybe that's what did it."

"That's *definitely what did it.* Somewhere in the Bible it says that one will put a hundred angels to flight but two praying together exponentially increases to *thousands* working on our behalf."

"No kidding. I didn't know that." Danielle shook her head in amazement.

Chapter Thirty-Nine

That night as Danielle lounged on the deck off The Pink Room, looking out onto the lush vegetation on the farm, she tried to focus on reading the Bible. She could not. Next, she tried to pray. She couldn't concentrate on that, either. She knew she should be grateful that she was here. It was an ideal place to recuperate. Still, she felt restless.

Unable to sleep, she arose in the wee hours, heading downstairs to the kitchen for a glass of water, maybe a snack. She poured a glass of water from the fridge. Drank it and peered inside the fridge to see if anything looked appealing for a snack. Nothing beckoned to her. She closed the door. As she was turning to leave, she was startled to discover Graham.

He stood in the doorway, clad in a white terry robe. He was strikingly handsome, no question about it. Her heart lurched. *Lord... I'm not supposed to feel this way. He's taken. Still, a part of her rebelled. She was every bit as good as Dana. Every inch as attractive despite being a bit older.* She heard the still, small voice speaking to her. She knew it was the voice of God. It was clear as a bell. *He's taken.*

Yes, Lord, I know he's taken.
Then back off.

But even as she heard the warning in her spirit, a negative force rose up within her. *You can have him if you really want him,"* it seemed to be saying. "What are you doing up at this hour?" She smiled at Graham.

"I was about to ask you the same thing." Graham yawned. "Good-night." He turned on his heel, heading back to the hallway leading to the master bedroom. He closed and locked the door behind him. He'd wanted a snack, but no way was he going to stick around with Danielle milling around the kitchen. She was bad news and he didn't trust her, despite wanting to help her in her darkest hour.

The next morning, Dana and Graham rose early, dressing in their usual Western garb. After breakfast, they headed to the barn together. It was barely past 6:00 a.m. "Hey Graham, I think our favorite colt looks better every day, don't you?" Dana fed him his special food, carefully measuring it.

"Actually, I don't like the way he looks." Graham was looking over the colt carefully, scrutinizing him to within an inch of his life. "It's his eyes. They don't look right."

Dana chided herself for perhaps missing something. *She* was the expert, after all. She sighed and began peering into the colt's eyes, assessing him, looking very closely at him."You know, you're right, Graham. His eyes don't look right." She was suddenly on high alert. "Now what?" She sighed.

"Let's not panic, honey. We'll go out to the track...see how he does today. Meanwhile, we'll ask the vet to meet us out there after lunch. We'll get his take."

It's so nice to have a man around the house, rang through her mind and heart. "I hope he'll be able to make it. It's not an emergency and we both know how busy he is."

"I'll call him right now. He might even be out at the track. Meanwhile, let's put the angels on the assignment and see if we can expedite this. If he's coming down with something, we might be able to nip it in the bud."

It was their lucky day. The vet was out at the track. Dana found him attending to another colt. "Would you check out our colt? He seems a little off, despite the fact that we've been feeding him the finest food available."

The vet glanced over at Dana. "Symptoms. What are the symptoms?"

"A slight decline in appetite. Not quite as spirited as he usually is."

An hour later, after all the tests had been run, the vet shook his head. "Keep me posted. Right now I'd say maybe he's just having a bad day or two. Forget about it. Get back to training. If anything changes, let me know. Certainly, there's nothing seriously wrong. Nothing to worry about."

Dana breathed a sigh of relief. "All right, back to work, guys." She smiled over at Jacob and Graham.

"Honey, I hate to kiss and run, but I need to get back to the farm. Let me say a quick prayer for you."

"Thanks, honey."

"Lord, we give you praise and glory for what you are about to do. We know that in all things we must glorify you and keep lifting up your name so that others might see you." He kissed her on the cheek, his eyes dancing with joy. *Lord, thanks for bringing Dana into my life. I'm crazy about that woman.* "Bye, honey, see you at dinner."

Dana's face lit up with joy. Every day that went by, the love they shared grew sweeter. Sweeter than the day before. *Thank-you, Lord.*

Today their colt was competing with another colt to get used to the dirt flying in their faces, used to racing and competing. The competing colt was serious competition. In fact, he was the winner in the first race between them.

Jacob patted the colt on his shoulder, whispering what a great race it was and egging him on to greater and greater success. "Fast. You must become fast. Like Lightning."

Chapter Forty

A wicked mood clamped onto Danielle. She had an uncontrollable urge to throw things. It was that evil spirit again. Acting up... directing her to do more evil deeds. But she wouldn't succumb. She had repented and now she had to try to make amends with Dana and Graham. Otherwise, it would be a very lonely life. They were the only family she had. And they meant everything to her. She padded out to the back porch. The sounds of the cockatiel chattering gaily and incessantly got on her nerves. She felt like swatting him. *Why should he be so happy?*

She decided to play a little game. *Sea Worthy*, the red cockatiel, had formerly lived on a boat with a captain in Florida. So Violet had told them. *Wouldn't it be fun to snatch him from his cage and drive off? That way, Graham, Dana and Violet would beseech her to return with the Cockatiel. And before she knew it, she would be a permanent resident at the farm. Then, all she had to do was stage a nasty indiscretion on Dana's part. Frame her and it would be game over for the marriage. She despised herself for being so devious. Particularly, since she'd been invited here to recuperate. But time was marching on. She was cunning. She could wrest Graham away from Dana if she set her mind to it.*

She sat on the back porch. She knew she looked great in the lime green top and pants. She'd just had her blond locks colored and cut. The mirror told her she looked fabulous. "Hey Sea Worthy... how you doin'?"

He chattered a mile a minute, amusing her.

Violet peered out the window, soon strolling outside onto the veranda. "Flirting with my baby?"

"Yeah, I am. Do you mind?"

"'Course not. Just don't run away with him." Violet smirked, peering directly into her eyes.

Does the woman read minds? Danielle felt a slow blush creeping over her face. *So much for that little scam. Next?* "The iced tea is refreshing. Thanks, Violet."

"Sure. Think I'll take a break and join you for a glass of iced tea."

"Yeah. Why don't you just do that?" *Darn her.*

They were still on the veranda sipping their iced tea when Graham strode back from the barn, the two yapping dogs accompanying him. He mounted the front steps of the veranda, striding to where Violet and Danielle sat. "Hi ladies. The tea looks refreshing."

"There's a pitcher of it on the table. Help yourself." She'd made a pitcher of iced tea and it stood on the glass and wicker table, which was flanked against the exterior of the house.

Danielle's eyes swept over Graham. She flashed him a bright smile. She was glad she'd had veneers done a few years back. And Botox had peeled off a few more years. She'd always been fanatical about maintaining herself. Still, it was a challenge to capture Graham's attention. She'd have to come up with a brilliant, unique scheme.

Graham continued on into the house instead of joining the women on the veranda.

If the mountain doesn't come to Mohammed. Mohammed must go to the mountain. She waited until Violet finished her break sipping tea on the veranda. Then, Danielle sauntered into the kitchen, plopping herself down at the kitchen table, where Graham sipped iced tea while peering at the news on TV.

He didn't acknowledge her as she entered the kitchen. Nor did he glance her way when she sat down at the table where he was seated.

I'll outsmart you. I'll outsmart Dana. I'll outsmart everybody. Just you watch. She didn't know what she was going to do. But she was certain she'd come up with a brilliant, unique plan. A plan that would deter Graham from his focus on Dana. Instead, transferring it to her.

It struck her like a bolt of lightening. She would pretend that she had multiple personalities that were controlling and obsessing her. That way, she could flirt outrageously with him, and simply pretend it was one of the multiple personalities controlling her. She could hardly wait to use her innate dramatic talent.

Out of the foggy mist of her mind, a plan began to emerge and take shape. A plan that would cause Graham to focus his attention solely on her. And when that happened, he would find her irresistible.

She waited until 5:00 in the morning. Then opened

the small, locked rollaway suitcase and put the camouflage outfits on the bed. *Red. Men were suckers for red. It spelled excitement. Drama. First, the red wig. Short, saucy and fun. It peeled ten years off her. Next, the low cut pink, slinky top with the matching slinky pants. The pink sandals with the small heel looked amazing.*

Before she'd lost her money she'd gone on a shopping spree, buying the best make-up available; which was Dior, in her opinion. She applied it with the new, false lashes and eyeliner....twenty minutes later and she was ready to make her move. "I look every inch the femme fatale. I can have any man I want." She spoke to the mirror, flashing a huge, confident smile. Finally, she was going to get what she'd always wanted. Graham.

Murdering Dana wouldn't be easy, and it would take Graham time to recover; but once he did, she would be right there nursing his wounds, holding his hand and sympathizing with his laments. Men often enjoyed woman a little older than themselves. It made them feel secure, somehow.

She dusted off the Beretta, carefully wrapping it in white tissue paper. She checked that it was loaded. A few more details and she would be ready to embark on her mission.

She knew it was Violet's day off today. Last night she'd driven off to visit her niece, mentioning that she wouldn't be back until much later. That's when she knew she had to implement her plan tonight. It was now or never.

She had a touch of nerves. And more than a touch of conscience. Still, she was determined to go through with her plan. Living in Dana's shadow was not her idea of the good life. She deserved a great guy and a wonderful life. Didn't God say he came to give life and give it to us more abundantly?

God forgives everything, even murder. She'd read David and Bathsheba's story in the Bible. David, after murdering Bathsheba's hubby, later repented of his wickedness and went on to a good life. Maybe she would repent, too. She would miss Dana, of course; and she was sorry in a way that Dana couldn't complete her mission of competing for the Derby again this year. But that was life. Nobody gets it all. And it was *her* turn to live the good life.

She would wait until Graham went to the barn to start the morning chores. And she'd make sure the boys had gone off to school. With Violet away, it was clear sailing. Dana and Jacob would be out at the track early. She would stand by until Dana returned from the track.

She usually returned home around 4:00 just before the boys hopped off their school bus. Graham was often out on the property doing any one of a myriad of chores. With Violet absent, and the boys not yet home, she would be alone with Dana.

The surprise element always worked best, according to all the suspense and mystery novels she'd read.

2:45 p.m. Danielle sips water from a tall glass in the kitchen. Poised and ready to roll, she takes one last glance at her hand-held mirror. "I look amazing! I am amazing. Forgive me God for what I'm about to do..."

She stepped out of the shadows, heady with success even before it happened. *I look fabulous in my pink outfit and the red wig!* She aimed her Beretta at Dana as she entered the front hallway of the mansion. "I'm sorry, Dana...I'm sorry you have to die...but either *I'm* going to have an amazing life...or *you're* going to have an amazing life." She smiled. "I win." She aimed the Beretta at Dana, but while she taunted her, a pair of undercover cops stepped out of the shadows. The sheriff grabbed her gun. "It's over, Danielle. You're headed back to prison."

"What? How did you know?" Danielle went into shock.

Dana shook her head, sadly. "Oh, Mother; you overestimate yourself and under estimate everybody else. There are hidden video cameras in your room; as well as throughout the house. It's all been filmed." She smiled, sadly. "The outfit looks amazing though. And the wig is flattering, but Danielle...." She shook her head. "Your wickedness never ceases to amaze me."

The sheriff handcuffed her as she writhed, screamed and cursed. "There's been a mistake!" Her shrill scream reverberated throughout the old mansion, eerily.

"No mistake, Danielle. We've been watching you on video the whole time you've been here, and we've been stunned and shocked at your wicked scheme."

"It...it was just a game! It was only a game...

"Yeah. Right."

"I'm going to plead insanity as a defense. The devil made me do it."

"Let's go, Danielle. You're going back to prison where you belong. Maybe after you've chilled out for many years, you'll come to your senses and realize the law of reciprocity. *"Cast your bread on the waters, and after many days it will come back to you."*

THE END

Don't miss book one, <u>Kentucky Cowboy</u>

Made in the USA
Middletown, DE
06 February 2019